He grabbed her and kissed the devil out of her.

Damn, but she felt good in his arms. And her lips were soft as they sighed against his. Soft and warm and sweet. "Sweet as sugar," he murmured, then pulled her closer and kissed her again.

At first she kissed him back, making a little purring moan and wiggling against him. Then he felt her stiffen. After a moment's hesitation, she shoved away from him, struggling and spitting like a puma cub caught in a net.

"How dare you!" she screeched, then hauled off and slapped the daylights out of him. . . .

SUGAR ANNE

Jan Hudson

FAWCETT GOLD MEDAL • NEW YORK

A Fawcett Gold Medal Book
Published by The Ballantine Publishing Group
Copyright © 1998 by Jan Hudson

http://www.randomhouse.com

Library of Congress Catalog Card Number: 97-94531

ISBN 0-449-15026-7

Manufactured in the United States of America

First Edition: March 1998

10 9 8 7 6 5 4 3 2 1

In loving memory of my mother,
Ruby Oliver Eddington

ACKNOWLEDGMENTS

Many people were helpful as I researched material for this book. I would like to thank the staff of Rosenberg Library in Galveston, as well as the archivists and staff of the historic collection there, for invaluable assistance with maps, photographs, newspapers, and mountains of other material from the period. For information on trains, I am grateful to John Dundee, executive director of the Railroad Museum in Galveston, and to Thomas Taber III, administrator of the Railroad Historical Research Center, an Internet source. The librarians and archivists at the Historic New Orleans Collection were of tremendous help in the hours I spent among their impressive holdings. The librarians at Nacogdoches Public Library and the Ralph Steen Library at Stephen F. Austin University were also supportive.

My special thanks to Jennifer Blake, a treasure who graciously shared her time and knowledge with me. I was blessed to have Jim Hudson as intrepid researcher, chauffeur, and general assistant. Thanks also to Mary Lynn Baxter, Susan Wiggs, Laura Devries, Anne Kolaczyk, Julie Kistler, Linda George, the terrific folks on Painted Rock, and to a special cab driver in New Orleans, a lady who boldly took us where others feared to go.

I drew on scores of sources for information, but the following books were especially helpful: *Galveston: A History,* David G. McComb; *Galveston,* Ray Miller; *Bob's Galveston Island Reader,* Bob Nesbitt; *The Fair but Frail: Prostitution in San Francisco, 1849–1900,* Jacqueline B. Barnhart; *New Orleans: A Pictorial History,* Leonard V. Huber; *Queen New Orleans,* Harnet Kane; and *New Orleans Architecture, Volume III: The Cemeteries,* Mary Louise Christovich, editor.

Prologue

Sugar Anne was sitting on a trunk in the empty front parlor, a bottle of laudanum in one hand and a bottle of brandy in the other, trying to decide whether to take the permanent way out of her situation or merely the temporary one.

She wasn't concerned about the letter that had arrived a short time before. She knew no one in New Orleans, nor did she recognize the handwriting on the envelope. Besides, she had other, more important considerations at present.

Outside a sharp-featured man from the Pinkerton Agency was watching the house. Why wouldn't those detectives believe her? Despite some silly file they had found in Edward's office, she knew nothing of his whereabouts. Nothing.

A voice called to her from the back of the house.

"I'm here," she answered, getting up and moving toward the caller.

Beatrice Ralston, her next-door neighbor and dearest friend in Chicago, beckoned her to the back hall. "Oh, Sugar Anne, I've just returned from Connecticut. Has everything been taken?"

"Everything. The house, the furniture, everything that Edward didn't steal. I'm left with only a few trunks of clothing and some personal mementos." She fell weeping into her friend's arms. "Oh, Bea, I've never been so glad to see anyone in my life. Dear God, I'm so lost and alone, and I don't know where to turn. I've become a pariah to my friends. There doesn't seem to be a soul who doesn't believe that I was involved in Edward's scheme. They think I'm to blame for their losing money in his fraudulent railroad stock business."

The words of comfort that she expected from Bea didn't come. Instead, her dear friend stiffened noticeably and moved from the embrace. "I'm sure that you'll come out all right. You were always resourceful. Even back in boarding school, you always seemed able to wiggle out of every jam you got yourself into. Don't you have relatives in Texas or somewhere?"

She was surprised by Bea's cool tone. "There's a cousin in Galveston, but I haven't heard from her in years. She may be dead by now. I was hoping that perhaps you—"

"Sugar Anne, I feared that you might expect more from me than I'm able to give. That's why I defied Robert and sneaked in the back way just now. You can't expect any help from me. He's forbidden me to consort with you, or even speak to you."

Stunned, Sugar Anne could only stare at the person she thought was her true friend. *"Forbidden?"*

Bea's cheeks reddened, and she glanced away.

"Surely Robert doesn't think that I'm a part of Edward's swindle?" When Bea didn't answer, what was left of Sugar Anne's heart almost broke. "Surely *you* don't think that I would deceive my friends, steal from investors?"

"Sugar Anne, what Robert and I feel is not the issue. Robert is president of the bank, and Robert says that our reputation must be above reproach. Robert says that a great many people are tarring you with the same brush as Edward. Why, Robert says that the Pinkerton Agency suspects—"

"Robert says! Robert says! What do *you* say, Bea?"

When Bea didn't answer right away, fury flashed over Sugar Anne. "Do you honestly believe that I have been a party to this duplicity? Don't you remember that while I was confined to bed with a terrible cough and a raging fever, Edward—the sorry scoundrel that I was idiotic enough to marry—not only stole my entire inheritance, but also cleaned out the safe and my jewelry case, took my furs, the paintings, the silver, everything he could carry, and left in the middle of the night with his mistress? What he didn't take, now the creditors have. I'm left with nothing. Nothing. Not even my reputation. And I'm innocent of any wrongdoing. Totally innocent. I'm the biggest fool of all."

Bea studied her fingers, which were laced in a tight grip at her waist. "I'm sorry," she whispered, then turned and hurried out the way she'd come.

Sick at heart over Bea's defection, Sugar Anne suddenly realized that her last hope was gone. She had clung to the anticipation of Bea's return, confident that her friend would help her in this time of despair. Now she grasped the depth of Bea's disloyalty; the moment the news had broken about Edward's embezzlement and flight from Chicago, Bea had "an emergency" and had to leave for Connecticut to care for her critically ill mother. Sugar Anne would wager her last pair of silk stockings that Bea's mother had never so much as sneezed.

"You snotty, self-righteous coward," she yelled after Bea. "You're a sorry excuse for a friend."

Energized by her anger, Sugar Anne stalked back into the parlor where the bottles of laudanum and brandy sat on her trunk.

"Hell and damnation!" she shouted. "Damn your conniving heart, Edward Allen Herndon!" Snatching up the brandy bottle, she hurled it against the wall. It smashed into smithereens, splashing liquor in a pungent, dripping stain on the wallpaper. "And damn you, Grandfather Jacob, for manipulating me into marrying the lying, thieving, whoring bastard!" The laudanum bottle followed. "And damn all my family for dying and leaving me alone! Damn! Damn! Damn!"

She fell to her knees, buried her face in her hands and wept.

A few minutes later, when the knocker pounded at the front door, Sugar Anne started at the harsh, hollow sound reverberating through the empty house.

Dashing the tear traces from her cheeks, she strode to the door ready to give that detective a piece of her mind if he'd come to harass her again. Instead of the detective, Mrs. Chapman's brother, Alfred, stood there. If not for Cora Chapman, her former housekeeper, Sugar Anne would have been in a more dire predicament. Warm, wonderful Mrs. Chapman, who had gone to run a boarding house for another of her brothers, had taken in Sugar Anne as a tenant. At least she had food and a temporary bed.

Alfred doffed his cap. "Ma'am, Cora said there was trunks to be fetched."

"Yes, thank you." Sugar Anne stood aside while the burly man entered. "These three and one in the parlor."

She waited stoically as Alfred loaded the trunks onto his empty beer wagon. When he offered her a hand up to the driver's seat, she thanked him as graciously as if he had been assisting her into the grandest carriage, for he was a kinder man than any of the fine gentlemen on Prairie or Michigan Avenues.

Somehow, some way, I'm going to find you, Edward Herndon, and make you pay for what you've done!

Head held high as the beer wagon rumbled down Grand Boulevard, Sugar Anne made her exit from Chicago society.

⋐ One ⋑

Oh, no. Please, no.

Her heart hammering wildly, Sugar Anne Spicer Herndon—no, not Herndon, her mind must erase that despicable name from hers—crouched in the shadow of wooden crates stacked alongside the Dallas depot. Her shallow breath sent quick puffs of vapor into the chill drizzle of the gray dawn.

The train, ready for boarding, hissed great billows of steam that hung low, turned the engine's wheels into hazy outlines, and crept across the platform toward her hiding place. The handle of a small leather satchel, containing various essentials, including the last of her money, her ticket, and the letter, was looped securely about the wrist of her black-gloved hand. That same hand was pressed against the top frog of her black coat trying to hold back the panic building inside her; the other hand gripped a heavy tapestry valise and her black umbrella with the ebony wood shaft.

It *had* been the Pinkerton man she'd seen sitting in the restaurant adjacent to the depot. She was sure of it. He'd had the same underslung jaw, the same sharp nose and prominent Adam's apple as one of the men who'd harassed her for weeks. He had reminded her of nothing so much as a weasel in gold-rimmed spectacles.

How could the Pinkerton man possibly have followed her here? She'd been so careful to lay false trails. She'd brought along only a few indispensable items, leaving her other belongings in trunks for Mrs. Chapman to ship to Mrs. La Vigne, her grandmother's cousin in Galveston. Sugar Anne had cautiously spent an extra day in St. Louis and another in Dallas, hoping that anyone who might be on her trail would assume that one of the towns was her final destination.

Remembering the seedy rooming establishment she'd just left, with its smells of cows and cabbage and crawling with who knew what kind of vermin, she shuddered. If her funds hadn't been so desperately low, Sugar Anne would have never sought out a place frequented by such loud, coarse-talking people, mostly men. Even with the washstand pushed against the door, she had been too terrified to sleep there. Instead, she'd spread a shawl over the lumpy mattress and lay staring at the water-stained ceiling, napping in short fits until departure time.

Why wouldn't those blasted Pinkerton agents leave her alone? Why did they keep hounding her? Why wouldn't they believe her when she told them that she didn't know where the money was?

Lifting her widow's veil for a better view, Sugar Anne peered around the crude board boxes and into the gloom. Squinting, she searched the dreary mist and watched each passenger board the train. The bespectacled weasel was not among them. Perhaps she was only imagining that she had seen him. Slumping against the crates, she breathed a sigh.

If she could only get to Galveston undetected, Trista La Vigne, her last remaining relative, would help her. And as badly as she hated to admit defeat, Sugar Anne desperately needed help. She was too exhausted to run any longer.

Her stomach grumbled.

And too hungry, she added. She had skipped dinner the previous evening so that she might have a hearty breakfast before the train departed. Now even that had been denied her.

A match scraped across a rough plank and flared. Sugar Anne startled, and her head shot up.

"You need some help, ma'am?"

Only his deep Texas drawl was comforting to ears long grown accustomed to hearing clipped speech. Everything else about him, from his boots to his wide-brimmed black hat, was big, dark, and menacing. He was too close, much too close.

He held the match to his thin cigar, and the light from the flame revealed his face, or what could be seen of it. He wore a full black mustache and had the beginnings of a beard, not a neatly trimmed beard of the sort Edward had worn, but a scruffy dark mess that simply hadn't been acquainted with a razor in a week or more. His hat was pulled low, and his light eyes squinted against the cigar smoke.

"Ma'am," he repeated, "you need any help?" He flicked out the match and tossed it aside.

She drew herself up into her best finishing-school posture. "And why would you presume to think I needed any assistance, sir?"

"I reckon it was because you were squatted down

behind those plow crates looking like a cornered rabbit. And it's part of my job to notice such goings-on." He lifted his hat. "Webb McQuillan, ma'am. Captain, Texas Rangers." He resettled his hat and drew back his coat to reveal a silver star on his vest.

Sugar Anne didn't know whether to be panicked or relieved. Everyone knew of the Texas Rangers' rough, tough reputation. At least he wasn't a Pinkerton detective, but had the Texas law enforcement agencies been alerted? Surely not. She was a long way from Chicago.

"Captain McQuillan." She nodded curtly and thought quickly. "Sir, the reason that I was . . . being discreet is that an unsavory gentleman seemed to be following me, and as a woman traveling alone, I was concerned. I believe that I've eluded him. Now, if you'll excuse me, I have to board the train."

"I'll see you safely aboard, ma'am." The tall Ranger threw scarred saddlebags over his shoulder, plucked Sugar Anne's valise from her hand, and offered his arm.

Short of wrestling her bag from him, she had no alternative but to accept his offer. In case that *had* been the Pinkerton man she'd seen, she didn't dare draw attention to herself.

She made no comment as he escorted her to the train bound for Houston. When they reached the steps of the coach, Sugar Anne stopped. "Thank you very much, sir. I'll take my valise now."

"I'll carry it on for you, ma'am. It's right heavy."

Still hesitating to make a scene, she lifted her skirts and climbed aboard. The car was more than half full, but she easily found a seat, leaned her umbrella against the wall, then discreetly arranged her bustle and skirts, placed her satchel beside her, and settled in for the long day ahead. He stowed her valise near her feet, then tossed his saddlebags beside it. When he slipped into the seat facing hers, she sputtered, "But—but—you—"

He lifted his hat again and gave her a very fetching, lopsided grin. "We seem to be going the same way, ma'am. I hope you don't mind if I join you. We've been plagued with train robbers along this route."

"*Train robbers?* Oh, my dear aunt Minerva!"

"Now don't you get in a tizzy, ma'am. I'll see that you don't come to any harm." He fanned back his coat to display a pair of extremely large shiny guns, one strapped to each side. "That's part of my job, too." He smiled slightly, as if amused by her shock.

And she had to admit that she was shocked. For the past sixteen of her twenty-six years, she had been living in places more civilized than Texas. Gentlemen of her acquaintance didn't carry firearms. Now, worry about train robbers only added to her long list of troubles. She looked Webb McQuillan up and down, from his black boots to the guns on his slim hips to the hard expression in his rather handsome blue eyes. It struck her that Ranger McQuillan could handle a half dozen train robbers. Easily.

Sugar Anne nodded. "Thank you, Captain McQuillan. I am grateful to have you as a protector until we reach Houston."

"You have relatives in Houston?"

"No. But I—I have friends there."

After the train pulled away from the station, Sugar Anne breathed a soft sigh and relaxed. She hadn't seen the weasel board the train. Perhaps, at long last, she was free of her tormentors.

She opened her leather satchel and removed a small, cheaply printed booklet from inside. The night before, she'd found two dime novels discarded in her room and had decided to bring them along to pass the time. They weren't her usual reading fare, but they would do. The first one was about a marshal in a wild western town.

"Would you like something to read?" she asked, offering the novel to him. "I have another."

He glanced at the cover, scowled, and shook his head.

A thought struck her, and she was suddenly mortified. "Oh, dear, please excuse me. Do you not read?"

"I read." As if to prove it, he unbuckled his saddlebags and pulled out a bedraggled book, opened it, and began to peruse the pages.

Sugar Anne could hardly help but notice the title: *The Law of Real Property.* "Ah, I see that you're reading about the law. Do you plan on becoming an attorney?" She tried to keep the rancor from her voice. She despised attorneys. Edward was one, as his father before him had been. Seymour Brown, the cad who was supposed to protect her property from confiscation but seemed more in cahoots with the shysters after her home, was another. Slippery snakes, one and all.

"I'm not exactly sure, ma'am. I haven't stayed in one place long enough to get much formal schooling, so I take correspondence courses from time to time. Well . . . the truth is, I take them most of the time. Lately I've been studying law and business procedures."

"Correspondence courses? How does that work?"

Webb squirmed. None of his comrades knew of his

studies, though he'd been taking courses for almost ten years. "You sure you're interested in this, ma'am?"

"Certainly I'm interested. Tell me."

He shifted in his seat again. "Well, there's not much to tell. With my job and all, I can't enroll in a university like regular folks, so I've located several colleges and universities that offer courses for people like me who can't settle down and enroll to get a degree but still want a college education. A couple of the schools are here in Texas, but most of the courses I've taken come from universities in Boston and Chicago. Instead of going to classes, my professor sends me instructions by mail, and I read and study on my own, then send my lessons back to him by mail."

"Fascinating. Simply fascinating. How do you take examinations?"

He shrugged. "If it's for a college in Texas, sometimes I go to the school if I'm able. Otherwise, I do those by mail too."

"Why, that's wonderful." She leaned forward and patted his arm. "Just wonderful. And at your age too. I've been thinking of returning to my studies as well. The exploits of Miss Clara Barton and Miss Florence Nightingale and Miss Amelia Bloomer absolutely fascinate me. I might become a teacher or a nurse . . . or perhaps even a doctor or an explorer—why not, I say? When I was a young girl, I—Excuse me, sir. I'm babbling." She turned and focused her attention out the window at the monotonous passing scenery.

"When you were a young girl—?" he prompted.

She laughed nervously and waved off the comment.

"No, tell me. I'd like to know, Miz— Ma'am, I don't recall you mentioning your name."

"Spicer. I'm Mrs. Spicer." She chuckled again and leaned forward to whisper, "When I was a girl, no more than twelve, I wanted desperately to run away with the circus and become an acrobat. I wanted to travel and have exciting adventures. Unfortunately, I'm too old for such things now." She returned her attention to the passing scenery; he opened his book and began to read.

After a few moments Webb looked up from the page to study the woman across from him. Exactly how old was she? Although he couldn't see any more than a vague hint of her features behind that black veil hanging over her fancy hat brim, he knew for a fact that she was a young woman. Sturges had told him that. She was young and pretty with brownish eyes and reddish hair. In fact, he had a small photograph of her in his vest pocket.

Dead tired from a sleepless night, Webb yawned. He set aside his law book, tipped his hat over his eyes, and slunk down in his seat. He needed to catch a few winks while he could. It would be a while before the train stopped, so she wasn't going anywhere. But just in case she decided to pull a fast one, he propped his boots on her valise. Though his makeshift bed was a far cry from the feather one he'd always longed for, Webb had slept in worse places most of his life. Much worse.

"Captain McQuillan," she whispered just as he was dozing off.

He opened one eye. "Yes, ma'am?"

"Are we truly likely to encounter train robbers?"

What was he to tell her now? Except for the one last

month, there hadn't been a robbery in this area for several years. But with the bad drought in '83 and the beef market dropping all to hell last year, a passel of cowboys were out looking for work where there was none to be found. Already a rash of rustling had broken out. It was only a matter of time before the hungry and idle boys turned to bigger kinds of meanness. "I reckon it's always better to be prepared, but odds are that we won't run into any trouble."

She leaned forward, the paper novel pressed against her breast. "How can we be prepared? Exactly what should I do if we're held up?"

"Keep your head down, especially if there's any shootin'. Get under the seat if you can. That's about the safest cover around. Usually train robbers aren't interested in killing passengers; they're after valuables."

"Valuables?" she asked shakily.

"Money, jewelry, watches, and such. It's best for a woman not to argue with a robber. Just hand over your valuables without a fuss."

"Without a fuss?"

"Yes, ma'am. Don't make a nervous man with a gun any more nervous."

She sat back in her seat, looked around furtively, then eased her leather satchel under her skirts. Exactly what was she carrying in that bag? Webb wondered. He'd have to check it out first chance he got.

He closed his eyes again.

Sugar Anne's stomach grumbled. Loudly.

Hoping that none of the other passengers had heard, she pressed her hand against her abdomen, trying to quell the noises. There wasn't a dining car on this train. She had asked the conductor earlier. But they would be stopping soon for dinner, the term the gentleman had used for the noon meal. She'd purchased an apple from the news butcher, but it had only blunted her hunger for a short while.

To check the time, she automatically touched the place on her bodice where her watch was always pinned. The watch was missing, of course. She'd sold it in Chicago, along with her pearls, the silver-backed brushes she'd bought for Edward's birthday gift, and the few other things that Edward had missed in his hasty flight. The watch had still been pinned to the dress she'd worn the day before, the pearls were at the jewelers for repair, and the brushes were wrapped and hidden in the attic.

If her gold wedding ring hadn't been on her finger, the scoundrel would probably have taken that as well; he had purloined all her other lovely jewelry. That floozy he'd run off with was probably wearing it now. When she thought of her grandmother's diamond brooch and earrings or her mother's emerald ring, she wanted to weep. And curse.

Damn that vile man! Why had she ever listened to her grandfather's dying plea to marry him? She would have been better off alone than with Edward. If it was the last thing she did in her life on this earth, she meant to track him down and make him pay. That letter she'd received from New Orleans had been a godsend. Edward was probably gone by now, but at least she knew where to begin her search.

But first, she had to get to Galveston and borrow money from Mrs. La Vigne. The two gold eagles and three nickels in her coin purse were all she had left, those coins and her gold wedding ring—which she planned to dispose of as soon as her masquerade as a widow ended. And she still had to buy food and her train ticket to Galveston.

She tucked her satchel more securely under her skirts and willed her stomach to cease its growling.

Sugar Anne had never tasted anything more wonderful than the pot roast, mashed potatoes, black-eyed peas, and slabs of corn bread dripping with butter. And she hadn't eaten pickled okra in years. It was delicious. She barely looked up from her plate until it was cleaned.

"I like to see a hearty eater," the robust waitress said as she whisked away Sugar Anne's plate. The woman, who appeared to be about forty or so, winked as she plunked a bowl on the table. "Peach cobbler and cream."

Embarrassed that she'd been gobbling down her food, Sugar Anne glanced across the table at Webb, who was smiling that amused little smile.

"I was right hungry myself." He leaned back, crossed his arms, and continued to watch her while his plate was cleared and cobbler placed before him. His smile grew wider.

Blast him! He was laughing at her. She lifted her chin and glared. "I would prefer, sir, that you didn't stare at me as if I had a bee on my nose."

He seemed to struggle to compose his face. He didn't achieve his aim. "Sorry, ma'am." He grabbed his spoon and began devouring his dessert.

As did she. More politely, of course.

They were sitting at a corner table with the captain's

back to the wall—a custom of the West according to the
dime novel she'd just read—and her back to the rest of
the patrons, which had worked out perfectly since she
had to lift her veil to eat. She preferred not to show her
face publicly any more than necessary, in case the Pinkertons managed to trace her journey beyond Dallas—if,
indeed, she hadn't mistaken their man, Sturges, she believed the weasel's name was.

When she glanced up again, the Ranger's bowl was
empty, his arms were crossed, and he was staring at her
once more. And grinning. Mrs. Effington, the old pinch-
mouthed headmistress at the Penworthy Female Academy, had instructed Sugar Anne, on the many occasions
when she had been called in for a stern lecture, that grinning was low and vulgar behavior. The following year,
Sugar Anne had been dismissed from Penworthy for
"riotous and rebellious conduct." Rather than feeling dis-
graced, she had been ecstatic to have gained her release
from "The Pen," a horrible place, the first in a string of
such places, each more severe than the last. Now, for the
first time in all the years since, she began to see merit in
Mrs. Effington's stinging words.

"Pray tell me, sir, what do you find so amusing
about me?"

"Those freckles across your nose. You don't look any
more than fifteen years old."

"Captain, I can assure you that I am a grown woman, a
decade and more past fifteen, and I find your comments
about my complexion extremely rude." She jerked her
veil back into place and started to rise.

He caught her hand. "Beg pardon, Miz Spicer. I didn't

mean any disrespect. Those freckles are cuter than a speckled pup."

"A *speckled pup*? Sir, I don't find that description any less impolite."

"Sorry. That's a common saying around here, and it's a true compliment. I think you're a right pretty lady. It's just that I hadn't seen you without that cover over your face, and I figured that you were older."

"I see." She picked up her satchel and removed her coin purse.

"Oh, no, ma'am. At least let me buy your dinner to make up for hurting your feelings."

"Lunch. Breakfast, lunch, and dinner at night. And thank you very much, although my feelings aren't hurt."

"Dinner. In these parts we have breakfast, dinner, and supper—if we're able to grab any grub a'tall—and I'm mighty glad your feelings aren't hurt."

The lanky Ranger rose from his chair and picked up his hat. He escorted her across the room and paid for their meal, and they went outside to walk a bit and "stretch their legs" as he said. In a few minutes they would begin the last segment of the fifteen- or sixteen-hour journey from Dallas to Houston. Sugar Anne's back, already exceedingly sore from her Chicago to Dallas jaunt, ached more with every mile. How she longed to travel in the kind of private compartment she had once taken for granted.

Well into the evening and long after the coach lamps had been lit against the dark, Sugar Anne awakened from her doze. The train had stopped. Although she was wearing her coat and had retrieved a woolen shawl from her valise for additional warmth, still she was chilled. How she yearned for her fur muff and lap blanket. Edward's paramour was probably wearing Sugar Anne's lovely warm muff this very minute. She shivered.

"Cold?" the Ranger asked.

"Yes. Very. I expected Texas to be warmer this time of year."

"Usually is. But Texas weather is unpredictable, except in July and August when it's always hotter than— 'Scuse me, ma'am. Summers in Texas are hot. Real hot. A norther blew through yesterday and brought the temperature down a right smart and put a nip in the air. Things will warm up in a day or two."

She hoped so. The clothes she wore were the warmest she owned. Edward had taken her sable coat *and* her fox cape. She tucked her fingers under her arms. "Did the stove go out?"

"No, but the fuel's low. We'll take more on here at this station."

"Oh," Sugar Anne said, craning her neck to see out the window. Steam from the engine, expanding into thick clouds against the frigid air, obscured her view of the lamplit surroundings. "Have we stopped for dinner?"

"Supper. I understand that we're running behind some, and they'll be bringing boxed suppers aboard for the passengers."

Sugar Anne noticed that a few people had gotten off the train and several others had boarded. Indeed they had picked up boxed meals, which were passed out shortly after they pulled away from the station. Extra fuel had been added to the stove, and the coach was soon warm enough for her to remove her gloves to eat.

"This looks very tasty," she said, peering inside the box at the food. She found two pieces of fried chicken, a biscuit, a large pickle, and a fried apple pie of the sort she hadn't eaten since she was a little girl in Galveston. Before her mother and father and grandmother and little brother, Jonathan, had died of yellow fever. Before Grandfather Jacob had sent her away to the first boarding school, when she was only ten years old.

Using a handkerchief for a napkin, she ate the chicken and the pickle but saved the biscuit and tart for breakfast. Captain McQuillan was kind enough to allow her to wrap these in a sheet of his newspaper. Even though she was drawing near her destination, she was still careful with her spending. One never knew what one might encounter in these parts.

The captain seemed little concerned with saving any of his meal until morning, for he was merrily munching on his fried pie when Sugar Anne glanced up.

And gasped.

She was staring down the barrel of a very large and very nasty-looking revolver.

⌒ TWO ⌒

When Mrs. Spicer screamed and dove for the floor, Webb dropping his pie and, cursing, went for his Colts; but the blamed woman, her head under the seat and her bustle in the air, had wrapped her arms around his ankles in a death grip. Before he could clear leather, he lost his balance and pitched forward on his nose. That's when the pair of train robbers started shooting, bullets began whistling past his coattail, and he lost control of the situation.

Cursing some more as he untangled his feet, Webb stood to face the bandits he'd let get the drop on him. He recognized the taller of the two as a cowboy suspected of rustling cattle in Tarrant County a few months back. With a scar across his eyebrow and another running from the side of his bottom lip to his chin, the trail-worn cowpuncher fit the description exactly. Ugly devil. Pete Beavers his name was. Rumor had it that he'd killed four or five men and was meaner than a javelina hog. The other one was a tow-headed kid who didn't look like he shaved yet. They were both nervous.

The boy stuck his gun against Webb's chin, which was about as far up as he could reach. "Don't even blink, mister, or you're dead. Unbuckle them guns and hand 'em over."

A strangled sound came from the floor behind him, and Mrs. Spicer grabbed at his ankles again. Thank the Lord he was able to free at least one leg before she got a good hold on it.

The boy's shaking gun poked Webb's chin, and his voice broke as he said, "Unbuckle them guns, I said. Right now."

Webb frowned. The last thing he wanted to do was hand over his Colts to this snot-nosed kid. His hand feinted to his holster buckle, then swooped upward. In one quick motion he grabbed the shaking gun and laid the butt hard beside the kid's head.

The boy crumpled to the floor, but Pete Beavers was smarter. Pete had snatched an old woman out of her seat and was holding her in front of him as a shield. His gun barrel was against her temple, and he stood too far away for Webb to do anything.

"Drop the shootin' iron and your own rig of .45s, mister, or granny here gets it," Beavers snarled.

The old lady began praying, and Mrs. Spicer tightened her grip on his leg. Worse, the boot that she clung to was the one with his four-shot house pistol in it.

"Come on," Beavers said. "I haven't got all day."

Reluctantly, Webb tossed the kid's gun on the seat and began to unbuckle his gun belt. He figured that this mangy rascal and the boy weren't the only bandits on the train. Usually their kind rode in gangs. Most of the men had probably hit the baggage car that held the safe, and a couple of others would be in control of the engine by now, with maybe another pair in the next car.

His eyes locked on Beavers and the old woman, Webb carefully laid his rig and peacemakers on the seat, but still within reach, and tried to shake Mrs. Spicer off his leg. She hung on tighter'n a cocklebur.

"All you ladies and gents, have your cash and your watches and your gold rings and geegaws ready when I pass amongst you," Pete Beavers said loudly. "And don't you go holdin' out on me neither." To Webb he said, "I'll start with you two. And don't twitch a whisker. Tell that woman to get up off the floor and open up her satchel."

"Miz Spicer?" Webb shook the leg she still clung to. "I think you ought to get up now."

She didn't budge.

He didn't know if she was stubborn as a mule or just plain scared to death. He tapped her shoulder. "Miz Spicer, you best get up before there's more trouble."

Still no movement.

Dammit, he'd told her not to make a nervous man with a gun any more nervous. Pete Beavers was worse than nervous: he was a mean son of a bitch. Some of the passengers could get hurt—hurt bad.

"She doesn't seem to be paying any attention to me," Webb said to the outlaw. "Maybe she's fainted."

Beavers's eyes narrowed. "Fainted my eye. I'll get her up." He shoved the old lady aside, strode across the aisle, and kicked Mrs. Spicer's rump. "Get up, woman, or I'm gonna shoot that bustle clean off your backside."

Webb took a menacing step forward, but before he could open his mouth, Mrs. Spicer, her umbrella clutched in both hands, came up off the floor like a swarm of mad hornets.

"How dare you, you nasty worm!" She whacked

Beavers's gun arm with a mighty stroke of her umbrella, and his revolver went flying. "I'll not give up my valuables to you!" She launched into the outlaw and thrashed him solidly about the head. "No man is getting the best of me again! Ever! Ever! Ever!" She punctuated each word with another whack of her demon umbrella or a smart jab with the tip of the shaft.

Beavers alternately protected his head with one arm—the other one looked broken—and tried to pick up his gun.

Webb kicked it out of the outlaw's reach, then snatched up his own .45, grabbed Mrs. Spicer around the waist, and pulled her back before she got hurt. "Whoa, ma'am. Easy now. I've got him covered."

Three of the male passengers rushed forward to help as the train slowed to a crawl. "You men tie up these two," Webb said as he strapped on his gun belt. "I'm going to check the baggage car."

When Webb got there, he found two men dead, the safe blown, and the money gone. The robbers were gone too. They'd probably hightailed it on hidden horses when the train slowed. Dammit! Afoot, Webb would never be able to catch them.

Starting back to the passenger car, he noticed a burning in his right flank. It smarted every time he took a step. He put his hand to the spot; it came away bloody. Dammit! He'd been hit earlier and hadn't even realized it.

What a hell of a note—getting shot in the butt *now*. He'd taken a few bullets before, and he figured that this wasn't much more than a graze, but it sure was a damned inconvenient time. Besides ruining his best pair of britches, it had thrown a kink in his plans.

No—hell no. Webb wasn't about to let a little crease in his hide foul up his big opportunity. He was determined to find that pile of money that had been pilfered from those highfalutin Chicago fellows. Still stinging from the railroad stock scam, the irate investors were offering a big reward through the Pinkerton Agency, and Webb meant to collect it.

The reward was a whole lot more than he'd made in his dozen years with the Rangers. It was plenty to buy a business in town, a snug white house, and that feather bed he'd been hankering for since he was a kid. He'd even have enough left over to put some more in the Waco bank and buy a sweet little gal a pretty gold ring like the one Mrs. Spicer—Herndon, rather—wore on her finger.

Yes, sirree. He meant to stick tight to that young woman until she led him to her husband—and the funds he'd absconded with. And he wasn't about to let those cute little freckles or that pretty smile or any other of her attractions deter him.

The Pinkertons were sure that Mrs. Herndon knew more than she let on. They figured that the wife would hang around Chicago for a while, acting all aggrieved and innocent, then meet Mr. Herndon somewhere.

Webb had taken leave from rangering to go after that reward. If he collected it, he'd turn in his star and settle down. He was thirty years old, and he hadn't had a real family or a place to call his own since he was five, since that summer when the Comanche raided his folks' place and—

He clenched his teeth and shook off the memory. He wasn't much of one to dwell on the past.

* * *

Sugar Anne saw the captain when he entered the car. She'd been watching for him. His face wore a pained, angry expression, even more harsh than usual. The conductor met him, and they exchanged a few words before the Ranger returned to his place. He took his seat and resettled his hat lower on his brow.

She leaned forward and asked quietly, "What did you find?"

"Safe blown, robbers gone. You faring all right?"

"I'm perfectly fine, thank you, sir. Except for my umbrella. Two of the ribs are bent."

"The way you went after that ol' boy, I'm surprised the thing held together."

"I'm not surprised at all. The umbrella shaft is made of ebony, one of the hardest woods in the world. It belonged to my grandfather, you see, and he always said that he'd repelled many a wharf ruffian with it. I'm only thankful that Ed—I mean, I'm thankful that I brought it along for protection. The ribs can be repaired easily."

"Hard wood or not, there was a lot of muscle behind those blows—surprising for a little slip of a lady like you. Sure stunned old Pete Beavers."

"I'm stronger than I look. I play tennis regularly—that is, I used to play often."

"Tennis?"

"Yes. I find that regular exercise keeps the body fit and the mind sharp. Pete Beavers, you say? Did you know that awful man?"

"No, ma'am. But I've seen a couple of posters on him."

"Posters?"

"Yes, ma'am. Wanted posters."

"What is he wanted for?"

"Rustling. Robbing. Murder."

"Murder?" Sugar Anne felt the blood drain from her face and her heart almost leap from her bosom.

"Yes, ma'am. I expect that you can file for the reward once we get to Houston."

"Reward?" Sugar Anne perked right up. "What sort of reward? And why would *I* file for it?"

"You're the one who brought Beavers down."

"I *did*? I don't recall that."

"Yes, ma'am, you did."

"I was so livid when that ruffian wanted to take my few dollars that I simply couldn't contain myself. I merely gave him a few good smacks with Grandfather Jacob's umbrella. Perhaps I contributed to his downfall, but I certainly didn't bring him down, not by myself."

The Ranger shrugged. "I'd say you had the biggest part in capturing him. Truth is, you licked the fire out of ol' Pete with that umbrella. The rest of us just helped a little after he was whipped. And the reward will be cash money, though I don't recall the exact amount. Couple of hundred dollars, I suspect. And I wouldn't be surprised if the railroad didn't throw a little something in the pot as well."

"Really?" She sat up straighter, and despite her efforts to squelch it, a big grin spread across her face, a grin so broad that Mrs. Effington would have surely suffered apoplexy had she seen it. Thankfully her veil was in place, concealing her vulgar behavior from genteel eyes.

"Yes, ma'am. 'Course, it will take a few weeks for you to collect—with the paperwork and all. If you'll give me the address where you're going, I'll file on the reward and have the money sent along to you."

Her grin died. Damnation! She wasn't about to give cousin Trista's address—nor any other address to which she might be traveling—to a Texas Ranger. But she surely could use the extra funds. And soon.

"Thank you very kindly, sir," she said sweetly, surprised to hear the hint of a drawl returning to her speech, "but I wouldn't think of troubling you."

"No trouble a'tall." He smiled and tipped his hat.

"You're very gracious, but I prefer to handle my own business. Did you know that the conductor was tied up during the robbery? He was. One of the gentlemen who came to our aid discovered him in some sort of closet in the next car. When the conductor was freed, they all took those trussed-up outlaws and tossed them into the same place. They'll stay locked up until we reach Houston. How long do you suppose it will take us to get there?"

The Ranger looked at his pocket watch. "I'd guess three hours."

"That long?"

"Yes, ma'am. Maybe longer."

The conductor approached the captain, and they held a whispered conversation. How rude, Sugar Anne thought. What were they discussing? She was too well-mannered to ask, but she did see several other passengers craning necks and staring at the two men. Obviously the others were as curious as she.

Every eye was on the conductor as he strode to the front of the car, turned, and announced, "Ladies and gents, the D&H Railroad offers its apologies for any upset you suffered from the recent events. Don't worry, though. You have no more reason for worry. Everything is under control. But because of our troubles and needin' to toss those sidewinders that were captured in the jailhouse, we're traveling straight to Houston with all due speed and no stops along the way. Near's I recollect, none of you was plannin' to get off before then anyways. That right?" When nobody spoke up, he gave a curt nod of his head and strode out the door.

Sugar Anne blew out a tiny puff of air, then said quietly to the Ranger captain, "I must say, this journey has been very exciting thus far. Do you know if anyone was injured during the robbery?"

The captain cleared his throat and repositioned his hat low over his eyes. "Don't believe that I heard the conductor mention anything about any of the passengers getting hurt."

Catching the slight evasion in his words, Sugar Anne narrowed her eyes. "Was anyone else injured? What did you find in the baggage car, Captain?"

"Safe blown, robbers gone."

"There must have been guards or train employees there. What about them?"

He resettled his hat again. "Well, ma'am, a couple of men came to some grief."

"Grief? Do you mean—?"

"Yes, ma'am."

"Oh, dear. Texas still seems to be as wild as people say. Perhaps I should have purchased a firearm of my own before I came."

"I don't know about that, ma'am, but I do know that it's not a smart idea for a lady to travel alone. Most parts of Texas are real civilized nowadays, but there are still some mean customers around who're up to no good. But I expect that Texas isn't the only place where you'll find such meanness. I've heard tales about goings-on in New York City and Chicago and St. Louis that would near 'bout curl your— Beg pardon, ma'am. I didn't mean to run on. Maybe you ought to rest a bit before we reach Houston."

The hat came down over his eyes, and Sugar Anne sensed that the conversation was closed—which was just dandy with her. She hoped to find a decent place to spend the night in Houston and had no desire to have her sleep interrupted by nightmares.

However, the evening's events had given her an excellent idea. Before she set out on the last stage of her search for Edward, she meant to arm herself with more than an umbrella. She would purchase a gun as soon as she arrived in Galveston—and learn how to use it.

Sugar Anne stifled another yawn as the train pulled into the station. From the captain's posture, she deduced that he was sleeping, so she leaned forward and touched his shoulder to rouse him.

He clamped a hand on her wrist and had his gun between her eyes before she could draw a startled breath. His face was pale, damp, and menacing. She suspected that at that moment her own looked the same—at least the pale and damp part.

"Captain! It's me! Sugar Anne Spicer!"

"Sorry, ma'am." He returned his firearm to his holster. "Old habits die hard. It's best to call a Ranger's name to wake him."

"I'll certainly remember that advice for the future, though I doubt that I'll ever have the chance to use it."

She chafed her throbbing wrist. "I was just going to tell you, sir, that we're coming into the station."

His eyes looked a bit glazed as he sat up and glanced around. "So I see. Is someone meeting you, ma'am?"

"No. I wasn't precisely sure when I would be arriving, so I planned to take a carriage to my hotel."

"Me, too. If there's one to be had. Sugar Anne Spicer, you say. Interesting name."

Sugar Anne was so furious that she had inadvertently disclosed such personal information that she jumped to her feet. "Yes, er— Well, good-bye, sir." She tried to pick up her valise, but his tall boots were planted firmly atop it, and the blasted thing wouldn't budge.

"I'll carry your bag, ma'am," he said, tugging at the front brim of his hat, then standing. "But we'd best wait until the train comes to a full stop and the departure steps are down."

"Oh. Yes, of course. I was merely stretching a bit." She sat back down. It was then that she noticed the blood in the captain's seat. Thinking perhaps she was mistaken, she flipped back her veil and looked again. It was blood. Fresh blood. And a goodly amount of it.

"Captain! You're injured!"

"A scratch, ma'am. Nothin' to worry about."

"A scratch doesn't bleed that much." She stood and glanced around. "Conductor!"

"Pipe down, ma'am. He's busy. A bullet just grazed my hide. It's not the first time. Doesn't amount to a hill of beans." He waved her off.

Sugar Anne didn't buy his explanation for one second. She grabbed his elbow and turned him so she could look at his back. When she saw the bloodstain that crept down his trouser leg, she jerked up his coattail and gasped. "Captain, you're badly wounded! How did this happen?"

He jerked his coat back down and mumbled something.

"Pardon?"

He rolled his eyes and said, "It probably happened when you screamed and the robber commenced with his shooting. You had me by the ankles, and I kind of got overbalanced."

"Oh, dear. It's my fault."

"Oh, no, ma'am. I should have been paying less attention to that apple pie and more attention to business."

"You're just being kind, Captain McQuillan. I acted like an absolute ninny. Your injury must be tended to by a physician at once." She glanced around again. All the passengers had departed. "Conductor!"

"Shhh, ma'am. Don't go bothering him. I'm just fine." He tossed his saddlebags over his shoulder, picked up her valise, and escorted her from the car.

After the porter helped her down the steps, Sugar Anne turned to wait for the captain. Even in the flickering lamplight, she could see that his grim face was pale and perspiring.

"Captain, I feel simply terrible about your wound. I think that you should go directly to—"

"No need for that, ma'am," was the last thing Webb said before his knees buckled and he keeled over.

Three

Thinking she heard a moan from the big bed, Flora Lamb raised herself up on her cot and listened intently. Only the sound of Trista La Vigne's soft, slow breathing met her ears, that and the rustle of dry palm fronds outside their upstairs window.

Needing to be sure, Flora rose and turned up the lamp that glowed dimly on the side table rather than use the harsh brightness of the electric chandelier that Trista had had installed last year. Chill seeped into her bones and made her shiver. Flora hated to admit her progressing years—and never did so except for nights like this when she was alone with her maker and her thoughts, and when her joints ached. Rarely did nights grow so chilly on Galveston Island this early in the fall, but the last two had been damnably cold. Some kind of unusual front, she'd heard Donald O'Toole say. She prayed that the weather would soon warm since, despite all efforts to be frugal, their supply of coal for the furnace was dwindling fast.

She tiptoed to Trista's bed where her oldest and dearest friend—and former employer—lay. For all the world Trista looked as if she were sleeping peacefully on an ordinary night. But, alas, she had been sleeping for the past twenty-one days, half rousing only when Flora or Phoebe or Mary propped her up and coaxed her to swallow a few sips of nourishing broth or eggnog or such—which they did often. Even so, Trista had shed a considerable amount of weight—not that she couldn't stand to lose a few pounds.

Flora brushed the gray tendrils from Trista's forehead and felt for fever. Trista's brow was cool. She slept on.

Letting one of the tendrils curl around her finger, Flora remembered all those years ago in San Francisco when these gray locks were the color of burnished copper— and her own were a softer, more natural shade of gold than their current hue, which was augmented from a bottle purchased at Mr. Brunsen's pharmacy.

"Oh, those were the days, Trista," Flora whispered. "Those were the days. Do you remember that gent who was so smitten with me that he bought me a carriage and a smart pair of palomino horses that matched my hair? Wonder what ever happened to that gent? Or those horses? I'm afraid Donald won't be able to keep up your carriage and horses if something doesn't happen pretty soon."

These days Donald O'Toole and his wife, Mary, were a godsend. They'd been in service in a fancy lord's house in London, but the couple had come to America to buy a nice farm and start afresh. Alas, some fast-talking louse had scammed the pair out of everything they had before their ship docked in Galveston, and they were left almost destitute, with no choice but to go back into service.

Trista, bless her tender heart, had taken the stunned pair under her wing, and they now lived over the carriage house, working until they could save enough to purchase a bit of land of their own. Mary was a fine cook, and Donald, who'd been a stable master in England, was the man of all trades in their household. A fine couple they were, staying on to help even when the money dried up. They were like part of the family, as were Phoebe and Willie, two other desperate strays that Trista had gathered to her bosom. Then there was Mr. Underwood, whatever he was. And all of them needing to be fed.

Flora rearranged the long braid over Trista's shoulder, tucked the down comforter closely under her chin, and patted the form that lay so still.

"That Richard Fitzwarren is a sorry bastard, he is. If he has his way, you'll be in an asylum and the rest of us in the poorhouse before this is over. I don't know what to do, Trista. I don't know what to do. Sugar Anne's telegram to you, coming out of the clear blue like it did, is bound to be the answer to our prayers—and we've been praying like old Billy Rip. I know that you've been heartsick about losing track of her. How she learned about our temporary money problems, I don't know, but she's on her way to help out. She should be here any day now." Flora chuckled softly. Old Jacob Spicer would turn over in his grave if he knew what his granddaughter was doing.

"I hope you don't mind that I signed your name to the telegram I sent her," Flora whispered. "Don't you worry one little bit, Trista. Sugar Anne will get things straightened out when she gets here. She's a bright girl, always was a sharp one, and with a bit of spirit to her, too. Reminds me right smart of you." She patted her friend again, then went to stand at the window and look out into the darkness and pray some more.

In no more than a minute, the Lord began to fill her with courage, then filled her right up to the brim and overflowing. Things were going to turn out fine, she knew it. Just fine.

Why, for goodness' sake, they weren't going to starve— not with all the red-blooded and ready men overrunning Galveston. Although Trista might not approve the idea, Flora knew that she could always earn a few dollars if need be. It had been several years since she'd plied her trade, but, by gosh, hers was a skill that didn't get rusty.

Content in her newfound peace, she stole back to the cot and slipped into the warmth of her covers.

Feeling hot, Webb stirred beneath his covers and opened his eyes. Where was he?

He was in a soft bed. And he surely did enjoy sleeping in a soft bed. But where?

By the dim lamplight, he could make out lace curtains and walls papered with big pink roses. A hotel room. He vaguely remembered Mrs. Spicer and somebody else taking him to a hotel, the doctor being called.

Webb moved; his rear end throbbed and stung like he'd been sitting in a big nest of bull nettles. Seems like he recalled the doctor putting a couple of stitches in his backside.

Wasn't the first time he'd been sewed up. And for sure, he wasn't about to let a bit of stitchery keep him from tailing Mrs. Sugar Anne Spicer Herndon to that sorry husband of hers and locating the embezzled money from Chicago.

Mrs. Spicer! Where the hell was she?

Cursing under his breath, he sat straight up in bed,

ready to hit the floor running. Then he glanced over to the side of the room. Soft lamplight glowed beyond a cloth screen. And he could see a feminine silhouette bathing from a wash bowl.

A *very* feminine silhouette.

He saw shadows of curvy breasts and a tiny waist and hips that swelled provocatively. And when she propped one leg on a chair to smooth a cloth over its long, slender length, he couldn't help but groan under his breath.

Webb realized that he hadn't kept the groan to himself when the figure abruptly stilled. He watched her throw on a wrapper; quickly he lay back down and closed his eyes tight.

"Captain?" she whispered softly.

He played possum.

Her soft hand stroked his brow, and he couldn't hold the moan that escaped his lips.

"Oh, dear, you're burning with fever. You need to take some of the medicine the doctor left for you. He said that we must beware of infection. Captain?" She shook him lightly. "Captain?"

He groaned again and opened his eyes a slit. "Water," he managed to croak pitifully. "Water." Matter of fact, he didn't have to try too hard to sound pitiful. His mouth was drier than three bales of cotton, and he felt swimmy-headed and hotter than the hinges of hell.

Webb hoped that Mrs. Spicer was one of those soft-hearted women who wouldn't go off and leave him in his hour of need. He figured that if he played his part right and kept acting real sick and pathetic, he could stick to her tighter than a tick without rousing her suspicions.

Hadn't she said how she admired Florence Nightingale? Maybe getting shot in the butt wasn't all bad.

"Here you are, Captain. This should soothe your parched throat." She raised his head and held a cup to his lips.

He drank greedily. He even took the foul-tasting concoction that she spooned into his mouth without making too much commotion about it. Then he drank some more water.

She felt his forehead again, and he groaned again. Louder this time.

"Oh, dear, I'm afraid that your fever may be very high. I need to look at your wound."

Webb frowned. He felt around under the covers and along his flank, then frowned some more. He was buck naked with a bandage on his butt. "Ma'am, I don't think so."

"And why not?"

"It wouldn't be proper."

"Of course it would be proper. I told you that I once considered becoming a nurse."

"Ma'am, there's a mile of difference between considering and becoming."

"Oh, don't be silly, Captain. I've had training. I worked as a hospital volunteer for years. Don't worry, I have a strong constitution." She didn't add that her training consisted of a two-week course and that the hospital was one for indigent women and children. She started to tug down the covers.

"Ma'am!" He grabbed the quilt and held it tight under his chin. "Ma'am, I don't have any clothes on."

"Don't you think I know that? Who do you think

helped the doctor cut your bloody britches off last night?"

"My britches! You cut up my best pair of britches?"

"They were hardly salvageable, sir, with a large hole in the seat and soaked with blood. How else could we tend your wound if we didn't cut your trousers away?"

"We? Who is 'we'?"

"The doctor and I. I told him that I had a modest amount of experience in nursing, and he was delighted to have my assistance. And you'd best be happy that I was present, Captain McQuillan. It was *I* who insisted that he wash his hands in lye soap before cleaning and suturing your laceration. It was *I* who removed the cigar from his mouth before its long ashes dropped onto your raw flesh."

For a moment Webb was speechless. When the content of her babbling sunk in, he was mortified. He gripped the quilt tighter. "Do you mean that—that you . . . ?"

"I am well acquainted with your bare backside? Yes. I taped the bandage in place. Don't concern yourself, Captain: I have glimpsed the male posterior before, and yours is nothing extraordinary. I promised the doctor that I would nurse you and see to your wound, and I intend to do so. After all, if it weren't for me, you wouldn't be hurt. If that wound gets infected and starts oozing, you will be in too sorry a shape to ever sit a horse. Now please turn over."

Accepting that he had no reasonable alternative, Webb gritted his teeth and turned over. He wasn't quite sure which irritated him more: the fact that she had examined his backside or that she had found it unremarkable.

* * *

Sugar Anne was hard-pressed to explain how it had come about, but by midmorning she was seated on the train for Galveston—and Captain McQuillan was seated across from her, on a plump pillow provided by the railroad company. Well, she couldn't just leave him in a hotel with no one to look after him, could she? She had promised the doctor that she would see to the captain's nursing, but she had to be on her way. She'd had no choice but to bring him along.

Besides, she had wanted to file for the reward, and after that her destination was no secret. Feeling fairly confident that she had eluded the Pinkertons, Sugar Anne had given the authorities Trista's name and address so that any remuneration would be sent to her cousin to help repay the amount Sugar Anne planned to borrow from her.

And as for the captain accompanying her, it was, after all, her fault that the captain had been injured in the first place, and for all his protestations about being fit as a fiddle, she didn't like his color or the redness of his wound. Hadn't he needed her assistance to descend the stairs at the hotel, and even to climb the few steps into the railroad coach?

In Galveston the servants in her cousin's household could take proper care of him. Too, he seemed to have grown dependent on her. Why, the brave man became absolutely panicked when she suggested any alternative that would separate them.

The first time she mentioned leaving him, Sugar Anne had been mopping his fevered brow. He had grabbed her wrist and, looking positively wild-eyed, said, "You can't leave me alone. I don't trust anybody but you to take care of me." He had groaned loudly then, and—well, what was she to do?

The captain had called for a clerk and sent him to the nearest mercantile for a new pair of trousers. Then he'd banished her from the room while the clerk helped him dress—as if she hadn't already seen all of his backside that it was possible to see.

Sugar Anne sighed. Perhaps it had been wise. To tell the truth, she'd fibbed about his backside being nothing extraordinary. It was taut and muscled like the rest of him—and as remarkable. Not that she had had all that much experience with male backsides above the age of eight or so. Although she considered herself a progressive thinker about the normalcy of the human body and its functions, actually she'd only seen one other bare, adult male posterior up close: Edward's when she had once lanced a boil. The despicable poltroon had carried on something awful with only a simple prick from a sewing needle. Captain McQuillan had been marvelously stoic during his far more serious treatment. Anyway, from what she could recall, Edward's derrière had been rather soft and uninteresting.

When the train lurched, the captain sucked in his breath.

Sugar Anne asked, "Are you all right, sir?"

He stretched his lips over his teeth in a parody of a smile. "Right as rain, ma'am."

She frowned. Right as rain? Nonsense. Total nonsense. Anyone with eyes and half a brain could tell that the man was seriously ill. His face was ashen, his eyes bright with fever, and his fingers gripped the armrest of his seat so fiercely that the color had left his knuckles.

He ought not to have come. She should have stayed another day or so at the hotel with him. At this point, another day or two wouldn't have made a great deal of difference in her plans, and the captain had insisted on paying for their room and meal, so money wouldn't have been a problem.

It was too late now. They were on their way to Galveston, she without that blasted veil that had annoyed her half to death. Since the captain already had seen her face and since a new group of passengers would be on the train to the coast, she had ripped the dusty nuisance from her hat and thrust it into her valise. Before they departed, she had wired Trista of the time of her arrival, telling her that she was bringing along an invalid and asking for a carriage to meet them—more for Captain McQuillan than for herself. As she recalled from her childhood, Trista's large, lovely home was only a few blocks from the train station.

Sugar Anne settled back into her seat and allowed those forbidden memories to slip into her mind, memories of an elegant older woman whom she'd first met in the cemetery by her family's vault. Sugar Anne had often sneaked away from her governess to go to the cemetery on Broadway and place flowers from the garden there and talk to Grandmère, Mama, Papa, and Jon. She was so lonely and missed them so much.

Mrs. La Vigne had been placing flowers there too when Sugar Anne approached. Trista La Vigne turned out to be Grandmère's cousin. "Wonderful!" Sugar Anne had said. She'd thought that the yellow fever had taken all her family except Grandfather Jacob.

Sugar Anne had talked with her newfound cousin for

quite a while and taken an immediate liking to her. But when she mentioned Mrs. La Vigne to her grandfather, he had flown into such a rage that she thought he might explode or drop dead on the spot. She was never, *never* to talk to that woman again, he had fumed.

When she had asked why, Grandfather Jacob had slapped her. Actually slapped her. She was so stunned that she'd merely stood there and stared at him. He was instantly contrite. She could see in his expression that he was horrified by what he'd done; though stern, her grandfather was not a physically violent man. In any case, he mumbled something about abominations and black sheep and demanded that Sugar Anne walk on the other side of the street if she ever saw that creature again.

Sugar Anne didn't see Mrs. La Vigne for several weeks, but when she did, she didn't cross the street. She waved, and they stopped to talk, then went to the ice cream parlor for a dish of strawberry ice cream.

After that they met frequently for a dish of ice cream—every Thursday afternoon after Sugar Anne's piano lesson. She grew very fond of her grandmother's cousin, who had a soothing voice and a lilting laugh and often told stories about when she and Grandmère were girls in New Orleans. Sugar Anne always ate her ice cream very slowly to draw out her time with Cousin Trista.

Unfortunately, one Thursday afternoon, Grandfather Jacob happened to pass by the shop and glimpse inside. Sugar Anne had seen him as well and sat paralyzed as he stalked inside and jerked her up from her chair. He didn't even acknowledge Mrs. La Vigne's presence as he marched Sugar Anne from the shop.

From that moment on, someone watched Sugar Anne every moment, even when she went to the cemetery. And shortly after that, she was sent to the Penworthy Female Academy and Mrs. Effington. She'd never quite forgiven her grandfather for that.

As a child she had loved Galveston Island. Now, when the train rolled onto the high trestle bridge with the choppy waters of the bay surrounding them on all sides, Sugar Anne became exhilarated rather than nervous. Every chug of the engine said, *Going home. Going home. Going home.*

Memories flooded her, wonderful flashes of memories that pierced her heart and made her breath catch.

Smells of cinnamon cookies and her mother's sachets and the salty air. The cries of wheeling seagulls. Laughter and warm sand between her toes. Jon's plump cheeks and shining eyes as he squealed with delight dashing from a wave or glimpsing the flutter of a butterfly's wings on Grandmère's roses. Riding on Papa's broad shoulders and snuggling in Mama's bed to drink cups of steaming chocolate as a special treat. And Grandmère's sweet smiles and warm hugs, even when Sugar Anne had been very naughty.

> Sugar and spice, and everything nice;
> That's what little girls are made of.
> Sugar Anne Spicer. No miss nicer.
> Papa's shining joy. Even without her front teeth.

Tickles and giggles. And love. So much love.

Sugar Anne blinked furiously and sniffed discreetly, then lifted her chin. Water under the bridge, as Grandfather Jacob would say.

* * *

By the time the train hissed to a stop at the station on Water Street, Sugar Anne thought that Captain McQuillan was looking positively ghastly. She asked for assistance from a burly passenger in a brown bowler who sat across the aisle. After the other passengers departed, she and the man were able, with some difficulty, to help the captain from the coach. Although he seemed barely conscious, the captain groaned several times during the detraining and muttered a goodly number of impolite words. She ignored them as the ravings of the ill and presumed that her assistant was well acquainted with such language.

As they alit from the coach, a middle-aged man, even sturdier than the man in the bowler, stepped forward and doffed his cap. He had a bulbous nose and kind blue eyes. "Miss Spicer?"

"Yes."

"I am Donald O'Toole, sent to fetch you to Mrs. La Vigne's house. May I help, ma'am?"

"Oh, yes, please. Would you assist this kind gentleman in getting the captain into the carriage? Gently, please. He's painfully injured. I'll see to our luggage."

The porter was nice enough to transfer her valise and the captain's saddlebags to the fine carriage that awaited them amid the hustle and bustle of the port town. Always vigilant, Sugar Anne kept the precious satchel looped over her wrist at all times; some unsavory types frequented the waterfront area, she recalled from her girlhood.

As soon as she had thanked everyone and tipped the porter a nickel, she paused a moment to savor the glorious afternoon before she stepped into the conveyance, to inhale deeply the nostalgia-laden air, to smell the saltiness suspended there and taste it on her lips.

For the first time in several days, Sugar Anne was warm. Soft sunshine banished the chill that had seemed to follow her from Chicago, and she held her face up to it. From their vantage point near the busy wharf, with its cacophony of sounds and activity from fowl and man and machine, Sugar Anne could see gulls drifting on the air currents, looking to steal a meal from the boats moored there.

Walls of baled cotton that had been unloaded from train cars and ferry boats stood waiting for the screwers, those brawny men who compressed and packed the bales efficiently into a ship's hold for transport. Crates of other merchandise, either coming or going, stood on the wharves as well. Further down, at the fruit importer's warehouse, dark men walked the gangplank from a moored ship, carrying great stalks of green bananas on their backs.

Her grandfather's office had not been far from the spot where she stood, and the ice cream parlor had been but a few blocks beyond. *Was it there still?* she wondered.

And what about Mr. Patrick's grocery store and her best childhood friend, Lucy? Were they still there?

Did the house in which she'd grown up still stand? Did a new family live there? Had another child found her secret hidey-hole in the attic or discovered the joy of sliding down the banister when no one was about?

Enough of this foolishness! she thought, shaking herself. The captain was in pain, and she was wasting time. Putting her reminiscences and questions aside, Sugar Anne stepped into the carriage, and they were off. She leaned back against the soft cushions, and as she again breathed deeply the bracing Gulf breeze and listened to the muted cry of scavenging gulls, the tension in her shoulders slackened, and a feeling of peace gently cloaked her.

I'm home.

Everything would be all right now.

⇐ Four ⇒

"She's *what*?" Sugar Anne asked, aghast at the news.

The woman, who had introduced herself at the door as Flora Lamb, said, "She's in a coma. Has been for these last twenty-one days. Or twenty-two it is today." Flora, who appeared to be in her sixties, had bright yellow hair, rouged cheeks, and wore a dress more suited for the boudoir than for receiving guests.

"But how can that be? I received a telegram from her less than two weeks ago."

Captain McQuillan groaned. He stood, barely, propped between Sugar Anne and Donald O'Toole in the foyer of the huge Gothic residence on Church Street.

Flora wrung her hands. "Oh, dear. Is this the invalid you wired us about?"

"This is Captain Webb McQuillan of the Texas Rangers," Sugar Anne announced as she nodded to the half-unconscious man. "He gallantly took a bullet while trying to foil a train robbery on our way here."

"A train robbery?" said Flora, her eyes growing even wider.

"Yes. We were set upon by a gang of ruffians, and I'm sorry to say that most of them got away—after they

48

killed two men and blew up the safe. But two of the outlaws were captured. They're in a Houston jail."

Sugar Anne was too modest to reveal her part in their capture. Besides, she wasn't totally convinced that she'd done all that much. She began unbuckling the Ranger's gun belt. "Unfortunately, the captain was wounded in the fracas, and I—er, I felt duty bound to see that he's cared for until he regains his health."

"We'd best get him right to bed," Flora said. She turned and bellowed over her shoulder, "Mary! Phoebe! Quick, come help us here."

Rapid introductions were made to Mary O'Toole, Donald's wife, a stocky, rosy-faced woman in her middle years who served as housekeeper and cook, and to Phoebe something-or-the-other, the maid who appeared to be in her late teens and within moments of delivering a child. While Mary seemed the stereotype of a competent, no-nonsense cook, Phoebe reminded Sugar Anne of nothing so much as a small comical spider—all spindly arms and legs extending out from a big middle—dressed in ill-fitting garb that included a floppy, oversized mobcap that reached past her eyebrows. Her watery blue eyes were overly large and suggested that she was somewhere between perpetually awestruck and panicked.

There was also a brief mention of a Mr. Underwood who was giving a lecture for Mrs. McLemore's reading club and a boy named Willie who was in school. Sugar Anne paid scant attention, for by the time that the barest social amenities had been observed, the captain had groaned again and sagged to his knees. Sugar Anne's arms shook from struggling with his dead weight.

"Here now, ladies, give us a hand," said Donald, "and

we'll carry him upstairs to his bed. This one's heavier than he looks."

Donald hefted the Ranger's shoulders and walked backward with him, leading the way up the steps while Mary and Flora each hoisted one of his legs. Sugar Anne kept to the middle, trying to prevent his rump from bumping the treads as they climbed. Phoebe, struggling with saddlebags and valise and the captain's hat, followed.

With a great deal of huffing and puffing, they soon had the captain ensconced in a soft feather four-poster on the second floor. It was a cheerful, well-appointed room with wallpaper painted with a profusion of Japanese scenes in pastel greens, blues, and burgundies with a touch of gold here and there. The draperies that decorated the windows overlooking the street were of deep green velvet with undercurtains of ivory. A patterned burgundy carpet covered the floor.

While Mary and Flora each tugged at a black boot, Donald stripped off Captain McQuillan's coat and vest. Sugar Anne laid aside his belt and a pair of large, heavy guns along with a wicked-looking knife Flora had found in one boot and another small gun Mary had discovered in the other. Good heavens! How did the man walk with so much artillery on his body? The weight of it was astounding.

Donald cleared his throat. "I'll finish the job, ladies. Why don't you run along now and have some tea."

Flora snorted. "We can help, O'Toole. It's not as if we ain't never seen—"

Donald cleared his throat again, more loudly, and cut his eyes to Sugar Anne.

"Oh, sure. Tea." But before she moved from the bed,

Flora gave the man lying there a thorough perusal. "Good-looking devil. Never did trust the handsome ones. They'll bring you to grief every time." She turned and shook her finger at Sugar Anne. "You mind what I say. Never trust the handsome ones. Homely men are a heap more grateful. Now let's have some tea."

"Tea would be lovely, but I must see to the captain's medicine first. And I think it would be a good idea to send for a doctor. I'm concerned about his weakened state, Mrs. Lamb, and we must be careful of infection."

"Just call me Flora. No Mrs. to it. Never married. Not many in my pro—"

"Dr. Aiken should be along in an hour or so to see to Mrs. La Vigne," Mary O'Toole said. "He can look in on the captain then. Why don't you freshen up a bit, Miss Spicer, and then come down for a spot of tea. Phoebe will show you to your room. Won't you, Phoebe?"

Phoebe, who clutched the captain's saddlebags over her belly like a shield, nodded.

"Thank you," Sugar Anne said. "What's wrong with my cousin? I don't understand—"

Flora patted Sugar Anne's arm. "It's all very complicated. We'll discuss it later. At tea. With scones. Mary makes the most delicious scones with currants. Though come to think of it, we may be out of currants. And not likely to have— But that will all change now. Thank the dear Lord you're here. I've been praying and praying hard." The aging, overpowdered woman hurried from the room.

Sugar Anne wrested the saddlebags from Phoebe and dropped them on a chair. "These belong to Captain McQuillan." She picked up her own valise and smiled at

Phoebe, who seemed to be frightened to death. "Which room is to be mine?"

"This way, ma'am. Just next door." Phoebe bobbed a clumsy curtsy and had to grab the heavy walnut chest to keep from overbalancing.

Sugar Anne closed her eyes, drew in a deep breath, and wondered what in the world she had landed herself in. She lifted her chin and straightened her back. Whatever was going on in this very odd household couldn't be any worse than the mess she'd fled.

"Oh, dear." Sugar Anne's cup rattled in the saucer. "Do you mean that the household is totally without funds?"

"That pig Richard Fitzwarren's got every penny of Trista's tied up and won't even pay the butcher's tab," Flora said hotly. "And the butcher is beginning to complain, let me tell you. He ain't the only one either. All the bills are overdue, nobody's salary has been paid, and the horses don't have feed but for another day or two. They'd have run out last week, but Donald O'Toole bought some with his and Mary's own savings. Donald says that maybe we can sell—"

"Wait, wait," Sugar Anne stopped her. "Let me get this sorted out. First, who is Richard Fitzwarren?"

Phoebe, who had come into the parlor and begun wielding a feather duster over the mantel, made a strangling sound.

"A sorry, good-for-nothing lawyer who ought to have his gizzard cut out and tossed to the gulls."

"Why does he have control of Cousin Trista's money?"

"Because he has some piece of paper that gives him

the power to act for her if she can't. *He* declared that since we aren't her blood kin, we have no rights. I don't believe that for one minute."

"Nor do I," added Mary O'Toole, bringing a plate of scones into the room.

"Have you seen this paper?" Sugar Anne asked.

Flora sighed. "No, but the chief of police has seen it. I called him in first thing. He says it's signed and legal and binding, but I don't believe it. Nothing on this earth can make me believe she'd sign all her business over to Fitzwarren. I never did give a tinker's damn for that ugly little fart"— Mary gasped and frowned severely, but Flora ignored the admonition—"and Trista was coming around to my way of thinking.

"She didn't tell me the details, but I knew that she wasn't one bit happy with the way he'd been handling some of her business dealings—had his hand in the till, if you want to know my opinion. I think she was fixin' to boot his butt out of her affairs. If that burglar hadn't snuck in and knocked Trista colder than a corpse, I think Mr. Peckerwood Fitzwarren would be out on the street by now instead of bringing us affliction. That's what I think. Now here we are without a penny to our names, and Fitzwarren's saying that Trista is never gonna come to and needs to be put away for her own good. For her own good! Have you ever seen one of them asylum places? Ain't nothing good about them. Nothing good a'tall. Praise the Lord for sending you, her only blood kin, to save Trista from that fate, and the rest of us from worse."

Sugar Anne's brow furrowed as she tried to follow Flora's rambling explanation. "You're not related to Mrs. La Vigne?"

"Me?" Flora said. "Heavens no. Well, that is to say, we're like sisters—she being the older, you understand. I, uh, used to be in her employ years and years ago, but when we left San Francisco, I became . . . Well, I guess you could say that I'm her companion and dearest friend."

"I see. Now, as I understand this, Mr. Fitzwarren, who is Cousin Trista's lawyer, has legal authority over her business affairs and funds?"

"That's exactly right, ma'am," said Mary O'Toole, who had remained quietly in the room. "Or so the chief says."

"She does have money then? Cash in the bank, income from investments and such?"

"Oh, for sure," Flora said. "Trista's loaded. I know that for a fact. She's got a big interest in some shipping company down on the wharf, and she's got lots of rental property around town, and she has money in two or three banks I know about. Maybe others. I don't have much of a head for business."

"And this lawyer has refused to release funds for the payment of her own household expenses?"

Flora gave a curt nod. "You've hit the nail on the head."

"Why, that's ludicrous!"

"What's 'ludicrous' mean?"

Sugar Anne turned to find the speaker: a tow-haired boy of about nine or so leaning against the door jamb and munching on a scone.

"Willie!" Mary scolded. "Mind your manners, young man, and don't go interrupting with your questions."

"Mrs. La Vigne said I was to always ask questions if I

didn't know a thing. Asking questions is the way we learn, she said. Mr. Underwood said that too."

"Indeed I did, lad," said a dapper older man with a gray Vandyke beard who stood behind Willie. "Please pardon our interruption."

"Might as well come on in," Flora said. "You, too, O'Toole. I hear you in the pantry." To Sugar Anne she said, "This here is Mr. Preston Underwood, who has his digs on the third floor. Willie here, Willie Jones, has a room up there too. Trista is sponsoring Mr. Underwood's scientific research and book writing. And Willie—well . . ."

"Mrs. La Vigne took me in and is reforming my ways so I can live a proper life among decent folks," finished Willie in a heavy Cockney accent. A broad grin spread across his freckled face. "You the one what's come from Chicago to save us from starvation on the streets?"

Mrs. Effington would have made tatters of the boy's fresh behavior, but his elfin features were so endearing that Sugar Anne could only smile. "I don't know about that, but I'm Sugar Anne Spicer, Mrs. La Vigne's cousin."

"Then you're the one. You gonna have ol' Fitz tossed out on his ear?"

Mr. Underwood cleared his throat and frowned at Willie.

The boy was not deterred. "It was a learnin' question, Mr. Underwood. Ain't you itchin' to know, too?"

Flora laughed heartily. "He's got you there, Mr. Underwood." To Sugar Anne she said, "Truth to tell, we was all just about to the end of our rope. The butcher I was talking about told Mary this very morning that there would be no more credit, not even for a soup bone, and I cleaned out my meager savings to pay the grocer what we owed him so that he wouldn't cut us off too. The Brush Electric Company has sent a notice that the electricity service will be terminated the day after tomorrow. Telephone, too—though we'll not likely miss that contraption overmuch. But winter's coming on soon, and there's no money for coal. There's no money for anything. Mary and Donald have been saints, but they can't keep working for nothing. And Phoebe—"

Phoebe again made a strangled sound and spread her hand across her belly. A single tear rolled from each of her wide blue eyes. "I can't take to the streets again."

"Nor will you while I draw a breath," Mary said, hugging the pregnant little maid against her.

"Or I," Flora said. "Sugar Anne, Trista was mighty proud of you when you and her first met after we moved here to Galveston. It near 'bout broke her heart when she lost touch with you, her only blood kin left in the world. And that damned Jacob—But he's dead and gone, I hear. Now you're back, and we're greatly excited to see you."

Sugar Anne, whose distress had been growing throughout this discussion, tried her very best to stifle a shudder. She had expected to arrive in a safe port herself, not be thrust into worse turbulence. She wanted to weep and curse and rail against fortune's cruel prank.

She didn't, of course. Instead she drew a deep breath, looked around the room at all the expectant faces, and twisted the gold wedding band on her finger. Flora, Phoebe, the O'Tooles, Mr. Underwood, Willie, and the two who lay unconscious upstairs: they all depended on her in this time of crisis.

Sugar Anne glanced at the lovely Spode teacup in her hand, at the fine English silver pot on the equally fine silver tray, and at the Gainsborough landscape above the mantel. Although she was no art expert, she was sure that the proceeds from the landscape or even the small Vermeer in her guest room upstairs would probably provide amply for the household for a long time. And the large house was filled with many such treasures.

She smiled. "I don't think you have any cause for worry. Why, I should think that this pair of candlesticks would pay the butcher for a year."

"I don't doubt it a'tall," Flora said, "for I was with Trista when she bought them, but Fitzwarren swore that he'd have the lot of us thrown in jail if one thing came up missing from the household."

"He controls it all, you see," added O'Toole. "Why, I've considered selling the horses just so they'd have grain aplenty, but the proceeds would have to go straight into one of the accounts that the lawyer's overseeing."

"Don't seem rightly fair to me," Willie piped up. "I'm in favor of coshing old Dickie on the noggin and tossing him in the Gulf. That'd solve our problems all right."

"Willie Jones!" said Mary. "What a notion! 'Tis sinful even thinking such a thing."

Though she'd stop short of murder herself, Sugar Anne found Willie's idea tempting. This Fitzwarren sounded as if he were cut of the same cloth as Edward Herndon. The pair of them would benefit from a good dousing in the Gulf—if she could locate that low-down Edward.

She considered the few coins remaining in her purse, then sat up straight and lifted her chin. She wasn't going to let a second scoundrel get the best of her.

"Unfortunately," Sugar Anne told the expectant group,

"the majority of my funds are . . . tied up at the moment as well, but never fear, we will deal with this situation. I shall go and speak with Mr. Fitzwarren the first thing in the morning. I'm sure that when the man finds out who I am, he will be reasonable."

≈ Five ≈

"Watch it, woman!" Webb McQuillan shouted.

"Stop your wiggling, man," Flora said, scraping his soapy cheek with a razor. "I've no plans to cut your throat. I've plenty of experience shaving a man."

"And plenty of experience doing other things, too, I suspect." Webb had seen too many an old bawd in his day not to recognize Flora Lamb for what she was.

"Hold your tongue, Ranger. You've no call to insult me. I'll remind you of who fed you your breakfast and who is holding the blade."

"Sorry, ma'am. I'm in a mean mood."

"Don't I know it. But I expect if I had a bullet hole in my rump, I'd be in a mean mood too. There," she said with a swipe of a wet towel, "you're done. And looking considerably better than when Donald and Sugar Anne dragged you in here yesterday afternoon."

"I feel considerably better. Or will when I get my pants on." He started to rise.

Flora pushed him back down. "You won't be gettin' your pants on today. The doc says that you need to stay in bed for a spell yet. Seems you lost a lot of blood and got a bit of poisoning to boot. That poultice that Sugar Anne put on you last night seems to have drawn it out some, though."

"A poultice? What poultice? She put a poultice on me?"

"Didn't I just say that? I reckon you pretty well missed most of yesterday with your fever and all. She'll probably slap another one on you this evening." She stood, picked up the bowl of shaving water, and studied his face. "A damned shame."

Webb frowned. "What?"

"With some of that brush off your chops, you're even better looking." She turned and left the room.

Webb ran a hand over his jaws and fingered his mustache. Not a bad job, he had to admit. He looked around the room again, trying to figure out exactly where he'd landed. He hadn't been able to get much out of anybody he'd encountered, but, he thought, stretching and hollowing out a new place in the soft mattress, they had a damned fine feather bed.

Trembling with rage, Sugar Anne stood in front of Richard Fitzwarren's desk and fought against the feminine show of tears that filled her eyes. "But, sir, I truly am Mrs. La Vigne's relative. She and my grandmother were first cousins and very close."

The shyster with a scrawny mustache, who reminded Sugar Anne of a plump little pig, merely sniffed his porcine nose. "And I say again, prove it. Where are your references? I know nothing about you. Anybody could waltz in here and make such declarations. I figure you're in cahoots with some of the rabble that hangs around her house."

"I can assure you I am not in cahoots with anyone."

Her reply sounded weak, even to her own ears. But she couldn't supply character references from Chicago; she didn't want anyone there to know she was here. Besides, who in Chicago would testify to her good character? Everyone thought she was a thief.

"So you say! Prove it, lady. Not that it matters. This power of attorney is what matters," he said, waving a sheet of paper in her face. "This document says that I have control over Mrs. La Vigne's affairs, and I say that if she's not recovered in another week, I'm sending her to a proper institution that handles her kind. That bunch of leeches at her place will be out on the street where they belong. And if anything disappears from the house, I'll have the lot of them thrown in jail. That goes for you too, missy."

How dare that oily, odious man treat her in such a condescending manner! If she could be a man for two seconds, she would sock Fitzwarren right in his snout. But if she had been a man, doubtless the detestable runt would never have spoken to her in such a fashion.

"How dare you! You are contemptible," she declared between clenched teeth. Anger boiling inside her, she leaned across the desk so that she could glare into his beady eyes. "I don't believe that document is authentic. I don't believe it for one minute. I think you are a liar and a cad!"

He looked as if he might explode. "I don't have to listen to that kind of talk from the likes of you. Get out of my office. I wouldn't doubt but you're one of the little maid's trollop friends sent here—"

Without thinking, Sugar Anne swung her satchel and smacked him a good one.

He yanked open a drawer, grabbed a pistol, and stuck it under her nose. "Out," he said. "Now. Or I will send for the police and have you taken away in handcuffs."

Fury and fear paralyzed her for a moment. Surely he wouldn't shoot her in cold blood. But he was an unscrupulous miscreant; there was no predicting what he might do.

"Very well, sir. You seem to have the advantage, but believe it when I say that you haven't seen the last of me!" She whirled and stalked from his office.

She hurried down the steps and, once she was on the street, drew in great gulps of air, trying to calm herself. "That pompous ignoramus," she muttered. "That— that—that fat little fart!" Fury rolled over her in waves.

Now she was absolutely sure that Cousin Trista, a very astute woman, never would have signed over so much power to such a man. She knew, just as surely as she knew that the sun would rise the next day, that Richard Fitzwarren was totally unscrupulous. Sugar Anne would wager everything she possessed that the paper he flaunted was a forgery.

But how could she prove it? And how could she prove her identity as a responsible relative? What a quandary!

In an effort to control her anger and frustration, she crossed the Strand, the street that was the primary business district of the city, and strode down two blocks. Dodging businessmen and shoppers, she paused only briefly when she passed her grandfather's former offices. Thinking of him and his manipulation of her life made her angrier still. He was the first in a long line of men who had made her existence miserable, and she was extremely weary of being put upon by the male gender.

She walked briskly down another block, then stopped abruptly.

It was still there. The ice cream parlor was still there.

For several minutes, Sugar Anne gazed in the window, remembering when times were simpler. Twice she started to move on but stopped. At last she marched inside, ordered a dish of strawberry ice cream, and paid for it with one of the remaining coins she had so prudently hoarded.

Sugar Anne handed the butcher her last gold eagle and said imperiously, "I believe that this should more than cover the bill, Mr. Schmidt, and I hope that there will be no further problems. Until Mrs. La Vigne recovers, I shall be responsible for the household. I am Miss Spicer. Perhaps you remember my grandfather, Jacob Spicer. He was one of the founders of this city."

The butcher bobbed his head. "Oh, yah, I remember him, *fraulein*. It was Mister Jacob Spicer that loaned me money to start my business eighteen years ago, and I don't forget it. Your credit is always good in Schmidt's Butcher Shop."

"Thank you, sir." Sugar Anne nodded and left the shop.

That was the last of them. Having that dish of strawberry ice cream had soothed her mood and cleared her thinking. The next thing she did was locate a fine jewelry store to do a bit of haggling.

With the money she received from the sale of her gold wedding ring, combined with what remained in her purse, she had paid off the most pressing bills and extended the household's credit by shamelessly dropping her grandfather's name. She had ordered feed for the horses as well. With only a little money left, she decided to forgo further purchases and pray for balmy weather. The coal would have to wait.

With her humor considerably improved and feeling rather proud of her day's accomplishments, Sugar Anne struck out for the big house on Church Street.

Webb awoke when he heard the rattle of dishes and the door easing open. He sat straight up and winced as he automatically reached for his gun on the bedpost. But his holsters weren't hanging there. After the first rush of alarm, he got his bearings, then relaxed and laid his head back on the pillow.

The little maid—Penelope? Petunia? Phoebe, that was it—waddled into the room carrying a tray laden with food and utensils.

"Good morning," Webb said.

"Oh!" Phoebe startled, and the tray made a terrible racket until she plunked it down on a table near the bed. "You near 'bout scared me to death. I wasn't sure you was awake yet. And the mornin's gone. It's afternoon. Flora said you should sleep till you've a mind to wake, but Mary said you needed some nourishment to heal proper. She sent me with this. It's a nice stew made from the last of the roast beef and what vegetables we had on hand. The bread's fresh. Mary baked it this mornin', and she's made a nice custard with raisins in it. I like raisins, don't you?"

"Yes, I do." He thought the girl shy when she came in earlier in the day, but when she got wound up, she was a talkative little thing.

"How's your fracas doing?" Phoebe asked as she lifted his head to add another pillow.

"My what?"

"Your fracas. Miss Sugar Anne said that you got shot in the fracas while you was on the train. I'll bet it still throbs right smart." She placed the footed tray across his lap and removed the plate cover.

Webb fought a smile. "My fracas is a whole lot better. Where is Miss Sugar Anne?"

"Out tending to business, Flora said. She's trying to talk to Fitzwarren and get things straightened out. I expect that she'll be back directly. Lordamercy, I hope she can set things right with the lawyer or we're in terrible trouble." Phoebe began to wring her hands. "I don't know what I'll do if I'm turned out on the street all alone and me more'n eight months gone. Starve, I reckon, if'n the nuns won't take me in, and I ain't Catholic."

"Where's the baby's father? Won't he help?"

"No chance of that. He may be in Liverpool or Charleston or one of them islands or maybe no further than Water Street for all I know—and without an inkling of what he left planted in my belly."

Webb frowned. "Do you mean—?"

"I mean I don't know exactly which sailor is the daddy. I was working down by the wharf about that time, though, so I figure it was one of them men off'n the boats that was in port. I was gettin' by okay until I started swelling up. Then business fell off. If'n Miz Trista hadn't felt for me and taken me in, I'd be dead by now for sure. She's a saint, that Miz Trista." Tears welled up in Phoebe's big blue eyes and trickled down her cheeks.

"Don't you have any family?" Webb asked.

She shook her head. "My papa left when I weren't no more'n a baby, and my mama died two years ago when I weren't but twelve. She sewed for a living, but I wasn't much good with stitches, so—" She shrugged and studied the floor.

"I see. Tell me about this Miz Trista."

Phoebe beamed. "Miz Trista, she's a saint like I said. Took me in and give me a job when everywhere else I tried chased me off with a broom. She's a fine rich lady that owns this big house. She's got more dresses than anybody I ever did see. And fancy hats and shoes to go with every one of them. And jewels, Lord amercy, she's got so many jewels that she keeps most of them in a vault built into the wall in the dining room. Oh, I wasn't supposed to let on about that vault, but I guess it's all right to tell you, you being an upstanding Texas Ranger and all, not that it would matter none, 'cause the only one who knows the numbers to open it is Miz Trista and her mouth's sealed for sure."

"Mine's sealed, too," Webb said. "I won't let on to a soul."

"Figured you wouldn't, being a law man. Anyway, Miss Sugar Anne and her are cousins. I heard Flora say that Miz Trista and Miss Sugar Anne's grandmother were girls together in New Orleans. Some burglar broke into the house when everybody was asleep and conked her on the head. Near about killed her. And did send her into a coma."

Webb tried to follow the little maid's prattle, but it was confusing. "Who got conked on the head?"

"Why, Miz Trista. Miz Trista La Vigne. She's been dead to the world for twenty-two—no, twenty-three days now." Phoebe proceeded to relate in great detail how concerned everyone in the household was, especially since the lawyer Fitzwarren seemed to have taken over Mrs. La Vigne's business. "That's why Miss Sugar Anne's telegram was a message from God, Flora said. Now she's here, everything will get straightened out."

"Phoebe!" Flora called as she bustled through the door. "You were supposed to deliver the man's dinner, not chew his ear off. The front parlor needs dusting."

"I dusted it just yesterday." When Flora scowled pointedly at her, Phoebe made an awkward curtsy, mumbled "Yes'um," and hurried from the room.

Flora, too, scowled at Webb's bowl of stew. "Dig in. Unless Sugar Anne gets things straightened out with that bastard Fitzwarren, it might be a while before your next meal." She wandered to the front window and pulled back the thin curtain to look outside.

Webb dug in. The stew was the best he had ever tasted in his entire life. And the bread was lighter than butterfly wings. He didn't stop until he'd scraped the custard bowl.

"Here she comes now." Flora dropped the curtain she'd held aside and hurried to Webb's bed. "You through? I'll take that tray on my way down. If you know any prayers, you best get to praying."

She grabbed the tray and was gone before Webb could ask what he was supposed to be praying about. Deciding to go downstairs and find out for himself, he eased out of bed and discovered in the process that, though it was still plenty tender, his setter was considerably improved. In vain he looked around for his pants. He hated to make his appearance in a borrowed nightshirt that flapped around his knees.

Dammit! Where were his pants? Had that infernal woman taken them to keep him confined to this room?

As Sugar Anne was removing her gloves, she heard a terrible roar coming from upstairs. "What in the world is that?" she asked Flora and Phoebe, who had met her at the front door.

"Sounds like the captain," said Flora. "He must have discovered that his pants are missing."

"And his boots," Phoebe added. "He sounds real put out."

"It's for his own good," Sugar Anne said. "His wound will never heal if he doesn't take proper care of it. Another poultice or two and a few days' rest will soon have him on his feet."

"All that stomping around up there, sounds like he's on his feet already," Phoebe said.

Sugar Anne started up the stairs. "I'll quiet him down. Doesn't the man realize that there is another invalid in the household?"

"If you mean Trista, he's not likely to disturb her," Flora said. "More's the pity. Did you see Fitzwarren?"

"I saw him." Sugar Anne sighed and handed her gloves and hat to Phoebe. "For all the good it did. The man is a scoundrel."

Flora cocked a well-drawn eyebrow. "Didn't I tell you? Is he still planning to toss us out?"

"I gathered as much, but don't give up yet. I plan to deal with Mr. Fitzwarren."

Sugar Anne hadn't a clue as to what those plans were, but she knew she wasn't going to give up easily. And, as a matter of fact, she did have an idea or two. While she was out, she had learned that her childhood friend, Lucy Malloy, was indeed still in Galveston, as was her father, now *Judge* Malloy. Lucy was married to a gentleman named Ticknor and lived in a grand house on Avenue O. She meant to call on Lucy the following day.

She lifted her skirt and started upstairs, then remembered to relay the message to Mary O'Toole that she was free to order food for the household from the grocer and the butcher.

Once she reached the captain's room, Sugar Anne tapped lightly on his door.

"Come in!"

She opened the door slowly and poked her head in. A thin cigar clamped between his teeth and a venomous look in his eyes, Captain McQuillan stood by the front window wearing nothing but his black hat and Donald O'Toole's striped nightshirt. The nightshirt strained at the shoulders and barely reached his knees. And very nice knees they were, she noted. Her breath caught when she also noticed that the stubble was gone from his face and his mustache was neatly trimmed. The man was unbelievably handsome.

Not that his looks made any difference to her, she told herself sternly, trying all the while to quell the flutter of her heart and the flush spreading up her throat.

"Where in the hell are my pants?"

"Downstairs. Since you won't have any need for them for a few days, they're being cleaned and pressed. There was blood on them. And Donald kindly agreed to polish your boots. Lord knows they needed some wax and a brush put to them."

"I'm much obliged, but I need my clothes *now*."

Sugar Anne tucked an errant curl into her chignon and smiled sweetly. "I'm sorry, Captain, but that isn't possible." She crossed the room and held back the covers. "Why don't you get back into bed and rest? Your wound is never going to heal if you don't take care of yourself."

"Godammit, woman, bring me my pants!"

"No. And may I remind you, sir, to watch your language? There are ladies in this house."

"*Ladies?* All I know about are an old woman out colder than a frosted frog, two ex-whores, and a—a—"

Fury boiled up in Sugar Anne. She planted her fists on her hips and jutted her chin out. "A *what*, sir?"

His jaw twitched as he clenched his teeth around his cigar and sucked a deep breath through his nose. "A pig-headed female with the face of an angel and the disposition of a cypress stump."

Her brows lifted and she touched her cheek with her fingertips. "The face of an angel?"

Whatever had possessed him to say that? Webb had meant to call her a thief. Thank God he'd caught himself or he'd be in deep trouble. Though she did have the face of an angel. And the body of a temptress. He hadn't been so fevered that night in the hotel that he didn't remember seeing her shape behind the screen. He'd thought about it a lot. He thought about Sugar Anne a lot. About the way she smelled; about the way a little dimple came at the corner of her mouth when she smiled; about the way her hair, the color of sweet-gum leaves in the fall, came loose from its pins and curled around her face.

But Webb also reminded himself that getting sweet on her would be crazy. Even if she had wormed her way under his skin while he wasn't paying attention, he knew that she was nothing but trouble. She was a swindler married to another swindler. Either condition was enough to stop him cold. He couldn't abide thievery, and he never messed with married women. Never.

Sugar Anne Spicer Herndon was nothing more than his ticket to prosperity, and he wasn't about to let himself forget that. That reward meant settling down in a snug little house with a soft feather bed; it meant being able to start a business and have a normal family life with a wife and kids and church on Sunday instead of living with his gun, sitting a saddle all day, and sleeping on the hard ground at night. That reward meant everything to him, and by damn, he didn't aim to spoil his chance at it by letting a beautiful face and seductive figure turn his head.

He sauntered across the room, leaned against the bedpost, and drew on his cigar. Then he lifted his chin and blew a long stream of smoke toward the ceiling. "I also said that you were pig-headed and had the disposition of a cypress stump. And I forgot to add a tongue sharper than bear grass."

He watched her swallow as if his words had balled up in her throat.

"That you did," she said softly. "And I suppose that if you want to call me names, I deserve them since it was I whose silly, cowardly behavior caused your present predicament. But, Captain, I would appreciate it if you would refrain from referring to the other women of this household in such disdainful terms. They've done nothing to merit your disrespect. In fact, they have gone beyond their duties to make you feel welcome here and see to your needs. Now, if you will excuse me, I'm going down the hall to look in on my cousin."

Why was it, when he'd done nothing but speak the truth, that he felt lower than a snake's belly? Didn't she know about Phoebe and Flora? Nobody with half a brain could be around those two for more than a couple of minutes without figuring out what they were. Was she that naive? Maybe . . .

Naw. It was part of her game. He frowned at her and asked, "What about my pants?"

She walked to the door, turned, and stuck her nose in the air. "What about them?" She slammed the door behind her.

⌒ Six ⌒

Webb McQuillan didn't take that kind of sass off *anybody*. Sod-pawing mad and ready to jump onto Mrs. Sugar Anne Spicer Herndon with both feet, Webb jerked open the door. She wasn't there. He poked his head out and looked up and down the hall. No sign of her. He cocked his head and listened.

Her soft voice caught his ear; she was speaking to someone in a room nearby. He started out after her, then looked down at his bare legs. Hell, he didn't even have his union suit to put on. Stalking back to the bed, he grabbed the fancy quilt off it, wrapped it around his middle, and went to locate that blasted woman who was driving him crazier than Larrabee's calf.

Webb was about to bellow out her name when he spotted her in a big room across the hall. Sitting on a bed all decorated with ruffles and lace, she was holding a pale hand in her own. Edging a couple of steps closer, he saw an old woman's head resting on a stack of pillows. Her face was deadly pale, and her gray hair was braided over one shoulder of her beribboned and embroidered gown.

This must be Mrs. Trista La Vigne, the comatose mistress of the household. He stopped just inside the doorway to listen. Sugar Anne's back was to him, and she seemed too wrought up to notice his presence.

"Oh, Cousin Trista, what am I to do now? I've taken what little money I had and paid off the most pressing creditors, but that won't make any difference if that contemptible creature insists on sending you to the asylum and turning the rest of us out. And how am I to catch up with Edward when I have no funds? You *must* wake up." Sugar Anne brought the frail hand to her lips. "Please, Cousin Trista, open your eyes. Please."

The old woman didn't stir. Webb saw Sugar Anne's shoulders droop and heard her soft weeping. That was his undoing. A big lump grew in his throat, and he wanted to gather her in his arms and comfort her. Dammit, a woman's tears could bring him to his knees, and it made him furious. "Where in the hell are my pants?" he demanded instead.

She bounded from the bed to face him, quickly wiping the tears from her cheeks. "Keep your voice down. Don't you know that this woman is terribly ill?"

"That woman wouldn't stir if you blew a steam whistle next to her ear. She's in a coma."

"She may be in a coma, but I've heard that people in comas can sometimes understand what's going on around them, so I would appreciate it if you would speak in a civil tone around Cousin Trista."

"Very well." One hand holding up the quilt, he yanked off his hat and held it over his heart, then said very sweetly around his cigar, "Where in the hell are my pants?"

"I told you that they were downstairs. There was blood

on them, and Mary washed the spots. As soon as they're dry, someone will press them."

"I had another pair in my saddlebags, but I can't locate my saddlebags. Where did they walk off to? And what happened to my extra pants and everything else that was inside them?"

"I believe your other clothes are being repaired and laundered as well. Donald said they were a mite trail worn. Come meet Cousin Trista."

"Meet her? How can I meet her? She's out colder than Job's turkey."

"Shhh. Come." Sugar Anne held out her hand to him.

Both of his hands were occupied, and he was in a quandary over which to free. Keeping the quilt clutched around his middle, he slapped his hat on his head, stepped forward, and took Sugar Anne's hand.

It was small and soft in his big calloused one. The bones felt as fragile as a sparrow's. He could crush her fingers with one stout squeeze if he'd a mind to. But he had no wish to crush her delicate hand. Instead, its very delicacy brought out strangely protective feelings, and he held it lightly, like a rare flower.

She drew him closer to the unconscious woman's bed. "Cousin Trista, this is Captain Webb McQuillan of the Texas Rangers. He's the one that I told you about, the one who was injured in the train robbery and is now recuperating in the bedroom across the hall. Captain, this is my grandmother's dear cousin, Mrs. Trista La Vigne."

"How do, ma'am," he said, feeling plumb stupid greeting a woman who was the next thing to dead.

Sugar Anne scowled at him and whispered, "Captain, your hat!"

Another dilemma. Did he drop her hand or the quilt? Her hand felt too good—to hell with modesty. Cousin Trista couldn't see a thing anyway, and after all her nursing, he didn't have many secrets left from Sugar Anne. He dropped the quilt and doffed his hat. "Pleased to meet you, ma'am, and I'm much obliged for the hospitality."

"I'll look in on you again later, Cousin Trista," Sugar Anne promised.

He could have sworn that the old woman's expression softened into a slight smile when he nodded to her. "Ma'am." He plunked his hat on his head and hitched up the quilt with one hand. "We need to talk," he told Sugar Anne. "Let's go to my room."

She tried to balk, but he held on firmly and pulled her along.

When they were inside his room, she tugged against his grip. "Captain, please. You're hurting me."

He dropped her hand quicker than a scalding pot. "Sorry. But we need to talk. I've been hearing tales about some lawyer and his dastardly deeds against your cousin. What's going on?"

"It's family business, sir. Nothing to concern yourself about."

"Bloody hell it's not! If the man's a crook, I'll take care of him. Have you forgotten that I'm a Texas Ranger? Now, out with it."

She heaved a great sigh. "Very well, but first you must get back into bed."

She removed the cigar from his mouth, and wrinkling her nose and holding the butt at arm's length, she disposed of it in a small china spittoon beside the washstand. Plucking the hat off his head, she set it atop a chest, then held back the sheet and waited. The stern look in her eyes announced that she would brook no opposition. After he climbed into the bed, she pulled up the cover and spread the quilt neatly over him.

"Okay," he said, "I'm in bed. Now out with it."

Heaving another sigh, she sat down in a chair nearby. "I'm not comfortable discussing personal business."

"We've established that. Tell it anyway. Maybe I can help."

She explained about Richard Fitzwarren, the paper that gave him power over her cousin's business, and his threats to everyone in the household.

"Hmmm. The first question is, is that paper genuine?"

"I don't know. That's what I intend to find out. When I was a child here, my best friend was Lucy Malloy— Lucy Ticknor now. Her father is a judge. I plan to call on Lucy in the morning to see if she and her father can help me."

"You want me to talk to Judge Malloy?"

"No, thank you," she said stiffly. "I shall tend to this myself, just as I tended to the household bills this morning."

Webb smiled. "Then we're going to have supper after all. Flora was concerned that the cupboard was bare, and she had no notion where the next meal was coming from." Sugar Anne didn't return his smile. In fact, she wasn't even looking at him. She stared at a spot across the room and was nervously worrying her hands in her lap. As he watched her hands, he frowned. "Where's your wedding ring?"

She quickly covered her bare finger. "It's gone."

"Gone where?"

"I—I sold it."

His frown deepened. "Sold it? Why?"

"To pay the bills, that's why. It took almost every cent I had to pay the butcher and the grocer and the electric company and the feed store and the others, and I—I—" She sprang from her chair and began to pace.

Almost every cent she had? Even though he'd heard her tell the old woman the same thing, it still sounded fishy to Webb. "Don't you have *any* money?"

Sugar Anne shook her head. "Not more than a dollar or two. I was coming to my cousin for sanctuary."

"But what about your husband? Didn't—" Webb cut his question short before he gave himself away.

She stopped and proudly drew herself up to her full height. "Unfortunately, when my husband—departed, I was left with very little."

"I see," he said, not believing a word of that tale—except the "departed" part. Her claim of being broke made no sense. Herndon had swindled millions. She'd probably blown what she had on feminine fripperies and pastimes and was down to the bottom of the pot until she hooked up with her husband again. She'd said plainly that she planned to catch up with Edward—which meant that she knew her husband's whereabouts. Which meant that Webb was sticking to her like a mustard plaster.

"Why don't you sell off some of your cousin's belongings?" Webb asked. "I imagine that the paintings and doodads in this room alone would buy steak and pork chops for a year."

"That painting would buy meat for far longer than a

year, but nothing can be sold without Fitzwarren's permission, and he's not giving it. He swore that if so much as a teaspoon was unaccounted for, he'll have the lot of us thrown in jail. Everything is in a muddle, and none of the staff has been paid their wages. Phoebe has nowhere else to go, but Donald and Mary can't stay on for very long without their pay. Mr. Underwood depends on the stipend Cousin Trista gives him, and Willie desperately needs new shoes."

"Whoa, there. Who is Mr. Underwood? And who is Willie?"

"I'm Willie, gov'nor. Master Willie Jones, Esquire." The tow-haired boy slouched in the doorway, gnawing on an apple.

"Willie! What are you doing there?" Sugar Anne asked.

"Eatin' this apple and learnin' a thing or two." He sauntered in and plopped down on the corner of the bed. "I'm just home from school, and I can do without new shoes." He held up his foot to show his scuffed and skinned lace-ups. "These still have a lot of wear in 'em yet. Toe's beginning to pinch a bit, but I can borrow Mr. Underwood's razor and cut the end out." He looked Webb over and said, "You've perked up since I saw you yesterday. And Mr. Underwood's a professor that studies bumps on the noggin. Why, he says that my larcenous tendencies show up right here." He tapped a spot on his head. "Foolishness, if you ask me."

"He studies bumps on the head?" Webb asked.

"Professor Underwood is a phrenologist," Sugar Anne explained. "Cousin Trista has been sponsoring his scientific research. He has a room on the third floor."

"Right next to me," Willie said. "He's teachin' me the proper way to talk for lettin' him feel my head and write in his notebook about it. He goes down to the jail and feels heads too. Mr. Underwood swears that lots of prisoners have this very same bump that I do. But I'm reformed, I tells him. I ain't larcenous no more."

"Flora tells me that Willie had a brush or two with the police before my cousin took him under her wing," Sugar Anne said.

Willie snorted. "A brush or two? I was one of the best pickpockets in London, but I landed in a bit of a pickle and the coppers nabbed me. I pulled a trick one of the older lads taught me, and I managed to get away and hide out till I could hop a ship. Ended up in Galveston, tossed out on the wharf for stowin' away, which was aces with me. Better'n gettin' me neck stretched. 'Sides, I liked the weather better here, and I had my trade."

"Picking pockets is a sorry trade," Sugar Anne said. "I'm surprised you didn't end up in jail here."

"Might would have, if I hadn't met up with Miz Trista. That mornin' I tried to cut her purse was my lucky day— though I sure didn't think so at the time. She grabbed me by the ear and near 'bout twisted it off. Took me in, she did, and reformed my thievin' ways. That was more 'n a year ago." He grinned. "Now I'm an upstanding citizen and the best speller in the whole bloody school."

"Willie!" Sugar Anne said.

"Well, I am. Got a certificate on my wall to prove it, if you want to take a gander."

"I was chiding you for your language, young man, not doubting your veracity."

The boy drew his brows together and looked at Webb. "Wha'd she say?"

Webb chuckled. "Best I can make out, she was getting on you for saying 'bloody,' not doubting your word about your certificate."

"Oh. Yeah." Willie nodded sagely. "Sorry about that, ma'am. Miz Trista was always remindin' me that I didn't live in the gutter no more and ought not to talk like I did. It just kinda slips out now and then."

"I understand," Sugar Anne said.

Willie leaned toward Webb and said quietly, "I don't like the way Fitzwarren's lordin' it over everybody and gettin' the ladies all upset. I don't aim to let him cart off Miz Trista to one of them booby hatches. Them's awful places. They carried me ma off to one when I was a tyke, no more 'n five. Never did see her again. Had to learn to fend for meself. Heard she died soon after. I couldn't stop them takin' me ma, but I'll not abide it a second time. I'm older and smarter now, and I know how to handle blokes like old Fitz, but I need a bit of muscle to help me. You game?"

"For what?"

"You and me can slip over to his place when it's good and dark and cosh him on the noggin with a brick. We'll tie him up, weight him down with a couple of heavy barrel staves, and toss him in the bay."

"Willie!"

"Sorry, ma'am, I forgot such subjects isn't for a refined lady's ears."

"The way I feel about old Fitz," she said, "I would almost agree to help you myself, but physical violence is not the answer. Besides, Captain McQuillan is a Texas Ranger, sworn to uphold the law, not toss people into the bay."

Willie's eyes widened and every freckle on his face seemed to stand out. "That the truth? You one of them lawmen?"

Webb nodded. "I am."

"With everybody callin' you Captain, I pegged you for an army man." He grinned fetchingly. "I guess you figured out that I was just joshin' about throwin' old Fitz off a pier?"

Even though he struggled to keep a straight face, Webb couldn't help but grin back at the little con artist who looked as innocent as an altar boy. "Sure. But if the fellow doesn't straighten up, we might have to do something serious like that to get his attention."

Willie's eyes grew wide again. "Blimey! And you a copper?"

Sugar Anne glared at Webb. "He was only teasing you, Willie—though I do understand that the Texas Rangers are a bit rough and unorthodox in their methods. Now come along. The captain needs to rest."

When Willie stalled, Webb looked at Sugar Anne. "I'm tired of resting. Let the boy stay if you won't."

Sugar Anne reluctantly agreed. When she left, he and the boy hunkered down for some real "man talk." After Webb primed him with a couple of slightly exaggerated stories of his wild exploits with desperados, Willie gave him the lowdown on everything that was going on in the household.

And Willie hadn't missed much.

The sharp little dickens had even spotted something

everybody else had missed: a broken watch chain. He'd found it on the floor near the spot where the unconscious Mrs. La Vigne had been discovered.

⇌ Seven ⇌

When she stepped from the carriage and started up the walk to Lucy's grand house on Broadway, Sugar Anne's nerves were frazzled. *Please, Lord, let her be home today.* This was the third morning that she had come to call. The previous two visits had been futile.

"Mrs. Ticknor is not at home," the snooty butler had said the first time. When she couldn't produce a calling card, he had also sniffed rudely and closed the door in her face.

But she didn't have a blasted calling card anymore. She'd once had beautifully engraved and embossed cards from the finest stationer in Chicago. Unfortunately, they identified her as Mrs. Edward Allen Herndon, and she had tossed the last of them into a chamber pot in St. Louis.

The second morning, the butler had stuck his generously sized nose in the air and repeated, "Madam, Mrs. Ticknor is not at home."

Again he had started to close the door in her face, but this time she was ready. She wedged her grandfather's umbrella in the opening and refused to budge.

"My good man, do not be rude to me a second time or

the mistress of this household will boot you out on the street! Mrs. Ticknor and I were childhood friends, and she will be most distressed to learn that you have treated me so shabbily."

"Beg pardon, madam, but truly, Mrs. Ticknor is not at home and is not expected until late this evening. Who shall I say has called?"

In her haughtiest manner, she announced, "I am Miss Sugar Anne Spicer. Tell her that I am visiting in town for a few days and that I shall call again in the morning." She had yanked the sturdy umbrella from the door, nodded curtly, and marched back to the carriage where Donald waited.

Now, on the third morning, she prayed fervently that Lucy would be home. If they were to stop that blasted Fitzwarren, there was no more time to waste. And she had to settle this business with Cousin Trista if she was ever going to find that scoundrel Edward.

Every day, with every mounting adversity she encountered, Sugar Anne heaped more piles of coal on Edward's head; every day she became more determined that he would regret his despicable acts against her and those who trusted him.

Pausing at the front door, she took a deep breath, then rapped the knocker. Childishly, she crossed her fingers behind her back as she looked skyward and whispered, "Please, at least grant me this one small favor."

An elegant, willowy woman opened the door. Like a cloud of gold, her hair was swept up in the latest fashion, and she wore a stunning day dress of cornflower blue the same shade as her eyes. Sugar Anne felt positively dowdy in her widow's weeds.

"Sugar Anne!" the woman squealed, throwing her arms wide. "Is it truly you?"

"Lucy!" she cried, embracing her. "Oh, how I've missed you!"

The pair hugged and laughed and cried and babbled greetings. "Just look at us, acting like children," Lucy said, dashing tears from her eyes. "But I'm overjoyed to see you. I couldn't believe it when Fletcher said that you had called. I would have tried to find you last night, but I didn't know where you were staying. Come in. Come in. Let's have some tea. And I want to hear everything that has happened since I heard from you last. You stopped writing after you went to Europe."

They spent an hour or more catching up. Lucy had married Richard Ticknor shortly after her debut and now had two children, a boy of six and a girl, four. Todd was in day school, and Mattie was out with her nanny. Richard was an importer/exporter—and doing very well, Sugar Anne surmised, if Lucy's house and its splendid furnishings were any indication.

Sugar Anne brought her friend up to date with an abridged and embellished version of her own doings, trying to make the scoundrel she'd married sound half as engaging as Lucy's Richard.

Lucy was beaming as she asked, "Did your husband accompany you to Galveston?"

Sugar Anne's gaze dropped to her lap. Should she tell Lucy the truth? She hesitated, remembering Beatrice Ralston. Bea had been her closest friend and confidante for years, but it had meant nothing in the end. Her repudiation still stung.

"No," she said softly. "I . . . lost Edward some months ago."

"Oh, my dear, I'm so sorry." Lucy swept Sugar Anne into her arms. "I should have noticed that you were in mourning. How tragic. I would be totally undone if I lost Richard. Bereft. Inconsolable. You're very brave."

Sugar Anne felt dreadfully guilty for allowing her friend to believe that Edward was dead. "I appreciate your concern, Lucy, but I've come to terms with . . . his departure. Tell me more about your Richard."

Lucy was easily distracted, for she was completely enamored of the man, who sounded as if he treated her like a queen; she proceeded to expound on his virtues. "I miss him so."

"Miss him?"

Lucy sighed. "Yes. Unfortunately, his travels often take him far away. I frequently accompany him on his business jaunts, but this time he has gone to South America, and he said that his destination was no place for a lady. He's contracting for bananas, I believe. He'll not return for another two weeks yet, and with his being away and with Papa's dreadful condition, I'm in a complete ruffle."

Lucy prattled on, but Sugar Anne didn't comprehend a word. The moment she'd heard "Papa's dreadful condition," a chill went over her and her mind locked. She put her hand over her friend's to stop her chatter. "Lucy, is something wrong with your father?"

"Oh, my, yes. He's had an apoplectic seizure. I've been at his side these past two days. The doctor insists that my father will recover, but he must have complete bed rest for some weeks. I've engaged a very competent nurse to tend him. Oh, it's so sad, Sugar Anne, seeing that robust man laid low. His speech is slurred, and he's lost control of part of his body. Why, one side of his face looks like that droopy old hound dog that Chester Brown used to have. Do you remember Chester? He's a mortician now."

"I see," Sugar Anne said distractedly. Her thoughts were racing. "Is your father receiving visitors?"

"Heavens, no. The doctor will barely let me stay for any length of time. He says that the judge must have complete quiet or he may suffer another attack—and another might take him from us."

"I'm so very sorry," Sugar Anne said. And she was. Not only for the judge, but for her hopes of thwarting Fitzwarren—at least through her contact with Lucy. She would have to come up with another plan. Swallowing the lump in her throat, she took her friend's hands in hers, kissed her cheek, and said, "Oh Lucy, seeing you has been more wonderful than I can ever express. I often remember what fun we had as children, and I hope we'll be able to get together for another visit soon."

Although Lucy hadn't been able to help, Sugar Anne had truly enjoyed seeing her friend. When this muddle with Edward was over, she would return to Galveston and spend a great deal of time with Lucy.

But the muddle was far from over, and time was speeding by. Sugar Anne rose.

"Oh, we must. We've barely begun to catch up, and I would love you to meet the children. And one afternoon you must accompany me to the ladies' croquet club. Remember how we used to love to play on your grandfather's lawn? What fun we had! And what fun we shall have again." Lucy laughed gaily. "You're just the ticket to cheer me. The Island has a wealth of activities to amuse us. Why, there is a marvelous program planned at the opera house this weekend, and you must attend with me. Where are you staying? I shall call on you tomorrow, and we will make our plans."

"I'm staying on Church Street with my grandmother's cousin, Mrs. La Vigne, who is also very ill. Perhaps you know her?"

Lucy blanched, and she glanced away. "We're, uh, not actually acquainted. I know *of* her, of course, but we don't . . . travel in the same circles. I—I wouldn't dare intrude on her household when she's ill. I—I hope you'll call on me again soon."

Sugar Anne had felt the sudden barrier go up between them when Cousin Trista was mentioned. Ordinarily she would have graciously ignored the reaction. She no longer had that luxury. "Lucy, do you find a problem with my staying with Mrs. La Vigne?"

"Why, dear me, no," Lucy said, much too blithely. "I only meant that *we* don't socialize with her. I mean, well . . . She's considerably . . . *older* than our friends, you see. We don't have much in common. And— oh dear, look at the time. I've prattled on much too long, and I must be getting over to Papa's to see how he's doing. I pray that he fared well through the night. Let me see you out."

Sugar Anne held her ground. "Lucy, there's more to this than you're saying. You never could lie worth a darn. Now out with it."

Lucy's face blazed pink. "Well . . . It's just that I've heard rumors."

"What rumors?"

"I—I've heard that some . . . individuals of questionable moral character reside in that household. Why, my friends would—I mean, Richard's good—I mean—" The clock chimed the hour, and Lucy acted as if its sound had brought a reprieve from hanging. "Oh, dear, I can't believe the time. I'm afraid that I must go relieve Papa's nurse now."

She escorted Sugar Anne to the door. "It has been grand seeing you. Please come again."

No further mention was made of the croquet club or the opera house. Sugar Anne managed a smile. "I shall." *When hell freezes over,* she thought. She knew a snub when she saw one.

Furious, Sugar Anne strode down the sidewalk toward the carriage. What a supercilious snob Lucy had become in the years since Grandfather Jacob had brought a struggling young attorney and his family to the Island and helped set him up in practice. Had it not been for Sugar Anne's grandfather, Stanford Malloy would never have become a success in business nor risen to his judgeship.

Though she had been no more than four or five, Sugar Anne remembered well that week when the family arrived. Mr. and Mrs. Malloy, Lucy, and baby Ellie had stayed with the Spicers for several days until a house could be found for them. Sugar Anne and Lucy had immediately become fast friends, with Sugar Anne delighted to share her bed, her toys, and even her clothes with the little girl whose dresses and shoes were a bit shabby.

When Sugar Anne had whispered this to her mother and asked if she might offer one of her dresses for Lucy to wear on a special outing, Mama had disappeared into the attic. She soon reappeared with a heap of outgrown frocks that fit the smaller Lucy perfectly.

The two girls had been closer than twin sisters until Grandfather Jacob sent Sugar Anne away to school, away from her home and friends and everything she loved. For several years they had faithfully written to each other, promising to remain friends for ever and ever.

Damn you, Lucy Malloy, for becoming so pompous and shattering my precious memories!

So what if Flora dressed gaudily and wore a bit too much rouge or if her hair was a tad too—colorful? So what if Willie had once been a pickpocket? So what if Phoebe had a shady background and was about to deliver an illegitimate child? Each and every one of them had suffered, and each was a good and loyal ally to Cousin Trista, who was a saint, a *saint*, to have taken them into her household!

As Donald helped her into the carriage, Sugar Anne set her jaw and fought back tears.

Blast it, I don't need your help, Mrs. Hoity-toity Ticknor! I'll find another way—just see if I don't.

Still fuming, Sugar Anne stormed inside Cousin Trista's house and began stripping off her gloves. It was bad enough that Lucy had slighted her, but when the next-door neighbor ignored her pleasant greeting as she stepped from the carriage, Sugar Anne became even more irritated.

"Pinch-mouthed old biddy," she muttered, slapping her gloves against her palm. "Stuck her nose in the air as if I were the privy barrel collector. Well, I'm sick to death of being snubbed by sanctimonious fools. *Sick, sick, sick.*

Every one of them can go burn in Hades for all I care. Gossips. Hypocrites. Vicious dimwits."

As she hurried to the stairs, she glanced toward the parlor, and her right foot froze in its downward motion.

There, for all the world to see, sat Webb McQuillan, with his longs legs stretched out on a delicate red velvet settee and clad only in nightshirt and boots. His heels were propped on one arm of the settee and his . . . well-muscled calves and . . . nicely formed knees and a—a goodly amount of . . . hard thigh were totally exposed. He smoked one of his slim cigars and casually perused the *Galveston Daily News* while Preston Underwood's fingers were buried familiarly in the captain's thick black hair. She didn't quite know what to make of the blissful expression on Professor Underwood's face.

Sugar Anne stepped into the room and cleared her throat. "Pray tell, exactly what is going on here?"

Without so much as glancing her way, the captain stuck the cigar in the corner of his mouth, squinted his left eye against the updraft of smoke, and turned the page of the newspaper. "I'm reading this article about the labor problems down at the wharf, and the professor is feeling the bumps on my head. I wouldn't be surprised if the screwmen's union and the Knights of Labor strike over this row."

"I cannot believe that you are sitting in the *parlor* in such a state of undress—and with your boots on the furniture. Have you no modesty, sir? No manners?"

Webb scowled at her. "Nope, especially when I don't have any pants. Nobody in the house will admit to knowing where mine are, and Donald refuses to supply me with any of his or visit Cohen & Schram for replacements. Hell, I offered to pay him double what the store is advertising them for on page three of this paper, but he wouldn't do it. Even Willie refused. I would have borrowed some from the professor here, but I figured that they wouldn't be much of a fit."

The professor tittered. A gentleman on the far side of middle years with sparse, dun-colored hair and a mustache as wispy as a baby's eyebrow, Preston Underwood's head barely reached as high as Sugar Anne's.

"Professor." Sugar Anne nodded a greeting to the phrenologist, who looked as if he spent too much time in jail feeling prisoner's heads or holed up in his attic rooms. "Find anything interesting there?"

"Oh, my, yes. Quite a departure from the protuberances and convolutions of the specimens I've been studying. Strong moral character here—sober, honest, loyal, a man of integrity. Intelligent," he added as he moved his fingers over the captain's scalp from front to back, "bold, energetic. Excellent business acumen, excellent. And such amativeness I detect here! Why—"

Underwood jerked his hands from the base of Webb's skull as if he'd been singed and averted his face from Sugar Anne. Had the man been blushing?

"Such—*amativeness?*" she asked. "I'm not familiar with the term, especially in reference to phrenology."

"Well, yes, er—uh—" Underwood stammered, completely flustered.

Webb craned his neck and peered over his shoulder. "Out with it, Professor. My hide's thick. I imagine that a lot worse has been said of me at one time or another."

"I would say that you have a very . . . Well—" The small man turned to Sugar Anne momentarily and said,

"Excuse me, madam." Leaning forward, he said to Webb *sotto voce*, "You have a very passionate nature. Virile as a bull." The whispered words seemed to hang in the air for the span of a gasp before reverberating off the walls.

Webb McQuillan threw his head back and hooted with laughter. "Damn right."

Sugar Anne's cheeks flushed, and her heart began thumping in a most peculiar manner. "If you gentlemen will excuse me, I'll leave you to your endeavors." With all sorts of unbidden and extremely earthy vignettes of a virile Webb McQuillan flashing through her mind, she turned to flee.

"Whoa, there, Miz Spicer. Aren't you forgetting something? Where are my pants?"

⌒ Eight ⌒

Damn, but she was one fine woman! Watching the twitch of Sugar Anne's bustle as she hurried from the parlor, Webb could verify the truth of at least part of the professor's nonsense about head bumps. At that very minute he felt like a bull in the pen with a half dozen receptive cows—all het up and primed to perform, but danged confused about where to start.

As many times as he'd tried to figure it out, he still didn't know exactly what it was about that redhead that kept him in such a condition. But she surely did. She was bossy and more hard-headed than a mule in clover; she had the disposition of a patch of prickly pears and was a damned larcenist to boot. He was constantly reminding himself that Sugar Anne was a *thief* and a bald-faced *liar* and—dammit all to hell and back—his ticket to prosperity.

But her smile was straight from Heaven, and she smelled so good, like gardenias, he thought, remembering the same sweet scent enveloping him when his mother used to hug him.

Mama.

God, so long ago. Two rings, a sachet, and a few of his mother's handkerchiefs tucked into a scorched biscuit tin were all that he had left of her. For the longest time he could open the tin and smell the memory of her there. Through the twenty-five years since the raid, the fragrance had faded, but he still kept the tin and its contents. Right now it was locked up in the safe at Ford Spencer's saloon in San Augustine.

Sugar Anne might smell like his mother, but it wasn't any kind of maternal qualities that had his nightshirt standing up like a lodgepole pine—unless you counted those full, ripe breasts.

"A lovely, spirited woman, isn't she?"

Webb had forgotten that Preston Underwood was still in the room. "That she is," Webb said. "That she is."

"When the two of you are together, the air fairly hums with electricity."

Webb chuckled. "We do seem to rub against each other like porcupines in a bramble bush, don't we?"

Preston tittered. "As an easterner, I am always amused by your Texas sayings. I presume that colorful phrase indicates irritation?" When Webb nodded, the professor said, "I wouldn't precisely define the phenomenon as irritation. Frustration, perhaps. There is an acute awareness between you, one so dynamic that I can almost see sparks flashing. If our Trista were awake, I'm sure that she would agree that her dear Sugar Anne and you are a perfect match."

"Whoa, Professor. You've loaded the wrong wagon. Don't make too much out of this thing. I admit that she's prettier than a handful of aces and a mighty desirable woman, but that's it. There's nothing between us—no flirting, no playing tickle, nothing—and there's never gonna be. No way. I'd rather pick cockleburs out of a skunk's tail than get mixed up with *her*."

Underwood smiled and gave him a look that said he didn't believe a word. "The gentleman doth protest too much, methinks."

"I believe that quote was about a lady, not a gentleman."

The professor's sparse eyebrows went up. "You know *Hamlet*?"

Webb should have merely nodded and kept his counsel, but his pride got the better of him. "I've read some of Shakespeare's work." He took a long draw from his cigar and blew a smoke ring toward the ceiling. "And some Pope and Goethe, among others. Professor, just because some folks around these parts talk a little rough or act as common as pig tracks, don't make the mistake of thinking that they don't have any sense."

"Oh, dear me, no, Captain! I would never think such a thing. I have observed your astuteness. I meant no insult. I was surprised that a—a lawman knew the classics. I mean—"

"Forget it, Professor. I know what you mean. And the truth is, I can't name many Rangers who'd know that Bacon was anything more than a slab of side pork. Say, do you reckon that our hostess has any good sippin' whiskey around? Or, hellfire, about now I'd even settle for a slug of rotgut if you could rustle up a bottle."

The scrawny little fellow jumped up like he'd just squatted on his spurs and made a beeline for a corner cabinet. He produced a handsome decanter and a glass, then poured a double shot for Webb and brought it to him.

"For medicinal purposes," Underwood said with a hint of a smile.

"Aren't you going to join me?" Webb asked.

"Oh, it's a bit early in the day for me."

"Naw, Professor. In old Paree it's way past time for a nip. Pour yourself one, pardner. And bring the bottle. I never cared much for drinking alone."

The professor didn't need more coaxing.

After their second round, Captain and Professor became Webb and Preston, old *compadres*. With his tongue greased by Cousin Trista's fine bourbon, Preston added to Webb's knowledge of Mrs. La Vigne, her companion, Flora, and a bit about a sorry sonofabitch named Jacob Spicer. Either Cousin Trista or Flora must have confided a passel of information to the phrenologist, or he was a slick one at keyholes, for Webb got an earful.

He suspected that if Sugar Anne knew what some of the folks in the household had blabbed to him about her relatives, she would've busted her corset strings. One thing that he did know for sure: acorns don't fall far from the tree. And from what he'd heard about her family, any lingering doubts he might have had about Mrs. Spicer Herndon's culpability in that Chicago scrape faded fast.

After their third round, Preston slurred, "Webb, my friend, did you know that I would very much like to examine Miss Sugar Anne's protuberances?"

"Wouldn't mind doing that myself, amigo." He filled the glasses again. *I'd like to examine every protuberance on her body. All night long. And that's the problem.* He knocked back the whiskey and turned to refill Preston's, but the professor was slumped in his chair, snoring softly.

About that time Phoebe lumbered through with a large feather duster and made a pass over the mantel with it. "The professor in his cups again?" she asked.

"Looks like it." Webb set his own glass on the table beside the decanter. "Does he have a problem?"

"I'll say. But not all the time. It's the queerest thing. He'll go along for a spell and be sober as a judge, then he'll go on a toot and get drunk as a fiddler's bitch. Usually settles for cheap rum or gin down at one of them places on Market Street. I've helped put him to bed once or twice. Now when his money's run out, far as I know, he ain't touched a drop. But Flora threatened him within an inch of his life if he got into Miz Trista's good stuff."

"Sorry," Webb said. "I didn't know. I'm the one who told him to get the whiskey."

Phoebe shrugged. "He's a grown man. I'll throw a blanket over him. Mary said lunch is ready. You comin' to the table in your nightshirt?"

"Guess I'll have to since I don't have any pants." He cut his eyes at her, imploring her to remedy the situation.

"And you ain't likely to till the doc says you can. He'll be here this afternoon. Take it up with him."

"What kind of costume is that?" Webb demanded as Sugar Anne entered the dining room.

"Excuse me?" she said, her tone matching his. Her navy velveteen jacket was quite stylish, and its matching skirt was buttoned back to reveal very full Turkish trousers draped over high-buttoned navy gaiters. "This is what a lady wears in Chicago to go velocipeding," she replied. The nerve of the man! A man about to dine in his nightshirt had no cause to comment, even if she came to the table in rags—which she certainly had not. "My trunks were delivered this morning."

"Guess so. Two men sweated half an hour to haul that load up the stairs. It wore me out just watching them."

"How you exaggerate, Captain. Of course, Phoebe can serve you your meal in your room, as she's been doing."

"I wouldn't think of putting poor Phoebe to any more trouble." As he held Sugar Anne's chair for her, he smiled devilishly—determined to embarrass her, she knew, but even if he chose to traipse about as naked as the day he was born, she wasn't going to produce his pants.

Flora joined them, and Webb seated her as well. Glancing about, Flora asked, "Where's the professor?"

"In the parlor," Phoebe piped up as she ladled the soup, "soused to the gills."

"Soused?" Sugar Anne asked.

"Yes'um. Soused."

The captain grinned again. "That means—"

"I know what it means, sir. The question is, what is the professor doing 'soused' at this hour of the day? Is the man a drunkard?"

"Oh, no, honey," Flora said. "Most times he's sober as a judge."

"Them's the exact words I said," Phoebe added as she carefully carried a bowl from the sideboard.

"So that's a velociped ing outfit," Webb McQuillan remarked, to distract her from the professor's condition, no doubt.

"This is what a modern lady wears to go bicycling."

"Bicycling?"

"Yes. A bicycle is a two-wheeled conveyance—"

"I know what a bicycle is," he said crossly.

As she spooned the savory chicken and rice soup into her mouth, his question hung in the air. She ignored it.

"Sugar Anne found the contraption in the carriage house," Flora explained. "Belonged to a young woman who was living here last year. She was a professor of sorts, too. Studied the mating of crabs or some such. She left it behind when she went back to Massachusetts— which was only right, since Trista paid for it in the first place."

"And you plan to *ride* the thing?" Webb asked. "In that getup?"

"I certainly do. I'm quite proficient. And I'll have you know that my outfit is the epitome of fashion." Or rather, she thought, it was fashionable the previous fall when she'd purchased it in Paris. "I have several calls to make this afternoon, and there's no need to have Donald drive me in the carriage. It will be more convenient if I take the bicycle. Besides, I need the exercise."

"Where are you going?" asked Webb, his tone gruff.

"Where I'm going is none of your concern, sir. But if you insist on being nosy, my first stop will be the police station. I just learned from reading yesterday's *News* that an old friend of mine is a lieutenant in the police department. We were neighbors as children, and I'm sure that he'll remember me and be able to assist me in tossing Fitzwarren out on his ear."

"And if he won't?"

"Then I'll try someone else. I've made a list." The list was a stroke of genius. The idea had come to her after she'd seen the captain reading the newspaper. She knew that prominent people's names were likely to be noted in the daily and that seeing them would prompt her memory of old acquaintances or business associates of her grand-father. That was exactly what had happened. She now had a roster of at least a dozen men of importance who should remember her—or at least Jacob Spicer.

"If you'll get me my pants, I'll go with you and help get the mess straightened out."

She lifted her chin. "No, thank you, sir. I'll handle my own business."

After donning her saucy navy velveteen hat with the red plume and her leather gloves, Sugar Anne set out for the police station, praying that James Yarborough would be in. She remembered James as a tall, skinny, jug-eared boy who had white-blond hair and stuttered. He was al-ways bringing her favors: starfish shells, sand dollars, colorful bird feathers, and such. Once he gave her a blackened coin he'd found on the beach. When it was cleaned, it turned out to be a silver piece of eight.

James's family had lived on the street behind the Spicers, and the backs of their properties had joined. Sugar Anne hadn't thought of James, who was two years older than she, in ages. She desperately hoped that he had remembered her—and fondly—for she needed his favors now.

Even though Donald had cleaned and oiled the bicycle, riding it proved to be rough going in several places. Al-though the Strand, the primary thoroughfare of the busi-ness district, was paved with wooden blocks, and most of the main streets were topped with oyster shell, many areas were pitted and rutted and others had patches of loose sand that made progress difficult.

On stretches where there was no pedestrian traffic, Sugar Anne wheeled smartly along on brick or cement sidewalks, which were in much better shape than the bumpy streets. She enjoyed the cool breeze against her cheeks and blessed it for carrying away the stench of the city's ditches. She rang her bell and waved to those who peered at her from porches or carriages, smiled and sometimes laughed out loud, feeling a sense of giddiness and freedom that she hadn't felt in a long, long while.

Since she had not ridden in quite some time, her muscles were protesting by the time she reached City Hall on the corner of Mechanic and Twentieth streets. Parking the bicycle beside the entrance, she unbuttoned her skirt so that it fell in soft folds to cover her trousers. She straightened her hat and fluffed its plume, then plucked her satchel from the basket attached to the handlebars and marched inside.

After locating the police offices, she announced to the uniformed gentleman sitting at a desk, "I would like to speak with Lieutenant James Yarborough, please."

The brawny man, who sported a generous mustache and side whiskers, didn't even stand to acknowledge her presence. He looked her up and down and said, "Lieutenant's busy."

Sugar Anne didn't like the way he squinted at her. She didn't like it at all, but she smiled anyway. "I would expect as much of someone in his position, but I'm sure that he will spare a few moments for me. Please inform him that Miss Sugar Anne Spicer, an old friend and former neighbor of his, is here to see him."

The policeman didn't seem terribly amenable to her request, but he heaved himself to his feet and ambled to a doorway where he stuck his head in and muttered something. Then he turned and, barely restraining a smirk, said to Sugar Anne, "You can come on back, ma'am. The lieutenant would be de-lighted to see you."

She lifted her chin and strode briskly to the door and past the insolent fellow.

When the man behind the desk rose, for a moment she was shocked speechless.

James Yarborough had grown into his ears. He was tall, almost as tall as Captain McQuillan, and far from skinny. His shoulders and chest were as broad and muscular as a dock worker's. But his hair was the same white-blonde shade as it had been when he was a boy and some of the children had nicknamed him Cotton. It looked lighter still against the deep tan of his face. She could see that James had matured into a very handsome man.

"Sugar Anne Spicer," he said in a baritone without a trace of a stutter, "is that really you?"

She laughed and held out her hands to him. "It is, James. It really is. It's been so long that I was afraid that you wouldn't remember me."

He took her hands in his, and his blue eyes crinkled with a wide smile. "I could never forget you. How long has it been?"

"Fifteen years at least. You've certainly changed."

"As have you. The little girl is all grown up and more beautiful than ever. Have you returned to the Island for good or are you just visiting?"

"Well, I'm not sure," she said. "You see I have a problem, and I—"

"Cotton, you gotta come quick," the brawny policeman shouted as he burst into the room. "The chief sent word that there's trouble at the Mallory wharf again, and things is fixin' to get out of hand. Wouldn't take much for all hell to break loose, chief says."

"Damnation!" James muttered. "Sorry, Sugar Anne, I have to go." He grabbed his hat and started for the door.

She hurried after him. "James, I must talk to you."

"Later," he said, flinging open the door and striding away.

She stayed on his heels. "It's important!"

"Tomorrow!" He crossed the street at a run and headed down the block.

Infuriated by the interruption when she was so close to help, she jumped on the bicycle and started after him.

James disappeared around a corner, and Sugar Anne's legs churned, pumping the pedals as fast as she could, chasing him. She was desperate for his support and determined not to be put off, but as she rounded the same corner at a high speed, she gasped at the commotion before her.

Two score or more of roughly clad men had drawn themselves into two groups, one colored and one white, and were shouting threats and vile words at one another. Some carried sticks, some bricks; others concealed more deadly weapons, she was sure. Tension, palpable and imminently volatile, sizzled, needing only a spark to burst into a lethal conflagration.

Unnerved by the proximity of such a menacing mob, Sugar Anne immediately tried to brake. But her foot caught in a tangle of navy velveteen, and her efforts were futile.

Though she fought fervently to stop the bicycle, she couldn't avoid colliding with one of the clusters of angry dock workers. Clutching the handlebars, she yelled,

"Look out, men!" as she plunged directly into the middle of the fray.

Sugar Anne screamed as she downed two or three of the fellows like bowling pins, then pitched, along with the bicycle, on top of the pile.

She screamed again, and the crowd exploded into a riot.

Bricks flew; sticks swung like war clubs.

The curses grew louder as fists smashed flesh and bone.

Sugar Anne tried to get to her feet, but she was jostled and shoved and very nearly bludgeoned. Somehow she managed to grab her satchel, and she began to crawl on her hands and knees between the brawling men, trying to make it to safety.

An enormous foot planted itself squarely on her satchel and halted her progress. Its owner was engaged in smacking two heads together while roaring like a bear and trying to shake off another man who'd jumped on his back. She wasn't about to leave without her belongings. Not only did the bag contain important documents with Trista's true signature, but the last of her cash was inside as well.

She tugged and tugged and implored the foot to move, but the immense boot stayed firmly planted, and to make matters worse, an unconscious man fell on her and flattened her against the wooden wharf.

"Get off me, you oaf!" she shouted. She shoved him aside and seized the brick he'd dropped when he fell. "Move your foot, sir!" she shouted up to the giant of a fellow who held her satchel captive.

He paid no more attention to her than if she were a gnat. True, he was busy with an attacker armed with a length of metal pipe, but she wasn't feeling magnanimous.

She brought the brick down hard on his toes just as his fist slammed his opponent's chin.

"Yeoow!" His foot went up, and he began to dance around.

Quickly, she began crawling away, but straightaway she ran into a pair of legs like tree trunks. She slowly lifted her gaze until she was looking up at James.

He was scowling. "What in the hell are you doing, Sugar Anne?"

"I'm trying to keep from getting killed."

He lifted her to her feet. "Dammit, woman, you've started a riot!"

"*Me?* Why, I haven't done a thing." Sugar Anne heard a familiar roar, and out of the corner of her eye spotted the huge man whose toes she'd bashed. "Duck," she shouted.

Unfortunately, James didn't react in time. Sugar Anne ducked, but the huge arm slammed into James's face and sent him flying. He landed in a small wooden cart.

Furious, and with her fingers still wrapped around the brick, she spun to face the attacker, who had turned from them to ward off a blow from another man with a stout stick. While his back was to her, she bashed the brick against his head.

The giant stood dead still for a moment, then went down like a felled tree.

When Sugar Anne realized what had happened, she dropped the brick as if it were blazing, and her hands flew to her mouth. "Oh, dear Lord, no! What have I done?"

She turned quickly to help James, but the cart had disappeared. Looking around frantically, she spied it rolling slowly down the pier with his unconscious body sprawled across it.

"James!" she screamed, running down the planks as the wheels of the cart went over the side.

When she reached the spot where he'd gone into the bay, she saw him floating facedown in the water. Calmly, she set down her satchel, removed the pin from her hat, laid the plumed creation atop the bag—and jumped.

☙ Nine ☙

Webb had been pacing the foyer, puffing a cigar and anxiously awaiting the doctor's arrival, so when the brass knocker sounded, he yanked open the door, expecting to throw himself on the mercy of Dr. John Aiken for a pair of damned britches.

For a moment he was too amazed by the dripping, bedraggled couple he saw standing on the porch to say a word. The only thing dry on Sugar Anne was her hat, perched on her head at an odd angle and with its red plume broken and drooping over one eye.

He hadn't paid much attention to the man with her until a brief glimpse shifted into a gawk. "My God. Cotton Yarborough. I thought that you were gonna settle down in Oklahoma when you left the Rangers last year. What are you doing here? And what happened to your clothes?"

A sopping wet Cotton Yarborough, looking as if he could bite through a ten-penny nail, scowled at Webb. "I was about to ask you the same question."

Webb glanced down at his nightshirt and boots, then stuck his cigar between his teeth and jutted his chin. "It's a long story. You first."

Sugar Anne rolled her eyes. "Blessed be, Webb McQuillan, you and James can stand on the porch and chat all day if you want, but please step aside so that I can go upstairs and get out of these wet clothes before I take my death. The day may be quite balmy, but I can assure you that the water was extremely chilly."

Webb stepped aside. "Exactly how did you get wet?"

Sailing past him, she said, "I jumped into the harbor to save James from drowning."

Webb's brows went up, and he smirked as he turned to the ex-Ranger and old friend. "That so?"

"Yep," Cotton said. "That was right after she started a riot between a couple of hotheaded union gangs on the wharf. The white and the colored screwmen working the cotton ships have been spoiling for a fight and just waiting for an excuse for a good free-for-all. She gave it to them."

"This I've got to hear," Webb said.

"Could we talk about it later? I've got to change clothes and get back to the station, or I'm likely to lose my job—if I haven't already. The chief is mighty pissed about this mess. I've tried to pass off Sugar Anne's part in it, but he's bound to find out, and my ass will be on the line for sure. Sonofabitch'd like to get rid of me anyhow. He thinks I'm after his job."

"Are you?"

Cotton only shrugged. "Say, I've got that demon bicycle of hers in the back of the buckboard I borrowed. Let me get it, and I'll set it on the porch."

"I'll give you a hand."

Cotton chuckled. "Without your drawers on?"

"Oh, hell, I forgot. Are you the former neighbor that Sugar Anne went down to see at the police station?"

"Yep. When I was about twelve or thirteen, I was crazy in love with her."

"And now?" Webb said brusquely, surprised by the harshness of his own words.

"Hell, man, I haven't seen or heard from her in more 'n fifteen years." He cocked his head at Webb. "How about you?"

"*Me?* Oh, no, not me. I—" Webb hesitated. He wasn't about to spill the beans about why he was hanging around Sugar Anne Spicer, alias Mrs. Edward A. Herndon. Even though he and Cotton were old trail buddies, that reward for recovering the money she and her husband had stolen might be too tempting to Cotton. Webb didn't intend to cut anybody in on it. "I got shot in a train robbery north of Houston, and Miz Spicer, who was traveling in the same car, has kindly been looking after me until I heal."

"That so?" Even though Cotton kept his mouth straight, his eyes were damned near laughing out loud.

"Did Sugar Anne get a chance to tell you about the trouble here?"

"She talked about it some, but to tell the truth, I was too danged aggravated to listen to much of it."

"How about we meet down at Josie's for a drink tonight after you get off?"

"Can't tonight," Cotton said. "I've been invited to supper here."

Webb's hackles went up. "Here?"

A possum-eating grin spread over Cotton's mug. "Yep. Sugar Anne invited me to supper."

"Dinner. Here we call it dinner." Webb slammed the door in Cotton's smug face and strode away.

Flora, who had been standing unnoticed in the parlor—unnoticed because she was crouched behind the Chinese screen and eavesdropping shamelessly—smiled as she heard Webb stomp up the stairs.

Well, well, well. She'd had a hunch that the captain was getting sweet on Sugar Anne. This proved it. The captain was jealous of that Yarborough boy. Good enough. Nothing like the interest of another young buck to set the juices flowing.

Everybody in the household thought that Webb and Sugar Anne would be a fine match, including Trista. Well, Trista hadn't exactly said so, but her friend had sighed when Flora had told her about the latest sparks between the pair of them over the dinner table.

Trista had been sighing a lot over the past couple of days, and she'd been making a few other little sounds and slight movements. Taking nourishment better, too. And Flora could have sworn that she heard Trista mumble something that sounded like "Sugar Anne." Maybe she was just imagining things—which was why she hadn't mentioned it to anybody and gotten up false hopes—but the captain wasn't the only one who anxiously awaited the doctor. Flora planned to discuss the matter with Dr. Aiken when he came, but she felt in her heart that Trista was coming around.

She brushed aside the front curtains to peek out. Young Yarborough was already gone, but another buggy was pulling up to the gate. It looked like the doctor was here at last.

* * *

"More potatoes, James?" Sugar Anne asked sweetly.

Flora giggled behind her napkin as she watched Webb glower at the guest. No two ways about it, the captain was jealous of Yarborough all right.

"Hell, he's already had three helpings," Webb grumbled.

"Captain!"

"Only two," James said, smiling brightly, "but those potatoes are delicious. And so is the roast beef. You've got a fine cook, Sugar Anne."

"Mary is a fine cook," Webb agreed. "She's made a lemon pie for dessert. She knows it's my favorite." Looking right satisfied with himself, Webb leaned back in the chair he'd appropriated at the head of the table and stuck his thumbs in his waistcoat.

He was also wearing a new suit, one with two pair of pants, Donald had informed Flora when he returned from Cohen & Schram with the captain's new duds. She noticed that his mustache was trimmed and his boots polished. Both the captain and James Yarborough were quite slicked up. Preston Underwood was too, for that matter, but Preston sat around so quiet that most of the time Flora forgot he was there.

"I'm right fond of lemon pie myself," James said when Phoebe served dessert.

James looked at Phoebe kind of funny again, as if he were still trying to figure out where he'd seen her before. The meringue shook as Phoebe placed the slice of pie before him. The girl had had a few run-ins with the local law, and Flora knew that being around him made her nervous. Willie, who'd had a few brushes with the police himself, had been banished to the kitchen for his supper. No need asking for trouble from that scamp.

When Webb had cleaned the last crumb of crust from his plate, he stood and bowed to Sugar Anne and to Flora. "Delicious, ladies. Cotton, let's you and me go out on the porch and have a cigar."

"I don't smoke," Cotton said.

"Join me anyhow," the captain said, giving the Yarborough boy the eye, "in deference to the ladies."

"Oh, for goodness sakes," Sugar Anne said, standing. "You've been here nearly a week, and you've never been concerned about stinking up the place with your cigars before. Let's go into the parlor for coffee and brandy. I have something to discuss with James."

"You young people run along," Flora said, giving Preston a kick under the table. "I'm going up to sit with Trista for a spell."

"And I, er, I have some material to read," Preston said. "If you would excuse me."

Flora and Preston left Sugar Anne with the two young bucks and headed upstairs.

When Flora settled herself in the chair beside Trista's bed, she was laughing softly. "Trista, if you was able, we'd sneak downstairs and watch that threesome. Webb McQuillan's hornier than a Mexican bull over Sugar Anne, and I suspect that Yarborough boy knows it and is getting a big kick out of playing up to Sugar Anne. 'Course I suspect that James has a sweet spot for her, too. Least ways, from what I understand, he was stuck on her when they was kids.

"That Sugar Anne is a pure-d mess. Pretty as a picture and feisty as she can be. She's something to be proud of,

Trista. I'll bet you a gold monkey that she can sweet-talk James into turning Fitzwarren out."

"Sugar Anne," came the soft whisper.

Flora stiffened, alert and staining her ears. "You did it again! You said her name. Wasn't my imagination a'tall. I *knew* it wasn't. I *knew* I'd heard you. Dr. John wasn't sure about it, but he said it was possible you might be coming out of your catalepsy. Oh, praise the Lord, Trista! Praise the Lord!"

Flora talked and wheedled for another hour, but Trista didn't speak again. Maybe she'd better wait a spell before she said anything to the others.

By the time Cotton Yarborough finally took the hint and left, Webb had chewed through three good cigars. Well, it wasn't exactly a hint that sent him packing. Webb had stood and said, "It's time for you to go home, Cotton. We'd like to go to bed."

Both of Cotton's eyebrows had gone up, and danged if the man didn't smirk.

"Captain!"

"Oh, tarnation, I didn't mean it like that."

"Like what?" Sugar Anne had asked.

"I didn't mean that we intended to go to bed together."

Her cheeks went pink. "Well, certainly not!" Turning to her guest, she said, "James, don't let this boor drive you away. It's been delightful talking about old times, and thank you for your promise to help."

"I've enjoyed myself, too. I can't promise anything, Sugar Anne, but I'll talk to the chief tomorrow afternoon if I get a chance or first thing Monday morning for sure."

"Thank you, James." She stood on tiptoe to kiss his cheek.

With another nudge or two, Webb was finally able to get Cotton out the door. When he turned to look at Sugar Anne, her eyes glistened with fire. Something about the way her chin jutted and the way her fists, planted on her hips, pulled the green silk of her dress taut across her breasts set him on fire as well. Before he knew what he was about, he'd grabbed her and kissed the devil out of her.

Damn, but she felt good in his arms. And her lips were soft as they sighed against his. Soft and warm and sweet. "Sweet as sugar," he murmured, then pulled her closer and kissed her again.

At first she kissed him back, making a little purring moan and wiggling against him. Then he felt her stiffen. After a moment's hesitation, she shoved away from him, struggling and spitting like a puma cub caught in a net.

"How dare you!" she screeched, then hauled off and slapped the daylights out of him.

Webb was stunned, as much by his behavior as hers. "What'd you go and do that for?"

"Because—because—" she sputtered, "you kissed me!"

"Damned sure did. And you kissed me back."

"I did not, sir! I don't go around kissing men. I'm a respectable widow in mourning."

Webb couldn't keep from snorting at that pronouncement.

Sugar Anne stuck her fists on her hips and her chin out. "And exactly what does that rude noise imply?"

He nearly spilled the beans then and there, came within an inch of spouting off that she wasn't anymore a widow than he was a wall-eyed coyote. Instead he said, "I don't know what you're talking about."

She imitated his snort. "That rude noise. That's what I'm talking about. Are you impugning my character, Webb McQuillan?"

"I'm not impugning anything, Sugar Anne, but for somebody who batted her eyelashes at Cotton Yarborough all evening, you've sure turned sanctimonious all of a sudden."

"Batted my—I did not! James is an old and dear friend."

"Is that why you kissed him?"

"I didn't kiss him."

Webb folded his arms. "Blame sure looked like a kiss to me. And I expect if you asked Cotton, he'd say it felt like a kiss to him."

"A tiny peck on the cheek for an old friend is not like—like—"

"Like this?" he asked. And damned if he didn't grab her and plant another one on her.

And damned if she didn't sigh sweetly against his mouth again.

It was the longest time before she pushed him away.

Her voice was husky when she murmured, "Don't do that again, Webb. Do you hear me?"

"I hear you," he said, but he kissed her again.

Kissing her ranked right up there at the top of the list of the dumbest things he'd ever done in his life, but he couldn't seem to help himself. Despite all his reasoning, she'd become a drug in his blood, and her mouth was like the lure of an opium den.

"Please," she whispered against his lips. "Please."

"Please, what, darlin'?"

"Please don't do this. Please, not now. I can't—"

The pitiful little whimper got to him. He kissed her nose, let her go, and turned away. When he heard the rustle of her skirts on the stairs, he opened the front door and went out on the porch.

He lit a cigar and blew a cloud of smoke at the moon and cursed himself for five kinds of fool. No, she wasn't a widow; the lady had a *husband*. A sorry son of a bitch of a husband that he meant to catch up with and put in jail for the reward. He didn't figure that Sugar Anne was going to feel any too fond of him when she found out that he'd been using her to trail Herndon.

And on top of everything else, he'd never dallied with a married woman in his life.

Damn it all to hell! He'd acted like a lame-brained jackass. He wasn't about to get mixed up with Sugar Anne. That was the last time he would ever lay a hand on her.

Still dazed by what had occurred downstairs, Sugar Anne fell back onto her bed and stared wide-eyed at the ceiling. Conflicting thoughts and emotions whirled inside her like a swarm of mosquitos.

Whatever had possessed her to kiss Webb like a wanton hussy? She'd denied it to him, of course, but she *had* returned his kiss—with a great deal of enthusiasm. And, though she was loath to admit it even to herself, she *was* a married woman until she could find a way to end that sorry situation.

But, oh dear heavenly days, she had never experienced feelings quite so delicious. She touched her lips, remem-

bering the feel of his against hers, and her breasts tingled.
Again.

Her eyes widened, and she sucked in a great gasp of
air as she wondered at the tantalizing feelings that rippled
over her body. Now she had an inkling of what all the
fuss was about, why poets extolled their romantic ideas,
why Romeo and Juliet had acted like such ninnies.

Neither Edward's rough kisses nor their other intima-
cies had ever left her in such a state. She'd found her husband's touch unpleasant, something to be endured on the
rare occasions he'd approached her. Truthfully, he'd
made her skin crawl, not tingle pleasurably, even on their
wedding night. He'd called her a cold bitch and had
plowed himself roughly into her despite her protests.

She'd been delighted when he'd stopped coming to her
bed after their first year or so of marriage. She was weary
of pretending and weary of feeling inadequate when he
constantly criticized her as a bed partner. Secretly, she
suspected that he'd found a mistress, and gossip later
confirmed it. In fact, he'd had a string of women. She had
ignored his affairs, shouldering the guilt and believing
her shortcomings as a woman had driven him to seek his
pleasures elsewhere.

Now she had another reason to despise Edward
Herndon. She had begun to realize that she might not be
a "cold bitch" after all. Perhaps it was Edward, not she,
who was lacking in *savoir faire*, for when Webb kissed
her, heat had flashed through her like a grass fire.

What a terrible time for the situation to arise! Her life
was too complicated to allow herself to be sidetracked
now. She had to deal with Fitzwarren and get on with her

business. Her primary goal was finding Edward, recovering her fortune and that of the others he had cheated, and restoring her good name.

Another sensual memory of being in Webb's arms flickered in her mind, and she gasped once more as warm swells rippled through her body, stimulating unbelievably intimate locations.

Rubbing her hand along one particularly heated spot to quell the ache, she only succeeded in fanning the flames. Jerking her hand away, she rose quickly and began undressing for bed. These new sensations that Webb had provoked made her very uneasy.

Webb.

Pausing, she sighed and hugged her nightgown to her as her imagination went wild. She could almost feel the tickle of his mustache . . .

No! she admonished herself. No. For a dozen excellent reasons, she couldn't let herself become romantically involved with this man. No, absolutely, positively not.

No.

∼ Ten ∼

Shortly before Sunday morning services, Donald stopped the carriage in front of the church for the four passengers to alight. The captain and Mr. Underwood stepped down first and turned to assist the ladies. Flora hadn't wanted to come, citing her need to stay with Trista, but the day was so glorious that Sugar Anne insisted that Flora get out of the house.

"You've hardly left her side, Flora," Sugar Anne had said, "and you would benefit from fresh air and a change of scenery. Phoebe and Mary will look after Trista while we're gone. Put on your prettiest hat and come along."

Sugar Anne hadn't counted on Flora's hat being such a garish shade of magenta or having quite so many colorful ribbons and plumes and bunches of fruit. She did concede that the hat was a perfect match for the expensively made dress she wore, which was a velvet and satin creation in the same blinding shade and of a cut more appropriate for a much younger woman. In the harsh light of the outdoors, Flora's rouged cheeks appeared to glow even brighter against the paleness of her powdered face.

Once, Sugar Anne might have been embarrassed to be seen with such an outlandish, coarse-looking person, but she had changed her attitude about many things over the past few months. In any case, she'd never been one to desert her friends over such trivial matters as fashion, appearance, or the opinions of others.

Not like some people she knew, Sugar Anne thought as she spied her former friend Lucy standing on the lawn with a stylishly attired group. Lucy was staring at the newcomers, her mouth agape. In truth, everyone gathered in front of the church gawked at them—or, rather, at Flora.

No one smiled. No one nodded. No one approached with kind words or Christian greetings. Several parishioners turned and hurried inside; the others remained standing like pillars of salt, eyes wide and mouths open like a row of Spanish mackerel at the fish market.

When she heard the quick intake of breath, Sugar Anne glanced at Flora. The rouged mouth was set firmly and her chin was up, but tears glimmered in her eyes as she held her worn Bible against her breast.

"I'm not feeling well, dearie," Flora whispered. "I think I'll have Donald take me back home."

Rage built inside Sugar Anne as she stood in front of the church with its magnificent stained glass windows, which, if memory served, Grandfather Jacob had donated as a tribute to the members of the Spicer family who had died in that last horrible epidemic. A great deal of Spicer money had gone into the original construction of this lovely stone building with its ornate trim and tall steeple. Sugar Anne's parents had been married there; she had been baptized there; the funerals of her family had been conducted there.

But donations and other claims aside, this was a house

of God. By golly, Sugar Anne had as much right to be there with Flora—or the basest bunch of toothless sailors from the wharf, for that matter—as any of the sanctimonious prigs standing about gaping!

"Absolutely not, Flora," Sugar Anne said. "I'm sure you'll feel much better once we're inside."

Webb smiled at Flora and offered her his arm. "I would be honored, Miss Flora, if you would allow me to escort you inside."

Sugar Anne took Mr. Underwood's arm, and the four of them marched up the steps toward the sanctuary.

As they walked past Lucy Malloy Ticknor, a perverse defiance made Sugar Anne smile brightly. "Why, good morning, Lucy. How delightful to see you here, dear friend. I'm looking forward to attending a play at the opera house with you. It was so sweet of you to invite me. Drop by Cousin Trista's on Tuesday, and we can make our plans."

Continuing to beam at the dumbstruck Lucy, Sugar Anne fluttered her fingers and strode on. Webb led them to seats at the front of the sanctuary amid the gawking and buzzing of the congregation.

Sugar Anne was thoroughly disgusted. She would have never believed that one garish hat and gown, no matter how tasteless, could create such a commotion. True, Flora's appearance, including her generous application of cosmetics, made her stand out like a sore thumb—she seemed more appropriately dressed for the stage than for a front pew in church—but these people must lead exceedingly dull lives if a gaudy garb and a heavy hand at the rouge pot sent them into such a fidget.

She suspected that of all the people in that fine church, Flora had the kindest, most loving heart.

When the sermon was over and the closing hymn had been sung, Sugar Anne stood, planning to make a fast getaway and vowing never to darken the door of that church again.

Unfortunately, their seats at the front required that they wait for those behind to file out. Until the way was clear, they were stuck. While they waited, Sugar Anne glanced at the parishioners lingering across the aisle. One gray-haired matron, tall, regal, and pinch-mouthed, stared unabashedly at Sugar Anne. Her brow was furrowed and her dark eyes narrowed. Utterly weary of such rude behavior, Sugar Anne pinched her own mouth, furrowed her brow, and glared back at the old biddy.

The matron laughed and her face transformed into total sweetness as she pushed her way toward Sugar Anne. "You must forgive me, my dear. You seemed so familiar, and I was trying to recall where we'd met. You're Madeline Spicer's granddaughter, aren't you?"

"Yes, I'm Sugar Anne Spicer. I'm sorry, Mrs.—"

"Southern. Mrs. Emmett Southern. Your grandmother, God rest her sainted soul, was my dearest friend. I haven't seen you in many years—it must be fifteen or more—but I remembered you when I saw that pugnacious expression. You called me Aunt Gaggie when you were a child."

"I did?"

Mrs. Southern laughed. "Yes. My Christian name is Gabriel, and Madeline called me Gabby. Gaggie was the way you pronounced it when you were a toddler."

A memory flitted through Sugar Anne's head, then

came again and began to take firm shape. She recalled accompanying her grandmother to tea at an immense house on Broadway that looked very much like a castle. And she recalled a lovely, laughing woman who hugged her frequently, smelled of lilacs, and fed her strawberry tarts.

A cascade of bright warmth rushed over Sugar Anne. "Aunt Gaggie! Now I remember." Beaming, she threw her arms around Mrs. Southern's neck. "How wonderful to see you."

Realizing that people would surely be staring—with good cause—at her exuberant behavior, Sugar Anne pulled away. "Oh, Mrs. Southern, forgive me. I didn't mean to make a spectacle of myself."

"You didn't, my dear. I'm delighted to see you after all these years and discover what a lovely woman you've become. Madeline would have been so proud." Mrs. Southern glanced at the rest of the party. "I don't believe that I've met your friends."

Sugar Anne introduced Flora, Webb, and Mr. Underwood to Mrs. Emmett Southern, who, if memory served her correctly, was one of the grande dames of Galveston society.

The matron couldn't have been more gracious in her greetings, including saying to Flora with a bright smile, "Mrs. Lamb, what a colorful, spirited hat that is."

Flora smiled happily.

Mrs. Southern linked her arm with Sugar Anne's. "Come, my dear, and walk out with me. I want to catch up on all these past years. I recall reading that your grandfather passed away some years ago."

Sugar Anne was so busy talking that she barely noticed

the gaping churchgoers whose astonished eyes followed her group as they left the sanctuary.

When they reached the curb, Mrs. Southern said, "Dear, we need hours to talk. Call on me tomorrow morning and we shall have plenty of time. I'll have Cook make strawberry tarts."

Sugar Anne smiled. "I would be delighted, Mrs. Southern."

"None of that," the old woman said, kissing Sugar Anne's cheek. "I'll always be Aunt Gaggie. Call about ten." Turning to Flora, she smiled and said, "I'm delighted to have met you, Mrs. Lamb. I insist on having the name of your milliner." She nodded to Webb McQuillan and Preston Underwood. "Perhaps you ladies and gentlemen will come to dinner one night this week. Tuesday? We can decide tomorrow, Sugar Anne." The gracious gray-haired lady stepped into a waiting carriage and waved goodbye.

Only by concentrating mightily and summoning up all the grace from the depths of her being did Sugar Anne refrain from turning to the supercilious congregation of hypocrites and sticking out her tongue at them. Instead, she linked her arm with Flora's and smiled. "Wasn't that a delightful sermon? Ah, here's Donald with our carriage."

Sugar Anne had just finished the last spoonful of her chocolate blancmange when Phoebe waddled into the dining room and announced: "Miss Sugar Anne, there's a lady here to see you. Says her name's—" Phoebe looked stricken. "I forget her name. But I think it's something like Clock."

"Clock?" Sugar Anne probed her memory. "Clock? I don't know anyone with a name like that. Ah. Could it be Ticknor?"

"Ticknor. That's it. Pretty lady with blond hair. I told her you was eatin' your Sunday dinner. She said she'd wait."

"Lunch, Phoebe. The noon meal is lunch."

"Yes'm. Anyhow she's waitin' on the porch."

"The *porch*? Phoebe, you should nev—" She looked at Phoebe's puffy, sad face and curtailed her criticism. After her abominable behavior, Lucy didn't deserve polite treatment, certainly not at the risk of hurting Phoebe's feelings by correcting her. "Thank you, Phoebe."

Sugar Anne went to the door and found Mrs. Hoity-toity Ticknor biding her time outside. Perhaps Phoebe had the right idea, she decided, and declined to invite her former friend inside.

"Yes?" she inquired, her tone deliberately frosty.

Lucy wrung her hands and looked positively ashen. "Oh, Sugar Anne, can you ever forgive me?" she asked.

"Forgive you for what?"

"For being such a flagrant, uncharitable . . . snob. For thinking more of social appearances than friendship. When I saw Mrs. Southern's behavior, I was exceedingly embarrassed by my own, and when I told my father about the incident . . . well, I thought that Daddy was going to have another seizure for sure. 'By the grace of God and the Spicer family did you have food in your belly and clothes on your back, Lucille Malloy!' he shouted at me. Of course his speech is still impaired and he didn't say it that plainly, but it was plain enough. And he only calls me Lucille when he is dreadfully angry. Oh, Sugar Anne, I'm such an arrogant fool."

Lucy fell weeping into Sugar Anne's arms.

"Shhhh, Lucy, don't carry on so. Come inside. Have you had lunch?"

Lucy shook her head. "I couldn't eat a bite. I'm too distraught. Please say that you forgive me. Please."

"Oh, heavenly days, Lucy, I forgive you. Now let go. You're bruising my arms. We were just having blanc-mange for dessert. Chocolate. Perhaps you'd like a dish?"

"Chocolate, you say?" Lucy dabbed her eyes on a lace handkerchief as Sugar Anne led her inside. "Perhaps I shall have just a taste."

Sugar Anne smiled. Girlhood wasn't so far away after all.

Webb leaned back against the railing on one end of the porch, smoking his cigar. Since he'd recovered from his wound enough to wear his pants, Sugar Anne had banished him to the outdoors for his smokes. Actually he didn't mind. It gave him an excuse to separate himself from the rest of that crazy assortment living inside.

Especially Sugar Anne.

She and that snooty friend of hers had made up, and Lucy had told her that her father the judge would get some of his cronies to intervene with Fitzwarren. Ever since her friend left, Sugar Anne had been flitting around like a horsefly looking for a place to land. She'd even hummed most of the way through supper. Dinner.

He could barely enjoy his roast duck and dumplings for all her smiling and humming.

Damned if he could figure that woman out. If he

hadn't known about the slick deal that she and her husband had pulled on that bunch of investors in Chicago, he would have sworn that she was too naive for her own good. If he hadn't known better, Webb would also swear that she didn't know that her cousin and her friend were a couple of old whores. Everybody else in town seemed to know.

It was clear from everything that he'd learned that Sugar Anne had come from an upstanding family. Maybe she'd taken a wrong turn like her cousin Trista had. Or maybe Herndon had duped her along with the money boys. Maybe—

Nah. The Pinkertons thought that she was in the scam up to her eyeballs. That crew didn't miss much, and he wasn't about to go questioning their judgment. Next thing you know, he'd start thinking that she was a lily white innocent and begin making up excuses for what she'd done.

He was just restless. Anxious to get things moving and collect that reward. The lawyer Fitzwarren seemed to be the biggest stumbling block now. Sugar Anne needed a grubstake to continue on her way, and if she didn't soon get some help dealing with that oily lawyer, either from Cotton or some of her fancy friends, Webb was going to have to step in himself.

The screen door slammed. Webb glanced over his shoulder and froze. His eyes narrowed as he watched Sugar Anne stretch, her dress drawing taut across her lush bosom. He sucked in a quick breath and damned near strangled on cigar smoke.

"Oh, dear," Sugar Anne exclaimed, rushing to beat his back while he had a coughing fit. "Are you all right?"

"Fine," he choked out as his eyes teared up. Dammit, why was she always posing and showing off her body like that? Didn't she know what that did to a man?

"These nasty things will kill you," she said as she plucked his cigar from between his teeth and pitched it over the fence and onto the sidewalk. "You smoke much too much. When I see what cigar smoke can do to nice parlor curtains, I shudder to think what it does to a person's body."

Webb scowled, bit back a sharp comment, and strode to the end of the porch.

His scowl didn't seem to faze her. She sashayed over to where he stood and picked a rose from a bush that twined around a trellis there. She held the flower under her nose and leaned against the railing next to him.

"Isn't it a lovely night? Absolutely glorious. And the moon looks like a huge silver dollar." She took a deep breath—he didn't glance at her bosom, but he imagined what happened—and said, "Doesn't it smell wonderful? I'd forgotten how wonderful it smells here."

"Smells like an overripe outhouse to me. Why don't they do something about a sewer system in this town?"

"Oh, you," she said, swatting his arm with the rose. "Ignore that. I meant the smell of flowers still blooming in November and the fresh scent of the Gulf breezes. I'd forgotten how much I love Galveston."

She laughed and the joyful sound of it rippled over his skin and out through the darkness, raising chill bumps on his arms and tugging at his insides in a funny way.

"You sound pretty happy."

"Oh, I am." She whirled in a circle like a child. "I was

sure that my whole life was ruined and that I had reached a dead end, but now I feel that there's hope."

He took another cigar from his pocket, but instead of lighting it, he simply rolled it between his fingers. "Want to explain that?"

She shook her head, then turned, leaned her back against the railing, and lifted her face to the moonlight. "I almost wish that I could stay here forever."

Right then, with the light making her face shine like a pearl, Sugar Anne was the most beautiful thing Webb had ever seen in his life. Her lips looked as full and sweet as ripe figs in the summertime. He licked his own lips and swallowed the rush of longing that filled his mouth. "Then why not stay?" he asked very softly.

"I—I have . . . obligations."

Those lips seemed to draw him closer as surely as if he'd been lassoed. "What kind of . . . 'obligations'?" The moonlight cast a quicksilver shimmer in her eyes as they met his. His nostrils were filled with the smell of her, the smell of gardenias and roses.

"Just . . . things."

Like magnets drawing together, their lips came closer and closer until her breath was warm against his skin. Something inside him went loco. He grabbed her and kissed her like a parched man grabs water, drinking deeply.

She kissed him back, and he went even crazier, crushing the rose she'd held between them as her arms went around him.

When she moaned against his mouth, he lifted her onto the railing and began batting dress and petticoats aside to get to where he wanted to go. She locked her long legs around him, and he moaned a time or two himself. He cupped one of those lush breasts that had been taunting him; he stroked its soft curve, and she wiggled against him. Damn, she was hot and sweet as cane syrup bubbling in the mill.

Aching to touch bare flesh and taste it with his tongue, he reached for the buttons at the throat of her dress. He had four of them undone when she went dead still.

"Stop!"

Before his brain registered her command, his hand slipped inside to caress the creamy swell, to feel the hardened nipple.

"Stop. Webb, stop! Dear God, please stop this instant."

He stopped, but his hand stayed inside her bodice. Her legs stayed locked around his waist; he could feel her warmth where she had writhed against his belly.

Then he felt her begin to shudder. She trembled like a newborn calf in his arms.

"Please," she whispered, her anguished tone almost breaking his heart. "Please don't do this. I—I can't—I mustn't. Please."

Slowly he eased his hand from the warm nest and carefully rebuttoned her dress. That done, he took a deep breath, clasped his fingers around her delicate ankles at his back, and gently drew them from him. He stepped back, rearranged her skirts, and lifted her from the railing.

"I'm sorry," she said. "I never should have allowed that to happen. I don't know what got into me."

He could have apologized right then too, should have apologized like a gentleman, but he'd never been much of a gentleman, and he wasn't sorry for a damned thing. "I know what almost got into you, and—"

"Damn you, Webb McQuillan! Damn you to hell!" She whirled and stormed into the house.

Webb winced when the door slammed. Goda'mighty, if he didn't get hold of himself, he was headed for a calamity.

He knew then that he couldn't wait for Cotton or anybody else. Bright and early the next morning, he aimed to take the bull by the horns.

⪻ Eleven ⪼

With his twin Colts strapped to his sides, his silver star pinned to his vest, and his black hat pulled low on his brow, Webb McQuillan strode into Richard Fitzwarren's office, ignoring the sour-mouthed woman who sputtered in his wake. Webb hadn't slept worth a damn the night before so his "don't-fuck-with-me" glower was as genuine as his fuse was short.

And speaking of short, he couldn't believe that the runt he found kneeling on the floor and cleaning out the safe was the bugbear causing all the problems. Fitzwarren jumped to his feet and glared at the bird of a woman, whose hairdo was coming undone. "I said that I was not to be disturbed, Miss Purvis!"

"Oh, Mr. Fitzwarren, I tried to stop him. I tried." The poor dithering woman was almost in a swoon. "I simply couldn't—"

"Don't blame her, Fitzwarren," Webb said. "I told her that I would announce myself." He removed the cold cigar stub from his mouth, spat a perfect arc into the brass spittoon beside the big desk, then stuck the stogie back in the side of his mouth and shot the lawyer his most menacing scowl.

He had to hand it to the little dandy; though he was no more than knee high to a popcorn fart, he didn't back down. Fitzwarren merely lifted his eyebrows and smoothed his sorry excuse for a mustache. "And exactly who are you?"

Webb spat again, and damned if he didn't miss. He never missed. Ignoring his miscalculation, he stared the lawyer straight in the eye with a glare that had been known to make rattlesnakes turn tail and run. "I'm the instrument of your doom, you thieving, egg-sucking little bastard. I know what you've been doing, and it's judgment day."

With a single fluid motion, he tucked both sides of his black coat behind his widow-makers, readying to draw and at the same time revealing the badge on his vest that he'd shined up special that morning.

For a minute Webb thought that the sawed-off polecat was going to pee in his pants. But he recovered himself enough to squeak, "I don't know what you're talking about."

"Mr. Fitzwarren, shall I send Edgar for the law?" Miss Purvis asked timorously, wringing her hands.

"Ma'am, I *am* the law. Captain Webb McQuillan. Texas Rangers."

"You're a—a ... *genuine* Texas Ranger?" Her eyes rounded to the size of dinner buckets, and he struggled to keep from grinning.

"Yes'um. Now why don't you sit down in that chair over yonder and be real quiet until your boss and I are done." When she didn't move, he gave her his best intimidating squint.

"Yes, sir." She scurried to a chair in the corner and slunk down in it.

Webb cut his gaze back to Fitzwarren, whose hand was inching toward the top desk drawer. "I hope you're not fixin' to go for any gun in that desk, lawyer." He touched the handle of the Colt on his right hip. " 'Cause I ought to warn you that I'm faster than double-struck lightning."

Fitzwarren jerked his hand away from its destination. "What in heaven's name is this about, man? Why are you here bullying me?"

"I told you that I'm here because you're a thief, a sorry, low-down son of a bitch who'd have to look up to see hell. I aim to put a stop to your swindlin'."

"Swindling?" Fitzwarren sputtered. "Sir, I have no notion of what you're talking about."

"I'm talking about your chicanery concerning the affairs of Mrs. Trista La Vigne—at whose home I am presently abiding, by the way. You might say that I'm a friend of the family." He rested his hands on the butts of his guns. "A very good friend. Particularly of Miss Sugar Anne Spicer, Mrs. La Vigne's cousin and only living relative. I believe that you've met Miss Spicer."

A sweat broke out on the lawyer's high forehead. "I can assure you that I'm involved in no chicanery, but perhaps we can talk about your concerns at another time." He pulled out his watch and checked it. "At the moment I'm late for an appointment."

When Webb spotted the watch chain, he smirked. "Well, well. Appears that you have a shiny new chain for that old timepiece of yours. Surprised that a man in your position wouldn't buy himself a new watch as well. That one looks a mite scratched up."

"This fine watch belonged to my father, sir. Now, as I told you, I'm late for an appointment, and you'll have to excuse me. Miss Purvis will show you out."

"I'm not ready to leave just yet." From his pocket, Webb pulled out the broken chain that Willie had squirreled away. "This looks like a better match on that watch of yours."

"Where—Uh, *what* is that?"

"It's the chain that was broken in the struggle that night you tried to kill Trista La Vigne. You left her for dead, didn't you?"

The lawyer went ashen. "Certainly not! Why would I do such a terrible thing?"

"For the money of course. You planned to kill her after you'd dummied up that power-of-attorney document. Only she didn't die. And now you're trying to ship her off to some sort of asylum and take over everything. It won't work, Fitzwarren."

The little bastard cut a quick glance toward the safe, then caught himself.

Webb strolled to the open steel door and saw what the lawyer had been up to. Stacks of cash and papers were stashed in a valise. "What have we here?" He reached down and picked up a handful of papers.

"See here! Those are my personal—"

Webb's glare cut him off. "These papers seem to deal with Mrs. La Vigne's business. You must have already got word from some of Miss Spicer's connections that your doin's were coming under scrutiny. Goin' somewhere, were you?" He fanned out a stack of bills and stretched his lips over his teeth in a parody of a smile.

"Why, yes—that is, no. I—I mean—"

"I believe you were right the first time. You are goin' somewhere. You're through, Fitzwarren. Now Miss Spicer's friends, Judge Malloy and Mrs. Emmett Southern and their associates, probably mean to have you arrested all neatlike so that you can have your day in court. But before that happens, you intend to skip out with everything you can carry, don't you?"

"Certainly not! I'm a respectable—"

"You're a pile of dogshit, Fitzwarren, and I'm here to see that you leave town right this minute with nothing but the clothes on your back."

"You—you can't do that!"

Webb grinned. "Sure I can." He pulled his Bowie knife from its scabbard, stuck the point under the lawyer's chin, and lifted him to his tiptoes. "I'm gonna give you till the count of ten—no, make that fifteen, I'm generous—to get out of here and be on your way to the railroad station. There's a train leaving in about twenty minutes, and I expect you to be on it. If I hear that you've taken one thing from Mrs. La Vigne or that you've set foot in this town again, I'm gonna find you."

He shoved his face in the lawyer's until their noses were almost touching. "And if I find you, I'm gonna slit you from balls to gizzard and fry your innards in corn-meal. That clear?"

Fitzwarren's eyes bugged out like a bullfrog's, and he tried to nod without skewering himself on the knife tip. "Very clear," he croaked.

"Good." Webb smiled. "One . . ."

The lawyer tore out of his office like the demons of perdition were after him. He didn't even stop for his hat.

Webb turned to the woman who cowered in her chair,

drawn up in a ball like a scared pill bug. "Ma'am, you don't have a thing to fear from me. Unless you were in on the thieving of Mrs. La Vigne's property."

"No. Oh, no. Merciful heavens, no." She sprang to her feet, looking totally indignant. "I would never . . . Never! I am an honest woman, sir. Ask anyone about Mirantha Purvis."

"Yes, ma'am. I will."

"Was Mr. Fitzwarren truly a thief?"

"That he was, ma'am. And a forger. Mrs. La Vigne never gave him her power of attorney. He was stealing from her and meant to have her put away so that he could keep right on stealing. She's been in a coma, you know, and she'd be in an institution in a day or two if her cousin hadn't come to town when she did and put a stop to his shenanigans."

"I suppose this means that I'm out of a job." Miss Purvis sighed. "And I haven't been paid for last week either."

"Ma'am, I can't speak for Miss Spicer, but it seems to me that she'll need someone who knows about how things run around here, especially till particulars get sorted out. Did Fitzwarren have other clients?"

She shook her head. "He wasn't much of a lawyer. And when he took over Mrs. La Vigne's business, he dropped his other clients and spent all his time on her affairs." She snorted. "All the time when he wasn't down at the Tremont playing billiards or drinking spirits at Toujouse's bar with the gentlemen in the silk hats and trying to be one of them. Although I tried to be a loyal employee, I wasn't very fond of Mr. Fitzwarren, you see.

I found him to be—" She touched her fingertips to her mouth as if to hold back the words.

"The rear end of a mule's papa?" Webb ventured.

She tittered. "Exactly. Good riddance." She hurried out to her desk.

Webb briefly glanced through the papers Fitzwarren was about to make off with. One was the phony power of attorney, which he promptly tore in quarters and put in his pocket.

"I'll be back shortly to look through these documents more carefully, Miss Purvis. First, though, tell me which bank Fitzwarren uses. And where does he live?"

Armed with that information, he strode through the door and started down the stairs. He met Cotton Yarborough on his way up. "If you're looking for Fitzwarren," Webb told his old compadre, "he's not here."

Cotton frowned. "Know where he went? The chief wants to question him."

"He was headed out of town."

"Hellfire! Judge Malloy sent word first thing this morning to haul his ass in and get to the bottom of those shady doin's with Sugar Anne's cousin. Galled the chief. He and Fitzwarren play pool together. Now, when I tried to talk to him about Sugar Anne and Mrs. La Vigne, he told me that everything was on the up and up and to mind my own damned business. But when Judge Malloy says 'Jump,' the chief jumps. Though I'm supposed to be real polite-like when I ask the lawyer to come down to the station."

Webb nodded. "Sounds like I had the right idea."

"What was that?"

"I visited him a short time ago. That was when he decided to leave town."

Cotton grinned. "You give him the business?"

Webb grinned back. "I put the fear of God into that little bastard. Spread it on thicker than fresh churned butter. And he lit out quicker than hell could scorch a feather."

Cotton laughed and slapped Webb on the back. "Damn, wish I could have seen that. I've always said that the reputation of a Texas Ranger is better than twenty boxes of bullets. Never will forget the time you scared the shit out of those three cowpokes in that Fort Worth saloon. When you tucked your coat behind your guns and said, 'I'm the instrument of your doom,' two of 'em fainted and the other one took off running. Heard he didn't stop till he got to the Oklahoma border. Where you headed?"

"Over to the bank to make sure Fitzwarren didn't make a detour. Want to come along?"

"Think I'll pass. If I saw him, I'd have to take him to the police station. I'd sooner let some other town worry about him." Cotton touched his hat brim with his finger and started off in another direction.

Webb stopped by the bank on the Strand, saw that Fitzwarren wasn't around, and took a minute to explain to the president that the lawyer wasn't to have access to any funds. He needn't have bothered. The president of the bank, one Alfred Southern, said that his mother's handyman had just relayed that same message from Mrs. Emmett Southern. Sugar Anne must have been doing more than eating strawberry tarts with the old lady.

When Webb arrived at the railroad station, the ticket

agent said that a hatless man fitting Mr. Fitzwarren's description had just left on a northbound train.

Good riddance, Webb thought as he walked back to the lawyer's office. He wanted to examine the documents that Fitzwarren seemed so anxious to make off with.

After an hour or so, Webb shoved the papers aside on the big desk, leaned back in the leather chair, and let out a low whistle. The old gal was loaded all right, but Fitzwarren was badly mismanaging things. He wasn't even a smart thief. Didn't appear to know much about business. In the same time that the lawyer had had control, Webb could have doubled . . .

Nah. He didn't even want to think about such things.

He began stuffing the papers and money into the valise that the lawyer had left behind. He would try to help Sugar Anne sort out everything another day. At least now there was enough money to run the household—and to finance Sugar Anne's trip to hook up with Herndon.

Being antsy about getting on the way was one reason Webb hadn't hauled Fitzwarren off to the pokey. An arrest and trial would have slowed up things considerably. Too, there was the matter of Webb's authority. Technically, he was on leave from the Rangers and had overstepped his bounds a mite.

Webb grinned. Good thing the lawyer hadn't known that.

Hot damn. It wouldn't be long before he'd have that reward money in his pocket and a soft feather bed of his very own.

⇐ Twelve ⇒

Sugar Anne had barely set foot on the porch when Phoebe dashed from the house. "Oh, come quick, come quick!" Phoebe cried, seizing Sugar Anne's wrist and dragging her inside.

"Phoebe, what's wrong? Is someone injured? Is it the baby?"

"No, no. It's Miz Trista! Praise the Lord, she opened her eyes and called me by name. She's sittin' up in her bed and eatin' a bowl of custard. Just come see if she ain't. She's returned from the land of the shadows. Come on, come on." Laughing and jabbering, Phoebe tugged Sugar Anne toward the stairs.

When the news finally sank in, Sugar Anne let out a very unladylike whoop, tossed her hat aside, and bounded up the steps two at a time.

It was true. Trista La Vigne, still looking more than a trifle wan, was propped up in her bed, eyes open. Flora sat beside her, feeding her from a dish.

"Cousin Trista," Sugar Anne whispered, her eyes misting as she stood and watched from the doorway.

"Sugar Anne," the old woman said, her voice rusty and

soft. She smiled, and the years fell away. "I wish this custard were strawberry ice cream." She held out a frail hand.

Tears streaming down her face, Sugar Anne rushed to her bedside and took the hand in hers. "You remembered."

"Of course." She rested her head against the ruffled pillows and smiled. "I could hardly believe my ears when Flora told me that you were here. How wonderful that you've come for a visit. I missed you so after you left Galveston. Every time I passed that ice cream parlor, I wondered about you, about where you were, and about the fine young lady you were becoming. Turn around. Let me get a good look at you."

Laughing, Sugar Anne did as Trista asked, glad that she was wearing her favorite day dress, an elegant design in a flattering shade of soft willow green.

"Beautiful," Trista said. "More beautiful than I ever imagined. Your hair puts me in mind of mine when I was about your age."

Sugar Anne plumped her fall of auburn curls. "I always wondered how my hair came to be this color when everyone else had black hair or blond. So it's a family trait after all."

Trista touched the braid at her shoulder. "Yes, though mine faded and turned gray long ago. I remember a cousin Andre who also—Oh, listen to me prattle. Come, sit by me. Tell me about your life. Why are you here? Oh, I have a thousand questions. Flora, I can't eat another bite. Let Sugar Anne sit here and talk to me."

"For just a few minutes now, Trista," Flora said. "You mustn't tire yourself. You've been through quite an ordeal. Why, it's a miracle . . ."

"Flora," Trista said gently, "thank you for your concern, but my—my only relative is here after years and years of my hungering to see her. I won't break."

Flora gave a resigned nod and rose. "But mind you don't tire yourself out. Dr. Aiken is coming by as soon as he can."

Flora need not have concerned herself. After about ten minutes of talking—mostly listening to Sugar Anne's tale of her life after she left Galveston—Trista's eyelids fluttered several times, and although she struggled to remain awake, she drifted off to sleep.

Sugar Anne hadn't told Trista the real reason for her visit, nor did she intend to just yet. Though she had poured out her problems with Edward to her cousin while she was in a coma, the retelling could wait a few days until Trista was stronger.

She bent and touched her lips to the old woman's brow, smoothed her covers, and tiptoed from the room.

Webb and Flora stood at the foot of the stairs talking. As Sugar Anne came down, Webb glanced up to her. "Is it true? Has she really come out of the coma?"

She nodded. "And she's as bright as a penny. Weak, of course, but she seems to have all her faculties. The doctor should be by shortly. Richard Fitzwarren won't be happy to hear the news. Mark my words, that rascal is going to jail."

Webb suddenly looked very uncomfortable. "Uh, I wouldn't count on it."

Smiling smugly, she said, "But you don't know about my conversation with Aunt Gaggie. It seems she owns the bank where Cousin Trista does most of her business, and her son is the president. Mr. Fitzwarren won't be able to touch a cent until a full investigation is conducted. Another of Aunt Gaggie's sons is on the Board of Exchange. He'll see to it that—"

"Whoa! Listen to me," Webb said. "He's gone."

"Gone? Who's gone?"

"Fitzwarren. He lit a shuck a couple of hours ago."

"But why? Where did he go?" Sugar Anne asked.

"Dirty, low-down scoundrel," Flora said. "He probably got word from some of his buddies that the jig was about up. Now, with Trista coming to herself, things will really be hot for that snake."

Webb shuffled his feet and turned his hat round and round in his hands, studying the band. Sugar Anne's uneasiness grew as she watched him fidget. "You know something that you haven't told us," she said. "According to Lucy, Judge Malloy told the chief of police to bring Mr. Fitzwarren in for questioning. The younger Mr. Southern was going to do what he could . . . What has happened to Mr. Fitzwarren?"

"He's on a northbound train."

"Oh, no. He's escaped!"

"Not exactly," Webb said. "I put the fear of God into him, and he left at my bidding."

Fury overcame her. "At *your* bidding? And exactly who made this any of your business, Captain McQuillan? I was handling things just fine."

He made that snorting noise again, the one that he seemed inordinately fond of. Her irritation grew.

"Well, I was," she said hotly. "If you had stayed out of it, he would be properly jailed by now—he'd have to pay the price for his dealings. I'll wager that you sauntered in, drew your six-shooters, and threatened to shoot large holes in the poor man if he didn't get out of town by sundown."

"You'd better be damned glad that I did. The 'poor man' was about to make his getaway with a suitcase full of cash, bonds, and that power of attorney. Another five minutes, and he'd have been long gone."

Her hand splayed across her bosom. "Oh, no."

"Oh, yes. His secretary, a Miss Purvis, seems a decent sort of woman. I don't think that she knew anything about Fitzwarren's doings. You might consider keeping her on, at least until you get someone to straighten out the mess he's made of Mrs. La Vigne's business affairs."

"I will need to find someone, won't I? I'll ask—Well, actually I won't need to do anything. Cousin Trista is alert now. She'll want to choose her own man."

"I doubt that Trista will be able to do very much for a while," Flora said. "You must remember her condition. We wouldn't want to worry her, now would we?"

"Oh, certainly not," Sugar Anne said. "I'm sure that things can wait a few days."

Webb rubbed his chin and looked extremely uncomfortable. "From the bungling of things that I saw in my quick examination of Fitzwarren's office, I'd say that you don't need to waste any time. I know that I've just studied a little business and law, but I have a head for this kind of stuff. If you don't want Mrs. La Vigne to lose a passel of money, you'd better get right on it."

"Sounds right serious," Flora said.

"It is serious."

"Think you could straighten it out, Captain?" Flora asked.

He shrugged. "I could try."

Flora glanced meaningfully at Sugar Anne. When Sugar Anne didn't pick up on the cue, Flora elbowed her sharply. "You know anything about running a business, the legal matters and such?" she asked.

Sugar Anne sighed. "Almost nothing. Captain, would you consider assisting us in this matter? Temporarily, of course."

"I'd consider it. Temporarily, you understand."

"Wonderful!" Flora said. "That's settled." She slipped her right arm through Sugar Anne's and her left one through the captain's. "Now, let's go eat. I believe Mary said we're having flounder. I'm just crazy about flounder."

While Dr. Aiken was upstairs examining Trista, the entire household waited in the foyer. Nobody said a word. Even Willie sat quietly on the bottom step. The only sounds were the ticking of the grandfather clock and the occasional muted hiccups from Phoebe.

"He's been up there a *real* long time," Willie finally whispered.

"An exceedingly long time," Mr. Underwood said.

Phoebe hiccupped again, then clamped her hand over her mouth.

"Phoebe, hold your breath!" Flora said.

"And count to fifty," Mary added.

"What you think's taking so long?" asked Donald.

"I'm sure that Dr. Aiken is conducting a number of tests," Sugar Anne said.

"Either that or they're playing checkers," Webb offered.

Willie's eyebrows went up. "Checkers?"

"The captain is teasing, Willie," Sugar Anne said.

"Phoebe, you're turning blotchy. Let your breath out before you faint. Go get a glass of water and drink it in ten sips."

"Yes 'um, but I don't want to miss nothing."

"It's not that far to the sink."

"Yes 'um." The girl clutched her belly and scurried away.

"Want me to go up and listen at the door?" Willie asked. "I'll be quiet as anything. They'll never know I was there."

"Thank you, Willie," Sugar Anne said, "but no, we'll wait until the doctor comes down."

They waited quietly for another few minutes, and the doctor came downstairs just as Phoebe returned. His brow was furrowed, his mood somber.

"Doctor?" Sugar Anne said, feeling anxious. "Is my cousin all right?"

"It's the strangest thing I've ever seen." Dr. Aiken shook his head. "She seems to be perfectly healthy—weak, of course, but healthy. Considering she was in a coma for so long, I expected more atrophy of her limbs."

"It was that Chinese oil," Flora said. "I told you that it would work real good. I learned all about them massaging oils and herbs from a China gal that worked in one of Trista's houses for a while. They called her the China Doll. She was—"

Webb coughed loudly. "Doctor, how long before she'll be up and around?"

"I've no way to estimate. She's the first patient I've ever had to survive so long in a coma. I would suggest that first she try sitting up for a while, perhaps on the porch if the weather is suitable. When she's stronger, we can evaluate further. It might be some weeks before she should try walking again. Miss Lamb, the oils and the massage seem to have been beneficial. I'd say to continue with them."

Flora nodded with satisfaction. "Told you they was good. Why, the China Doll told me they kept her rheumy old great-grandpa going until he was a hundred and two. Now, I remember one customer she had—"

"What about her diet?" Mary asked, stepping in front of Flora. "Should she have anything special?"

"Not that I can think of. Nourishing meals without much spice or rich gravies."

"But Miz Trista's right fond of rich gravy," Phoebe said.

Dr. Aiken lifted his hands. "Then feed her what she wants. Captain McQuillan, happily it seems that I'm not likely to be returning to this house for a few days. I'll have another look at that wound while I'm here." The doctor smiled. "That's a right nice pair of pants you got on there. New?"

Once the doctor and the captain had gone upstairs for the examination and the rest of the household had dispersed, Sugar Anne went to the back parlor to write notes to Lucy and Aunt Gaggie. Thanks to their intervention—and to Webb's, she grudgingly admitted—Fitzwarren's brazen criminal activities had been curtailed.

With Cousin Trista recovering and her fortune intact, Sugar Anne could breathe a sigh of relief. In no time at all, she would track down Edward. Her reputation would be restored and her own inheritance safely back in the bank. She hoped that Beatrice and Robert Ralston and the rest of that bunch of fair-weather friends in Chicago would choke when they learned of her innocence and her valor in recovering their investments.

Yes, her luck had definitely turned.

⫷ Thirteen ⫸

Webb scratched his signature on the sheaf of papers, then handed it to the secretary. "Thank you, Miss Purvis. You've done a fine job. I'd be much obliged if you'd take that letter to the Willis & Jones Company to the post office right away."

"Yes, sir." Miss Purvis, who'd turned out to be indispensable in straightening things out, said, as she edged out of the office.

When the door closed, Webb stretched, then leaned back in the soft leather chair, propped his well-shined boots on the desk, and pulled a thin cigar out of his pocket. He ran the cigar under his nose and inhaled the aroma of fine tobacco fresh off a ship from Cuba. He'd bought a whole box from Heidenheimer's only an hour after the cargo was unloaded at the wharf the afternoon before.

Now this was the kind of life a man could get used to. Sitting in this chair was a hell of a lot more comfortable than sitting a saddle for hours on end. Though he wasn't quite ready to trade in his best cowboy hat for a tall silk one, he liked wearing his new suits and clean shirts, and he was getting mighty fond of that soft feather bed at Trista's house and of Mary's fine cooking.

He wouldn't have minded staying on as Trista's business manager—what she'd insisted on paying him was beyond his wildest dreams—but there wasn't a chance of that happening, especially when Sugar Anne found out that he'd duped her.

Webb lit his cigar and blew the smoke toward the ceiling. Damned shame. He sure did like it here. Liked the people; liked the town; liked what he was doing.

Liked it a lot.

Probably too much under the circumstances. But he enjoyed depending on his brain instead of his trigger finger. Maybe he was going soft, or maybe he was just getting too old for rangering, but he'd spent the last twenty years on his own, going from pillar to post, and he was past ready to settle down and enjoy a few comforts.

Sugar Anne pushed the wicker invalid chair up the ramp that Donald had fashioned and paused on the front porch. "Tired?" she asked Trista. "Shall we go in or do you want to sit out here for a while?"

"Oh, outside, please. The weather is so glorious, and our walk didn't tire me a bit. You're the one who did the pushing. I thought that Flora would be along by now. Where did we lose her?"

"She wanted to stop in at Mrs. Cautier's and look at the new hats. She'll be along." Sugar Anne wheeled the chair around until Trista was facing the street. "Want some tea?"

"Tea would be lovely, some of the new blend that was just delivered. Ask Mary to bring it out to us."

A while later, as they lingered over a second cup of tea, Trista said, "I thank God every day that you came back into my life. Not only have I missed you terribly, but if you hadn't come, I would have been locked away in a sanatorium by now, and poor Flora and the others would have been turned out to fend for themselves. It's a miracle, truly a miracle."

Sugar Anne squirmed. She hadn't told her cousin the true reason for her coming to Galveston nor the full extent of Edward's perfidy. Now was the perfect opportunity. Although she wasn't completely recovered, Trista was much stronger, mentally sharp certainly, and able to stand and walk a step or two unassisted. Dr. Aiken continued to be amazed; Flora continued to insist that the credit lay with the Chinese oils and herbs she used to massage Trista's back and limbs each day.

"My dear," Trista said as she brushed cookie crumbs from her lap, "there is something I must tell you, something important, and I don't know quite where to begin."

Smiling, Sugar Anne said, "And I have something important to tell you as well. You go first. And I believe that Grandfather Jacob used to say to begin at the beginning."

Trista's head fell back against the high-backed invalid chair, and she closed her eyes. "Ah, yes, Jacob. I suppose it begins with him." She sighed deeply, then after a few moments' silence, she began to speak again.

"When I was sixteen, I was sent to live with Jacob and Madeline in New Orleans, to be a companion to Madeline and care for her during her pregnancy. My branch of the family was the poor one—not that Madeline's side was enormously wealthy by any means, but they were comfortable, and Jacob was earning a fair living as well.

"Although Madeline was several years older than I, we got along famously, and I was delighted to have new dresses without patches and a few delicacies to eat. This was her third pregnancy—the two earlier ones ended badly—and she was determined to be very careful. She spent most of her time in bed, taking every precaution. I was happy to be at her beck and call, for she was such a sweet soul and I loved her dearly.

"Then a terrible thing happened." She heaved another deep sigh, then shuddered. "I suppose the only way to put it is to come straight out with it. Jacob . . . seduced me."

"Oh, Trista, no!"

"Yes, my dear, he did. Not on one occasion, but on several. I was terrified, and I had nowhere to turn. He told me that if I went to the priest or to the authorities with my tales, he would deny the charges, and he was, after all, a respected man in the community. Besides, as he reminded me, such accusations would devastate Madeline and perhaps even cause her to miscarry."

"Why, the old bastard!" Sugar Anne blurted out as she sprang to her feet. All of her old anger and resentment had rushed to the fore with Trista's revelations. "Perhaps I should be ashamed for calling my own grandfather names, but he was a self-serving, manipulative tyrant. He kept me stuck away in boarding schools and on his deathbed made me vow to marry Edward Herndon, who was the scum of the earth! No wonder he didn't want me to associate with you." She dropped to her knees in front of her cousin. "Oh, Trista, I'm so sorry that he did such a thing to you."

"There's more to the story, child. Much more. Madeline did miscarry, and I became pregnant."

Sugar Anne gasped, horrified at what she was hearing about her grandfather, but not doubting for a moment the truth of it. "How devastating for you. How terribly frightening. What did you do?"

"Jacob sent me away to a convent to have the child, then he and Madeline adopted the baby boy."

"The baby boy?" Sugar Anne felt the blood drain from her face. "My—my father?"

Trista nodded. "Madeline never knew the true circumstances of the child's birth. She was only told that his mother was a young, unmarried girl of good breeding. They moved to Galveston soon afterward. Jacob gave me a goodly sum of money and told me never to contact them again. I don't think anyone here knew that your father was adopted. Madeline treated him as her own."

As Sugar Anne knelt beside Trista's chair, she took the frail hands in hers. "Then you're my . . ."

"Grandmother. Yes, by blood I am. But Madeline was the grandmother of your heart. I remember how you used to speak of her after you'd lost her, when you were just a child. She loved you very much, and you loved her."

Sugar Anne laid her head on Trista's lap. "I did. I adored her. She was so sweet and kind and full of warm hugs. I miss her still. Grandmère and Papa and Mama and Jon. I miss them all. Jon would have been a grown man now." She looked up at the sad, lined face. "You never even got to see Papa, did you?"

Trista shook her head. "I promised Jacob that I would never interfere in your father's life and never speak to Madeline or see her again. I kept my vow. Oh, I heard about him through various means. I knew that he had married your mama, and I knew about you and Jon, but I never tried to see him or Madeline. Only when I heard of their deaths after that terrible yellow fever epidemic did I come to Galveston. I wanted at least to tell my son and my dear cousin good-bye, to say a prayer over my grandson and my daughter-in-law."

"That's why you were at the cemetery that day when I first met you."

"Yes. I was saying good-bye to the strangers who were my family." Trista stroked Sugar Anne's hair as if she were a child to be comforted. "Have I disturbed you, my dear?"

"No. Yes. Well, I mean, of course it disturbs me, but perhaps not in the way you think." She took Trista's pale hands and kissed each in turn, then smiled up at her. "I'm very happy to discover that I have a second grandmother. I'm angry and shocked to learn what Grandfather Jacob did to you—you, a young girl under his protection. His behavior was unconscionable. Unconscionable! He should have been boiled in oil or something equally vile. When I think—"

"Shhhh." Trista smoothed her hair back. "It was a terrible thing, I admit, but had it not happened, neither you nor your father would have been born." She smiled so sweetly that Sugar Anne's heart almost broke. "And I'm very, very glad that you were born. Just look at you. You're a joy to behold in my old age."

"Was it awful after he sent you away? Did your family treat you terribly?"

"I didn't return home. I couldn't face my poor mother, and they didn't need another mouth to feed, especially a girl who was ruined and not worthy to be any man's wife."

"But where did you go? What did you do? You were only, what? Seventeen?"

"Ah, seventeen. Was I ever really so young? I felt a great deal older at the time. I stayed in New Orleans for a brief spell, spying on Madeline and the baby as they walked in the park, watching them like a poor child with her nose pressed against the glass of a toy store.

"When I learned that they were moving to Galveston, I was heartsick because I knew that I couldn't follow. Galveston was too small a place for me to remain undetected. I stayed in New Orleans for several years, then about the time that gold was discovered in California, I took a ship to San Francisco. I was bright and determined, and there was a great deal of money to be made in San Francisco in those days. By the judicious use of the money that Jacob had given me and some I had accumulated myself, I was able to do very well. Under the tutelage of a few influential and very astute . . . acquaintances, I amassed a small fortune. I learned that money is power if a woman is to survive in this man's world. Never forget that, my dear."

"I'm not likely to, I assure you. Lately I've learned a few lessons of my own. But we'll discuss those another time. Now I want to hear every detail of your life in California."

"No, my dear, you don't, nor do I want to tell it all. I did some things that I'm not proud of, and the past is best left alone. It would shame you to know."

"Oh, I can't believe that. I'm a modern woman, Cousin Tris—, I mean . . . Grandmother. I'm not easily shocked or shamed."

Trista laughed. "You're an innocent lamb, Sugar Anne, and I'd prefer to keep it that way for the present. I love hearing you call me Grandmother," she said, cupping

Sugar Anne's cheek, "but for Madeline's memory, Trista will do. Now what was the important matter that you wanted to tell me?"

"We'll leave it until later. Here comes Flora and she looks in a stew. And you, my dear, need to rest a bit before dinner. I'll find Donald and have him carry you upstairs."

"Flora, are you sure?" Trista asked, glancing toward the door of her bedroom to make sure that it was closed.

"Of course I'm sure. My eyesight may be dimming, but I'm not so blind that I wouldn't recognize the man who's been living under this very roof. That's why I shooed you and Sugar Anne along. I didn't want her to see the captain with that actress."

"How do you know that she's an actress? Perhaps she's a business associate or something equally innocent."

Flora rolled her eyes. "I swear to God, Trista, for a woman who's seen it all and knows masculine nature better than anybody I ever met, you act like you're getting soft in the head in your old age. Maybe that knock on the noggin did more harm than we figured.

"I know she's an actress because not only is she very beautiful, but she carries herself like a woman accustomed to the stage. She glides like her feet were on rollers, and she holds her chin up real high—to show off her neck, I expect. She's got one of the longest necks I ever saw. Swan necks, they call them if my memory serves. 'Sides, didn't I see her picture on the playbill down at the entrance to the Opera House? She's an actress all right—and up to no good. Woman like her can turn a man's head.

"I told Sugar Anne not to fall for a handsome man. Told her you never could trust 'em. 'Give me a plain one every time,' I told her. Now he's going to break her heart."

"Oh, Flora, calm down," Trista said. "And stop pacing. What makes you think that Sugar Anne cares what Captain McQuillan does and with whom?"

"I didn't tell you that I saw them kissing. Sugar Anne and the Ranger, I mean. And it wasn't just a friendly little peck like she gave that young police lieutenant. It was a serious kiss. You know Sugar Anne isn't the kind of woman to go around giving out samples without it meaning something. And the way that they look at each other. Haven't you noticed?"

"Well, I suppose that I have noticed an attraction between them."

"An *attraction*? It's more like a case of dynamite waiting to explode, but now this actress has come into the picture. Captain's too virile a man not to take what's freely offered. And they were going up the steps to Mrs. Glenn's boardinghouse—I hear Mrs. Glenn specializes in renting her rooms to actors and actresses. I don't expect that they were going to her room to have a spot of tea."

Trista wrinkled her brow and shook her head. "No, I don't suppose they were. But there's nothing that we can do about the captain's conduct. Men will have their pleasures."

"I expect it would break Sugar Anne's heart if she knew he was carrying on with another woman."

"Then we won't tell her, will we? At least not yet. Let's see how things work out between them. Nothing may come of it, and we don't need to borrow trouble."

"If he hurts our Sugar Anne," Flora said, her fists planted on her hips, "I say let's give him the business. Just like we did with that fancy banker who beat up Consuelo and broke her arm. Bind his wrists, hobble him, and tie him to a lamppost. I'll never forget that old banker standing there on the corner of Kearney Street and Sutter, naked as a jaybird with a big red bow tied around his tallywhacker." Flora broke out into a cackle. "Lord, I've never laughed so much in this life, especially when his wife took the buggy whip to him before she cut him loose."

"Let's hope that things won't come to that, Flora, but I surely wouldn't relish seeing my grandchild hurt. I told her, you know. This afternoon I told her about Jacob and about her father."

"How'd she take it?"

"Very well." Trista's smile lit her bedroom nearly as brightly as the new electric chandelier. "In fact, I would say that she was pleased."

Flora hugged her old friend. "See, I told you that gal had something more to her than a pretty face and nice manners. What did she say about the rest of it? About the parlor houses and your profession in San Francisco?"

A fierce silence filled the room. It got so quiet that Flora could hear the ticking of Trista's fancy little porcelain clock. "You didn't tell her, did you?" Flora asked.

"Not yet, but I will. Soon."

"See that you do. Secrets have a way of coming out at the worst time you could imagine."

Hoping to hell that nobody saw him leaving the boardinghouse, Webb tipped his hat to Amanda and told her good-bye. She laughed and kissed his cheek. He'd been afraid that the Pinkerton Agency was getting impatient with him and was going to put one of their regular operatives on the case. After the appointment with his old friend, he felt reassured and considerably relieved. In fact, there was a spring in his step as he started down the walk.

Then he stopped abruptly.

Leaning on the gatepost and peeling a banana, Willie Jones grinned at him. "Evening, guv'nor."

"Willie! What are you doing here?"

"Waitin' for you. Saw you go in a while back and thought we might walk home together when you was done. That was a fine-looking lady you was with. Nothing puts a smile on a man's face like a nice visit with a light skirt."

"Whoa, pardner. She's no light skirt, and the lady and I were discussing business." Webb frowned. "And exactly what do you know about light skirts anyhow? You're only ten years old."

"I know plenty. Me ma was in the profession like Phoebe was. Just 'cause I ain't old enough to partake don't mean that I don't know what goes on. Ain't much I don't know about, growing up where I did."

Webb hurt for the kid who'd grown up much too fast. As bad as his own childhood had been, he'd been a danged sight better off than Willie. He ruffled the towhead's hair. "You're too wise for your own good, Willie. But the truth is, I really was talking business with the lady. Even so, I'd as soon you didn't mention seeing us together."

Willie tossed the banana peel among some rosebushes,

stuck his thumbs in his belt loops just the way Webb did, and winked knowingly. "You don't have to worry about me, Cap'n. My lips is sealed."

⇜ Fourteen ⇝

Webb almost spewed his soup all over Trista's fine lace tablecloth. Instead, he managed to swallow it before he bellowed. "You're planning on doing *what*?"

"I am going to buy a gun," Sugar Anne repeated, enunciating very clearly, "and learn to shoot it. I thought, since you are an expert in firearms, you might assist me, but if you're not interested, I'm sure that James Yarborough will."

"No, absolutely not! You don't have any business with a gun."

Sugar Anne blinked twice, then scowled at him as if he were a turd in a punch bowl. "I don't believe that my activities require your approval, Captain. If I wish to buy a pistol, I will buy a pistol."

Trista discreetly dabbed her lips with her napkin; Flora cut her eyes back and forth between the two of them; Preston kept his attention fixed firmly on the oysters in his soup.

Willie, the scamp, sat grinning openly at the pair. "Now, she's gotcha there, Cap'n."

Webb glared at Willie, but it didn't stifle the boy's grin. Willie only winked and grinned wider. Sugar Anne continued with her soup as if he hadn't said a damned word. Hell's bells! She didn't pay him any more attention than a horsefly. Turning her loose with a gun would be a travesty. She was liable to shoot somebody dead the first thing.

"Guns are serious weapons. They should be respected."

Sugar Anne rolled her eyes. "I am quite aware of that. But after our experience on the train, I realized that a woman needs protection, especially in some less civilized places. Therefore, I am determined to buy a gun and become proficient in its use."

"No way I can talk you out of it?"

"None."

"Then if you're hidebound determined, why don't you try out my four-shot to see if you can handle it? It's a small gun suitable for a lady."

"Thank you very much, Captain. I would appreciate it. When can we practice?"

"How about sometime toward the end of next week?"

"How about tomorrow?"

Knowing when he was whipped, Webb said, "You want to go out early in the morning before I go to the office?"

She smiled so brightly and so warmly that he dang near missed his bowl with his spoon. Lordamighty, it ought to be a sin for a woman to have such a potent smile. He hoped that she made her move for Herndon pretty soon or before long she'd probably sweet-talk him into teaching her how to fight with a knife.

"Tarnation, Sugar Anne!" Webb shouted. "Wait till I move. You blame near shot my hat off again!" He stood about a dozen paces away from her on the deserted strip of beach he'd selected for their training exercise.

She was extremely nervous, and his yelling only made her more so. "I'm sorry. It was an accident. I don't seem to be very good at this."

"You're not telling me anything new. We've been at it for an hour, and you haven't hit a single can, but I've got two damned holes in my hat! You ready to give up yet?"

"Absolutely not! And watch your language, sir. I mean to practice until I can defend myself. Step aside."

"You're enough to make a preacher cuss," Webb mumbled as he moved away from the targets.

She raised the small pistol and pointed it at the first can perched on the piece of driftwood. After taking careful aim, she held her breath and fired.

"Did I hit it that time?" she asked eagerly. "Did I hit it?"

"Depends on what you were aiming at. You missed all four cans, but you blew hell out of that sand crab over yonder."

"Oh, no," she wailed. "This is ridiculous. I'm beginning to wonder if I'm cut out to be a marksman. Perhaps I should consider a knife."

"No!" He strode toward her. "You just have to learn to keep your eyes open and on your target. Here, let me help you."

Webb stepped behind her, pulling her close against him while he helped her take aim, as he had done several times that damp morning. He was so close that she could feel the beat of his heart and smell the bay rum warmed by his body. Holding his arm alongside hers, his fingers closed around hers as she gripped the gun.

Her mouth went totally dry, and her own heart began pounding like a sledgehammer against her chest. Since she'd long ago scared off the gulls and pelicans with her wild shooting, the place was utterly quiet, save for the rhythmic wash of waves onto the shore. She was sure that he could hear the thuds of her heart and the odd pattern of her breathing.

Learning how to shoot wasn't what distressed her so. Never in her life had Sugar Anne been so totally aware of a man. How could she concentrate when she felt every rugged cast and jut of his masculine presence?

"Are you ready?" he asked, his words reverberating next to her ear. His deep voice was unbelievably seductive. Even the chill Gulf breeze couldn't cool her skin, which seemed blistering hot.

Ready? Ready for what? Her brain was like a dish of Mary's bread pudding.

"Now just point the gun like you're pointing your finger. Keep your eyes open. Sugar Anne?"

"Hmmm?"

"Are your eyes open?" His lips left the side of her ear to brush against her temple.

"Open? My eyes?"

"Mmmm."

"Uh, I'm not sure." Her voice was quivery, and she felt herself tremble.

His mouth traveled downward, and the tip of his tongue touched her earlobe, then his teeth gently nipped it.

She sighed. "They're closed now."

Gently he turned her until they faced each other. He lowered his head until their lips met. It was heaven. Pure heaven.

The tide could have gone out and come in a thousand times, and she wouldn't have known it. She was lost in the delicious sensation of Webb's kiss, the oak-solid strength of his arms as they enfolded her.

She was becoming lost. Lost in sensations. Wonderful sensations of hungry lips and questing hands and a hard body pressing against her. She wanted to throw off her garments and pull him after her into the ocean and feel the water and his virility engulf her, swallow her up in pleasure. Ah, she ached with the desire.

While her arms curled around his neck, drawing him closer, at the same time she struggled with all her might against the temptation to abandon herself, squeezing her fists to fight . . .

A sharp blast rang out. She gasped.

"Dammit, woman! Dammit all to hell! You've shot me!"

"Oh, no! Dear Lord, no! Where?" Sobered, Sugar Anne dropped the gun, jerked away, and began an instant examination of his body, patting arms, chest, buttocks, lap.

He grabbed her hands. "I don't think you drew blood this time, but maybe you can hang my hat over the mantel as a trophy." He stalked to a spot a few feet away and looked down at the black hat that had been on his head only moments before. A third hole was chewed out of the brim.

"Amazing," Sugar Anne said as she examined her targets. She'd hit every one. "Absolutely amazing. James, you're an excellent teacher."

James Yarborough grinned. "True, but I think your new spectacles have improved your aim."

She thought so, too. Even without the distraction of overwhelming physical attraction to her instructor, her first shooting lesson with James hadn't gone any better than the one with Webb. She'd been thoroughly disgusted with her lack of progress. But that evening, watching Flora put on her spectacles to do a bit of embroidery, Sugar Anne had an idea.

The very next morning she called on an oculist, a Dr. Dyer, on Market Street. After considerable testing with several of his charts, he declared her to be somewhat myopic. How odd that she'd never noticed the problem—but then her vision was excellent for reading and sewing and such.

Luckily, the doctor had a pair of eyeglasses that were just the ticket. Unfortunately, they were rather ugly, but since she only needed to wear them when she was shooting, she purchased them and went on her way, confident that the problem was solved.

And it was. In fact, she found that she had a real knack for shooting. Her proficiency with the firearm she'd bought at the gunsmith shop gave her a new confidence in herself.

"James, I'm exceedingly grateful for your assistance. To repay you, I insist that you come to dinner tonight. Mary's promised to do Yorkshire pudding."

"You won't have to twist my arm. You sure Webb won't mind?"

Taken aback by the question, she asked, "Why on earth would he mind?"

"Well, I kinda got the idea that the captain was sweet on you and had staked you out as his property."

Fury washed over her. "*His property?* I can assure you

that I am no man's *property*, least of all Captain McQuillan's. Need I remind you that I'm a mar—a newly widowed woman? I'm not casting about for another husband! The men in my life have done quite enough damage already, and I'm not anxious to tie myself to another."

Nose in the air, she whirled and marched to her bicycle, which had been repaired and was good as new except for a slight wobble in the front wheel.

"Men!" she groused as she mounted and pumped the pedals furiously toward home. "Men!"

His *property*. Staked her out, indeed! Why, the captain had barely noticed her in the past three days—even after she had purchased a fine new hat for him from the funds Trista had repaid her and had it custom fitted. He had avoided her as if she were tubercular, barely speaking to her, even at meals. He directed his remarks to Trista or Flora or Mr. Underwood, even to Willie or Phoebe. Rarely to her.

Surely a few holes in a hat didn't merit such cool treatment. And why should she care anyhow? Men were such fickle, undependable creatures, good for nothing but heartache.

Her father had been a good sort, she supposed, but he'd died and left her. And just look at her own grandfather, the cold, contemptible seducer. He'd abandoned her emotionally at the nadir of her life, shipping her off to boarding schools instead of offering her any sort of solace or affection. Worse, he'd manipulated her into a loveless marriage with a scoundrel of the worst sort. And Edward. She knew no words to describe his depravity in taking her inheritance and coldly leaving her to face the indignity and suspicion that she had endured.

Men! Bastards one and all, who couldn't be counted on when the going got tough, who kissed you passionately one minute, then tossed you aside over a silly hat.

Men! She didn't intend to lose another moment's sleep over any of them, especially Captain Webb McQuillan. On Monday morning, just four days away, she planned to be on a train to New Orleans. She meant to find Edward Allen Herndon and deal properly with him. If he gave her any difficulty, why, she would whip out her new pearl-handled pistol and show him exactly how fine a marksman she had become.

She could just picture the scene. Edward would sneer superciliously when she put on her eyeglasses; she would call him some sufficiently vile name, then draw her gun, take aim, and shoot a candle from its stick to prove that she meant business. Coward that he was, he would reveal the whereabouts of his loot before she was finished with him and his paramour. Sugar Anne could hardly wait to see Bea Ralston's face when she returned to Chicago with the stolen money.

Her desire for retribution burned like a fire inside her.

First, though, she had to gain Trista's blessing. And her financial support. One thing, then another had delayed Sugar Anne's confiding in her new grandmother. She planned to remedy that as soon as she arrived home.

"Oh, dear heart, you were left with nothing?" Trista said.

Sugar Anne shook her head. "Only my clothing and the few things I mentioned. What Edward didn't steal, the creditors claimed. My friends deserted me, and the Pinkertons hounded me unmercifully until I eluded them and came here."

"But surely they didn't believe that you were involved with your husband's scam?"

"Yes, they did. Edward left behind some documents in his office that incriminated me in his thievery. Oh, the file was supposed to be hidden, then simply overlooked in his rush, but you can be sure that it was a vicious and deliberate act intended to draw attention away from his escape and focus it on me."

"What sort of documents?"

"I've never seen them, but I understand that they showed that large sums of money were moved in and out of a bank account in my name and with my signature. The signature looked like mine, and probably was—I was always signing some paper or the other. Edward took care of all the business, and fool that I was, I trusted him. The documents were highly suspicious, I'll admit, but the police couldn't prove that any of this was done with my knowledge. The Pinkerton Agency wasn't quite so generous."

Tears began to trickle down Sugar Anne's cheeks as she recalled her despair when friends deserted her and she became a pariah. "They treated me as if I were nothing more than a—a common streetwalker. You can't imagine."

Trista opened her arms to Sugar Anne, who fell against her, weeping. Patting her back, Trista whispered, "Oh, but I can, child. I know how cruel people can be. I know very well. Now dry your eyes."

Sugar Anne dabbed at her tears. "I'm sorry to be such a ninny. I usually handle this better. I'm a very strong woman."

"I'm sure that you are, but even strong women are

entitled to a good cry now and then. Now, put the whole ugly mess from your mind. Your home is here now, and everything I possess is yours. You might be surprised to discover how much I'm worth, and how much you'll be worth some day. Much more than Edward made off with, I'm sure."

"Oh, Trista, no. I couldn't take— I mean—"

Trista smiled. "You're my only living relative, and I'm an old woman." With a flourish she gestured across the parlor, encompassing the furnishings, the paintings, and other lovely works of art. "I have always intended that all this be yours. It's in my will. I've made provisions for Flora and the others, of course, but the bulk of my estate will be yours."

Sugar Anne teared up again. She blotted her eyes and tried to smile. "See what you've done?" she asked as tears continued to flow.

Laughing, Trista pulled her close. "Heart of my heart, I'm so glad to have you back."

Sugar Anne sniffed and pulled away. She sat for a moment worrying the handkerchief in her lap, trying to find the right words.

"Dear, what's wrong? Don't you like Galveston? Are you unhappy living with two old painted ladies and the odd assortment I've collected?"

"Oh, no. Never that. I adore all of you. And only Flora wears paint." She drew a deep breath. "It's just that I've made a vow, and I need your help. Financially."

"You have only to ask."

"You may not say that when you hear my plan. You see, I know where Edward is. A letter came on the very day I vacated my house in Chicago."

"A letter?"

Sugar Anne nodded. "From the Hotel Dieu. In New Orleans."

Fifteen

"Cotton, get your damned dirty boots off my desk," Webb said, scowling at the grinning man who was casually taking his leisure. "And I don't recall telling you to help yourself to my cigars."

"I didn't figure you'd mind, us being old Ranger buddies and all," Yarborough said, puffing intently to light the expensive Cuban-made. He leaned back in the client chair and blew a perfect smoke ring toward the ceiling. "Man, this is the life. Having a fine office, living in a big house. Do you eat all the time like we did last night?"

"Yes, just not as much as you shoveled in your mouth. I swear to God, you ate like you hadn't had a decent meal in two weeks."

"I hadn't. Not like that. It more than made up for those shooting lessons I gave Sugar Anne."

"Let me see your hat."

"My hat?" Cotton asked. "Why do you want to see—" He laughed. "Oh, I get it. Sugar Anne's improved a lot since then. It was the spectacles that did it."

"What spectacles?"

"Oh, she didn't tell you? Seems that she couldn't hit anything because she couldn't see good, least not at a distance. Since she went to the doctor and got those eyeglasses, she can hit a redbug on a fence post. We were out practicing this morning, and she didn't miss a single time. She's a determined little thing once she sets her mind on something. I told her that I wouldn't be a bit surprised if she won that turkey shoot the week after next."

Webb was growing more irritated with Cotton by the minute. "You got a reason to be here besides yammering about turkey shoots? I got work to do."

Cotton's brows went up. "You sure got a burr in your blanket this morning, my friend. I just dropped by to find out if you mind me asking Sugar Anne to go to the Opera House for tonight's performance. They're putting on that Japanese thing tonight and tomorrow, and she's been talking about wanting to go. Tonight they're supposed to give out some kind of Japanese gewgaw to the ladies, a fan or some such, I suppose. I figured that if you didn't care, I'd get a couple of tickets."

The words flew all over Webb. Before he knew it, he was on his feet, his hand balled into a fist, and he damn near swung at Cotton. "You figured wrong. If Sugar Anne wants to go to the Opera House, I'll take her. You got that? Now get the hell out of my office!"

Cotton's eyes widened, and he puckered up and let out a low whistle. "You're downright touchy about it. Yes, sir, I do believe you're more'n a little sweet on our Sugar Anne."

"Either way, it's none of your damned business. Now get out of here. I've got work to do." He opened a drawer, grabbed a sheaf of papers, and slapped them on his desk.

Cotton slowly unfolded from his chair and stood.

"Guess I can tell when I'm not welcome," he drawled, but he was grinning from ear to ear. He was chuckling when he strolled out the door.

As soon as he heard Cotton's boots going down the stairs, Webb went to Miss Purvis's desk.

"You know anything about some Japanese thing going on at the Tremont Opera House tonight?"

She tittered. "Yes, sir. There's a performance of the new operetta, *The Mikado*. It's quite excellent. I saw it myself last evening, and the *News* gave it an outstanding review."

He reached into his pocket, pulled out a fold of greenbacks, and peeled off one. Handing the bill to the secretary, he said, "Go get me two of the best seats they got."

"Yes, sir. That will be parquet or the parquet circle. I'll go right away." Miss Purvis quickly donned her coat and hat.

"And, Miss Purvis, I'm gonna be out of the office for a spell. I—I need to locate Miz Spicer. I'll likely be back sometime after dinner—I mean lunch. You won't let me down about those tickets now, will you?"

"No, sir. Absolutely not. You can count on me, Captain McQuillan. Tessie Anderson is in charge of ticket sales, and we're very good friends. I'll see that you have the best seats available."

Webb left Miss Purvis to lock the office, and he went in search of Sugar Anne. It would be just like Cotton to ask her out anyway—just to get Webb's goat. He wasn't about to let that happen. It would be a cold day in hell when Cotton Yarborough got the best of him.

He strode down the block to the livery stable and picked up the horse he'd hired for as long as he stayed in

Galveston. The gelding wasn't near the horse Sam was, but his favorite horse was stabled back in Dallas. And at the rate this case was going, he thought as he mounted the roan, he might not be back in Dallas until next Easter.

When he got to the Church Street house, he didn't see any sign of Cotton. When he went inside, he didn't see any sign of Sugar Anne either. He found Flora and Trista in the parlor playing a card game.

"Sugar Anne around?" he asked.

"Oh, Captain, you startled me," said Trista. "I wasn't expecting you at this hour."

"I'm taking an early lunch," he said, then felt like a danged fool. It wasn't even ten o'clock yet.

"I see." Trista smiled and tried to cover it with a cough and a hand to her mouth. "Sugar Anne is off visiting with Lucy. You missed her by not more than ten minutes. Is there something that I can help you with?"

"No, thank you, ma'am. I think I might just mosey on by there. Cotton Yarborough hasn't been here, has he?"

"Not this morning. I believe that Sugar Anne met him for a shooting lesson earlier, didn't she, Flora?"

"That she did. I hear tell she's getting quite good with a pistol. It's the spectacles. But I swear, they're the ugliest ones I ever saw in my life."

"Yes, well, excuse me, ladies." Webb jammed his hat on and strode out the front door.

A few minutes later, he felt like a fool again when the fancy butler came to the door, but he gutted up and said, "I would like to speak with Miz Spicer. She's here visiting, I believe."

Fancy Pants looked down his considerable nose. "And whom shall I say is calling?"

Something about the man's attitude chapped Webb's ass, and he wasn't in a very good humor to start with. He fanned his coat behind his guns and let his silver star flash. "Captain Webb McQuillan. Texas Rangers."

He had to hand it to the butler: the old toot didn't bat an eye. "I'll inform madam. Wait here." And damned if he didn't close the door in his face.

In a minute or two, Lucy Malloy opened the door; by that point he was getting nervous. He'd turned his new hat round and round in his hands a hundred times as he stood there waiting.

"Captain, what a pleasant surprise," she said. "Do come in."

"I don't mean to interrupt your tea party, ma'am. I just need to speak to Sugar Anne for a minute."

Sugar Anne was right behind Lucy, looking alarmed. "Webb? Is something wrong? Trista? Phoebe?"

"*Phoebe?* Oh, no. Nothing like that. Everybody's fine. I, uh—I just came by to ask if you would do me the honor of allowing me to escort . . . I mean, you want to go to that Japanese thing at the Opera House tonight?"

She just stared at him for a minute, then said, "Yes."

"Good. I'm getting tickets." He put on his hat, whirled, and strode away.

Lucy closed the door and turned to Sugar Anne, bewildered. Then they both broke into giggles.

"Is he always like that?" Lucy asked.

Sugar Anne shook her head. "He usually growls a lot."

"He certainly is a handsome thing. And sooo . . . virile looking."

"Lucy Malloy! And you a married woman."

Lucy giggled again. "I'm not dead. What are you going to wear?"

"Oh, dear, I haven't given it a thought. How should I wear my hair?"

Flora took over as dresser and insisted on doing Sugar Anne's hair for the theater. Sugar Anne was a bit anxious about the arrangement, but Flora, under Trista's tutelage and at Trista's dressing table, turned out to be a genius with comb and curling iron. Sugar Anne's coiffure was a complex, exquisite design of curls and braids.

Flora had chosen a deep blue velvet dress with a richly embroidered bodice; it was adorned with a matching satin panel and rosette clusters that gathered a short train. It was an elegant ensemble, and Sugar Anne longed for at least a strand of pearls to wear at the neck.

"You need—" Trista began. "Wait. I have just the thing." Using her cane, she slowly made her way to a chest and opened its top drawer. She returned with a velvet box. Inside was a sapphire and diamond necklace and matching earrings. "These should be perfect."

They were. "Lovely," Sugar Anne whispered. "Absolutely lovely."

"I declare," Flora said, "I haven't seen those in years and years. I believe that's the set John Henry—"

"Flora, I believe you need another pin in that curl right there behind her ear."

"Right you are. There you go." She patted her handiwork. "You're gonna knock the captain's eyes out. He's waiting downstairs. Let's go get the verdict. Trista, you want me to get Donald to carry you down to the parlor?"

"No, I'll watch from the top of the stairs." She hugged

Sugar Anne. "You look so beautiful. I hope that you have a grand time."

Sugar Anne fetched her cloak from her room. When she started down the stairs, Webb was waiting. The look in his eyes sent an unexpected thrill through her, an excitement she hadn't felt since she was a debutante. It made her feel young and carefree and desirable again. And worth the two hours she'd spent getting dressed.

She wasn't the only one who had spent extra time dressing, Sugar Anne thought as the carriage bumped along the street. Webb looked quite dashing in a very fashionable new evening coat and a fancy white shirt that emphasized his sun-browned handsomeness and startling blue eyes. His hair was newly cut, his mustache trimmed, and his scent had a heady, masculine overtone. She was sure to be the envy of every woman at the theater.

"Have I told you how pretty you look?" Webb asked.

She smiled. "Yes, but a woman never tires of hearing such things."

"Well, you're pretty as a picture. Prettier, even. And I like the way you smell. Like gardenias."

"I'm surprised you recognize the scent."

"My mother had a gardenia bush growing by the back door. She sure did baby that bush to keep it green and blooming. Said it reminded her of home. And she used to put little bags of dried petals in her handkerchief box."

"I see. You've never told me much about your family."

"Not much to tell. They were all wiped out in an Indian raid on the Texas frontier when I was five. I was taken captive and lived among the Comanche until I was eleven."

"Oh, I'm so sorry." Sugar Anne touched his arm. "I

know what it's like to lose your family like that. Mine were all taken by yellow fever when I was nine. But at least my grandfather was left to look after me. Was it awful? Having to live with the savages, I mean?"

"Oh, I don't know. It wasn't too bad, and I learned a right smart amount. From what I've heard about Jacob Spicer, the Indians were probably a lot kinder. They were sure kinder than the old hellfire-and-brimstone preacher and his family that I landed with afterward. The only thing good that came out of that was that I learned to read and do arithmetic, and I found out I had a head for education. I slept in the barn and wasn't treated much better than a plow horse. I worked my tail off on that farm, and hated every minute of it. I took off when I was fifteen. Been more or less on my own since then."

"You've done very well."

He shrugged. "Better than some, I guess, but not as well as I'd like."

"And what would you like?"

"Oh, to settle down and have a nice family and a nice house and a respectable place in the community." He chuckled. "And a soft feather bed."

"I hope that you get everything you want."

He cleared his throat. "Yes, well, uh, looks like we're here."

As Donald pulled the carriage up to the front of the brightly lit theater, Sugar Anne's excitement sparked. Elegantly dressed ladies and gentlemen were making their way into the Opera House on Market and Tremont.

"I can hardly wait," Sugar Anne said. "I adore the earlier work of Gilbert and Sullivan, and this is their newest.

I hear it's a grand production. Are you familiar with their operas?"

"No, can't say as I am. Never had much opportunity for such entertainments."

She almost laughed at his pained expression and the unsaid words that hung in the air: "nor interest." Smiling as he helped her down from the carriage, she said, "I think that you might enjoy this."

"The main thing is for you to enjoy it," he said, then turned to give Donald instructions about picking them up.

The wind, now blowing from the northwest, swirled her hem about her ankles. She held the hood of her cloak with both hands to keep her hairdo from being mussed, and they hurried to the protection of the lobby.

Webb nodded to several gentlemen of his acquaintance, and Sugar Anne acknowledged a few of the ladies whom she had met through Lucy or Aunt Gaggie. How different was this cordial reception from the one at church that first Sunday. She held her fan to her lips and chuckled.

"Something funny?"

"I'll tell you later," she whispered.

After they were seated in a grand private box with plush carpeting and rich furnishings, Sugar Anne said, "I'm impressed. How on earth did you manage a box? I understand that they're usually reserved for a few select patrons."

He tried to look blasé, but a small grin ruined his effort. "When Miss Purvis went to pick up the tickets, she discovered that Fitzwarren had reserved this box for several performances. Next Friday night we can come see *Zo-Zo, the Magic Queen,* and the Friday after is *Romeo and Juliet.*"

"Oh, I would love—" She stopped abruptly when she realized that she would be gone Monday and with no idea of when she would return. "We shall see."

Having put her wrap aside, Sugar Anne retrieved the lorgnette Trista had lent her. Her own, an intricately embellished gold one, had, like everything else she cherished, flown the coop with Edward. Holding it to her eyes, she scanned the grandly appointed playhouse as the seats filled. Anticipation permeated the air.

"What's that contraption?" he asked.

"The lorgnette? It's something that ladies use in the theater, rather like a spyglass. Want to look?"

Webb shook his head. "I'll take your word for it. I hear you got some spectacles."

"I did. They're incredible. Not very attractive, I'm afraid, but incredible all the same. James says that my shooting has improved two hundred percent. It seems that I've a knack for hitting targets, and I hardly ever miss now. I practice early every morning. Would you like to come along tomorrow?"

"Maybe I will."

The overture began, and Sugar Anne clutched his arm. "There, it's about to start."

The curtain rose, and the stage burst into life. Sugar Anne was soon caught up with the songs and frolic and the story of Yum-Yum and Nanki-Poo and Ko-Ko; she was thrilled by the lovely Japanese costumes that fluttered across the stage like silk flower petals. She especially loved the performance of the actor who played

Pooh-Bah, and noted that Webb laughed at his comic lines and songs as frequently as she did.

By the time the cast took its final bow and the curtain fell, she had been transported to another world. Her troubles had vanished, and her heart was light. Still smiling and with the remnants of a melody dancing through her head, she turned to Webb. "Wasn't that glorious?"

"You know, it was right enjoyable. Not at all what I expected. But then, I've never been to an opera before. Truth is, I sorta had the impression that a bunch of fat people sang songs as loud as they could in some foreign language."

She laughed. "Sometimes that's not far from wrong. But Gilbert and Sullivan do light comic opera. I think you might enjoy some of their other work. *H.M.S. Pinafore* is very popular." She stood, and Webb helped her with her cloak.

When they arrived outside, Sugar Anne looked around. "Where's Donald?"

"He's not due yet. I thought we might get some supper before we went home."

"I'd like that." She caught her hood with one hand and tried to manage her skirts with the other. The wind was blowing much harder than it had earlier.

"Here, let's get out of this blow. The restaurant is right around the corner."

It was one of Galveston's finest, open late to accommodate the theater crowd. The waiter led them to a corner table where a bottle of wine sat chilling in anticipation of their arrival.

Secluded behind a pair of potted palms and a latticed screen, the spot was gently lit by candles that cast a flickering reflection on the crystal glasses. Quite a romantic setting, she thought. A pity that she wasn't in a position to enjoy a courtship with Webb.

Lucy was right. He was a very handsome and virile man. And, she had to add, a man of character, so far as she'd seen. Different, certainly, from the worm she was married to. She sighed silently. There's the rub. No matter how she tried to forget it, she was still a married woman. And this was not a suitable time for romantic notions. Not until she had dealt properly with Edward.

The words to "Let the Punishment Fit the Crime," a catchy tune from the opera, kept flitting through her head. As she sang the chorus silently, she realized that her entire life was at a standstill until she found Edward and saw that he was punished.

No, romance was out of the question until her difficulties were resolved.

Still, it would be wonderful to be loved the way that Nanki-Poo loved Yum-Yum, by a man willing to die for the love of you, willing to risk all for only a month in your arms. Staring at the flame of the candle, she could almost imagine—

"Champagne?" Webb held out a crystal glass to her.

She took the wine and sipped it. "An excellent vintage," she said. And when the bubbles tickled her nose and her palate, she laughed.

How could one not be gay with champagne and caviar, a handsome man with his magnificent blue eyes focused on you, and such a delightful setting? The opera had buoyed her mood to an enchanting lightheartedness. For one night, she decided, she would forget Edward and simply enjoy herself.

They laughed and told amusing stories, drank more champagne, and dined on delicate fillets of trout and puffy rosettes of potato, and ate something sinfully rich and saucy for dessert—a confection of peaches and brandy and caramelized sugar and cream. And drank more champagne.

By the time they finished, they were the only ones left in the restaurant, and Sugar Anne found that she adored resting her head against Webb's broad shoulder. And everything seemed exceedingly funny.

"I believe you've had a mite too much champagne."

"A mite too much? I? Certainly not. I never drink to excess." She giggled.

"It's time for us to go. Poor Donald has been sitting outside waiting for over half an hour."

"Ohhhh," she said, out of pity for poor Donald. "But I hate to end the evening. I've had such a glor-i-ous time."

"Maybe we could drop Donald off and take a ride down along the beach. Would you like that?"

She would have agreed to anything that seductive voice asked of her. "I would adore that," she said breathily, stroking his forearm, which seemed very taut beneath his sleeve.

Webb paid the bill to a sleepy-looking gentleman with a bald head and huge mutton chops. A shame he couldn't transport some of the hair on his cheeks to the top of his head. When a picture of attempting such a relocation with scissors and a glue pot rose in her mind, she got the giggles again.

As soon as they stepped out the door, the wind grabbed Webb's hat, and he chased it half a block before he caught it. Keeping her back to the brisk currents, Sugar

Anne laughed as he ran, and she clapped loudly when he captured his prize. "Hooray!" she shouted as he trotted back to the carriage.

He grinned. "Couldn't lose my new hat."

While Webb helped her into the carriage, Donald said, "Bit of a stiff breeze tonight. From the northwest, it is. Don't wonder that we'll feel more of a chill tomorrow."

"You might be right," Webb said, "but then again you never can tell about Texas weather. I remember bunking down under a big old oak tree one hot summer night, and when I woke up, a blue norther had come through and the icicles on the branches reached all the way to the ground, like bars on a prison. I had to wait two days for them to melt till I could get out."

Donald let out a deep roar of laughter. "Oh, Captain, get on with ya! I'll not fall for one of your tales."

Sugar Anne laughed too, snuggling close to Webb, nuzzling his lapel and savoring the wonderful maleness of his scent, of his very presence.

When they neared home, Webb said, "It's late. I suspect we should postpone that ride along the beach until another time."

"Noooo," she protested. "It's not that late, and I'm not a bit sleepy."

"It's awful windy."

"You promised."

"That I did. Donald," he called, "I promised Sugar Anne a ride along the beach. You go on to bed, and I'll unhitch the horse when we get back."

Donald protested, but Webb insisted.

Webb helped Sugar Anne into the driver's seat, climbed up behind her, and took the reins. With a couple of clicks of his tongue and a light snap on the reins, they were off. It was even breezier in their new perch, but she didn't mind. Her hood had blown back, and the wind through her hair was quite exhilarating.

Being well after midnight, the town was relatively still, and as they approached the beach, they found it quiet as well. The roller-skating rink where Sugar Anne and Lucy had taken her children the day before yesterday was closed. The electric pavilion was dark. Nothing much stirred except the waves washing in, their rhythm evident in the ebb and flow of whitecaps glistening in the moonlight.

"Let's stop," she cried. "Right here. I'd like to get out, take off my shoes, and run on the sand."

He chuckled. "Now I know that you've had too much to drink. Woman, not only are you wearing your fanciest dress, it's near 'bout the middle of November. You can't go running barefoot on the beach, especially at night."

"Of course you can. It's not that cold." She rapped him gently with the Japanese fan she'd been given at the theater. "Stop. You don't have to go barefoot if you're such a sissy."

He shook his head, but he stopped. By the time he shed one boot, her shoes and stockings had been thrown into the back of the carriage, and she was off.

"Dammit, wait, Sugar Anne!" He scrambled with his other boot and his socks. He tossed them, along with his hat, onto the carriage floor and took out after her.

Holding up an armload of gathered skirts to free her legs, she ran like a deer, laughing as she ran. He soon caught up and trotted beside her.

After a few moments, she stopped, thrust her arms

upward, and whirled around in a flurry of velvet and satin. "Oh, I do love it here. I've missed Galveston so much." She threw her arms about his neck. "Isn't this a wonderful place? Don't you just love the feel of wet sand between your toes? I find it very . . . sensuous."

Dark as it was, he could see that her face was radiant with exhilaration. Her eyes glistened as brightly as the glimmer of moonlight on the diamonds at her neck and ears. Despite every promise he'd made to himself, he could no more help kissing her than he could control the tides.

With the winds battering them and whipping loose strands of her hair across their faces, they kissed a kiss of soul-deep hunger.

She clawed at the buttons on his shirt and slipped her hands inside to stroke his skin. He groaned and found the swell of a breast to knead.

"You know what I want?" she asked, her breath ragged.

"What?"

"You'll be shocked."

He chuckled as he nuzzled her ear. "I don't shock easy."

"I want us to strip off all our clothes and run naked into the water and make passionate love in the sea." She reached for her bodice and began unfastening it.

Desire speared him with a red hot poker. He ached to rip every stitch off her and take her in the sand, but reason held him back. "Sugar Anne! Are you crazy?"

She laughed and turned her back to him. "You'll have to help me with some of the hooks."

She was half out of the top of her dress; her back was

creamy white and smooth. Just a taste, he thought, just a taste, as his lips and tongue slid over her warm flesh.

Lordamighty! he thought, coming to himself. He started trying to do up the hooks, but Sugar Anne was opening them faster than he could keep up with her. "Whoa! Dammit, Sugar Anne! Whoa!"

She turned to face him. "I'm not your horse. Are you going to help or not?"

"Not. We can't strip naked right out here in the open."

Sugar Anne looked up and down the deserted beach. "Why not? Who's to see?"

"Why, anybody could come along. This is a public place. I know you're drunk now. Drunker than Cooter Brown. I was plumb loco to let you drink all that champagne. Come on. I'm taking you home."

Her bottom lip went out. "Don't you want to make love to me in the Gulf of Mexico? I think about it all the time." Her arms snaked around his waist. "I think about you touching my bare skin with your big hands, and I think about the water and—"

"Good Lordamighty!" Before he changed his mind, he unlocked her arms, grabbed her elbow, and marched her back to the carriage. He didn't stop to put his boots on; he just plunked her in the seat, grabbed the reins, and took off.

Didn't want her? Hell's bells, his britches were about to bust from wanting her. He wanted her every hour of every day. Her face deviled him when he tried to sleep; his dreams deviled him when he finally did. Now that he knew the feel of her soft breast in his hand and the taste of her sweet skin, it would be worse.

Drunk or not, it was hard for him to deny what was freely offered. Real hard. Damned hard.

But he couldn't stoop that low. He couldn't take her body, then do her dirt when he walked off with the reward. Hell, he'd wondered more than once lately if the reward was worth it. He was real tempted to come clean, to tell her everything and let the chips fall where they may.

And the more Webb was around her, the more sure he was that Sugar Anne hadn't had anything to do with stealing any money. He'd near 'bout bet his star on it.

What a mess he'd gotten himself into. What a mess.

"I believe you're shy," she said, sighing and laying her head on his shoulder.

He snorted at that one.

"You're a true gentleman," she said, "a man of character."

He snorted again.

"You can't deny it." She wrapped her arms around his middle and snuggled closer. "Only a man of character would protect me from my base instincts. I know the difference. You see, my husband was a real son of a bitch."

Webb bit the inside of his mouth to keep from agreeing. "Oh?"

"Umm-hummm. And he said I was a cold fish. But I'm not, am I?"

He cleared his throat. "I wouldn't exactly say so, no."

"Oh, look, the sun's coming up." She held the blowing strands of hair away from her face and pointed to her right. "Isn't it beautiful? Don't you just love dawn?"

"The sun? It's not more than two o'clock. Daybreak's not for several hours yet." He squinted in the direction she'd pointed. A bright glow lit the horizon. "Wouldn't be the sun anyway. That's north."

They heard distant bells clanging.

"Oh, my God," Webb shouted. "It's fire!"

⌒ Sixteen ⌒

"Fire?" Sugar Anne cried as Webb slapped the horse into a faster pace. Her heart was in her mouth. Fire evoked horrifying images. "Where?"

"Hard to tell from here," he yelled over the wind and the noise of their conveyance, "but I'd guess down by the wharf; maybe it's one of the warehouses. Close to the Strand, probably not far from the Opera House, and damned close to the office. With this gale, it's going to be hell to put out."

They were heading north, against the wind and in the direction of the encroaching fire. By the time they crossed the wide expanse of Broadway, although they were still several blocks from the conflagration, great red and orange flames billowed high in the sky and spit showers of sparks like bursts from rockets on the Fourth of July.

Sugar Anne heard the fire roar, like an immense furnace, as it consumed homes and businesses and belched its black and foul-smelling swells into the air. The area was thick with wind-borne smoke. Bells clanged and alarms rang; shouting people, quickly belting robes and finger-grooming hair, spilled out of their lovely homes and onto their lawns. Panic was etched in their faces.

As they pulled into the alley behind the house, Donald was clattering down the wooden steps from the apartment over the carriage house, hitching up his suspenders. "What's doing, Captain?"

Webb pulled to a stop and set Sugar Anne down. "Come on," he called to Donald. "Looks like the business district is on fire. Let's go."

"I'm going too," Sugar Anne said as she tried to climb back into the carriage.

"No, you're not," Webb said emphatically, lifting her away. "You're staying here, and I don't have time to argue about it. Wake the others. You drive, Donald, while I get my boots on. Hurry, man!"

"My slippers!" Sugar Anne shouted as the carriage started to move.

Her shoes and stockings sailed from the carriage as the horse galloped away.

Webb had never seen anything like it. They had cut over and gone north on Twenty-third Street, then turned east on Strand, one street south of Water Street and the harbor. The office, near Twentieth and Strand, was untouched. The fire raged further east and south, though it was hard to tell in the smoke and confusion, and the horse was too skittish to proceed.

"You stay here, Donald. I'll go by foot and find out what's going on."

Webb ran until he saw a crowd gathered; among them stood a familiar tall, blond-haired man. "Cotton!" he shouted over the din.

Cotton, his face smudged with black, trotted over to him. "The devil has turned hell loose on us, and the fire department can't handle it. There's not enough water pressure, and those damned little seashells keep plugging up the hoses. With this wind, it probably won't stop until it reaches Broadway."

"What started it?"

"Near as we can tell, something from the Vulcan Foundry at Sixteenth and Strand. The wind is whipping the flames south, away from the harbor and toward town. A block on Strand and another couple on Mechanic Street are about gone, three blocks on Market are burning, and Postoffice is starting to go."

"My God, that's only a block from Church Street and Trista's house."

Cotton nodded and gestured toward the flames. "I don't think it will spread that far west, but I don't know. Hell, I don't know beans right now. I figured our new fire department could handle anything. They can't hardly do no more than spit on the flames and watch the town burn. It's too big, just too damned big. We're moving out everybody in the second, third, and eleventh wards."

"Where's that?"

"That covers most of the area between Thirteenth and Twenty-first Streets down to Broadway. Not Mrs. La Vigne's house, but it's damned close. If I were you, I'd move them out to be on the safe side—somewhere south of Broadway." He gave Webb a few more details, then said, "I've got to go. It's getting close to the county jail, and I may have to man a bucket brigade or move prisoners."

"You need any help?"

"We need all the help we can get."

Sugar Anne had everybody in the big house up and was helping Trista dress when Mary ran in. "Donald's back," she said, her chest heaving. "The captain says we're not in immediate danger, but to clear out just to be safe. Said we might go to the cemetery down on the south side of Broadway, where it's open. They think Broadway's too wide for the fire to cross, but Donald says the town is burning something fierce and sparks is shooting everywhere. Three blocks of Postoffice, from Sixteenth to Nineteenth, are aflame and the wind is driving it south across the Island. He says the poor souls are screaming and crying and trying to escape carrying what they can. An awful sight, he says."

"Dear Lord," Trista said, her hand splaying across her chest. "So close. We must take what we can. Mary, find Mr. Underwood. Tell him to gather his papers, then to take down the most valuable paintings and put them in the carriage. You pack up the best silverware. Here, Sugar Anne, is the combination to the safe." She scribbled on a piece of notepaper. "Take a valise and put everything from the safe into it, then don't let it out of your sight. Go, go, and send Willie to me."

For the next few minutes, the household was total confusion as everybody ran this way and that, selecting the most valuable and portable items.

"Forget that blasted mirror, Flora!" Trista shouted. "Don't bother with hats! Take the diamonds. We can buy a thousand hats with them. Dear heavens, I pray that the banks don't burn!"

Donald carried Trista downstairs. Flora, brandishing a bag of treasures in each hand, followed behind.

It was light as day outside with the flames blazing a path closer and closer, crackling and rumbling as they came. Thick swarms of fiery sparks flew through the sky and over the housetops only a few blocks away. The air had grown warm, and smoke strayed into the alley by the carriage house, hanging low and hiding from the fierce winds.

Less than half an hour after Sugar Anne gave the alarm, Trista, Flora, and Mary were seated in the carriage, and every square inch around them was packed with paintings and bags of jewelry and other valuables. Donald would drive, and Mr. Underwood would sit beside him.

Donald had hitched the buggy as well and tied Webb's hired gelding behind it. Mr. Underwood wasn't much of a hand with horses; Sugar Anne insisted that she was perfectly competent to drive the buggy. She and Willie and Phoebe would follow them.

"Phoebe!" Sugar Anne looked around frantically. "Where's Phoebe?"

"Why, I don't know," Mary said. "I knocked on her door and called to her."

"Did she answer?"

"Yes, and I told her we was to leave right away. She called back she was coming."

"I'll get her," Sugar Anne said. "You go ahead. I'll meet you at the cemetery."

"We'll wait," Trista said.

"No, no, we'll be only a minute behind you."

"She's probably in the privy," Willie said as the carriage pulled away.

Sugar Anne rolled her eyes. "Right." She ran to Phoebe's room off the kitchen and banged on the door.

Nothing.

She rapped sharply again and heard a muffled cry. "Phoebe?" she called, pushing open the door. "Phoebe? It's Sugar Anne. We have to leave immediately."

"Oh, Miss Sugar Anne," Phoebe groaned. "It's my time. I'm dyin'."

"Nonsense. You're not going to die, not if we hurry and remove ourselves from the path of the fire."

"No!" Phoebe wailed from the cot where she lay. "It's the baby. It's comin'."

"Oh, dear merciful heaven. *Willie!*"

Willie came running at her scream. "Yes'um?"

"What do you know about birthing babies?"

"*Me?* Nothin'."

"I was afraid of that," Sugar Anne said as Phoebe let out an awful shriek. "You'll have to go for the doctor. Do you know where he lives?"

"On Winnie Street, about six blocks over that way." He cocked his head toward the east.

"Hurry, run quickly and see if you can find him. But be careful. Please, be careful." She turned to Phoebe, knelt down, and brushed the damp hair from the terrified girl's face. "Shhhh, Phoebe, I'm here. Everything is going to be fine, just fine. Don't you worry one bit. Willie's gone for the doctor."

Phoebe moaned again, even louder this time. "I'm dyin', Miss Sugar Anne. I'm dyin'."

Webb and the other men ran from house to house a block ahead of the flames, checking to see that the occupants were gone and helping roust the stragglers. His eyes watered and his lungs burned from the smoke. Twice he'd used his hands to bat out a spark that threatened to catch his clothes on fire.

"Ma'am," he told the frightened woman who didn't seem to understand English very well, "you have to go. The fire is almost upon us here."

"My father," she said, weeping. "My father. He cannot walk."

Webb hoisted the wizened old man, who clutched a big family Bible in his arms, onto his back and ran with him toward the City Park, dragging the wailing woman after him. He glanced over his shoulder just in time to see the roof catch and burst into flame.

At the park, hundreds of people milled around with their meager belongings, dumbstruck and covered with soot. He left the woman and her father with friends they found, then stumbled away and dropped to the ground to rest for a minute.

Some kind soul offered him a dipper of water from a bucket. Webb drank it gratefully, then pushed himself to his feet and went back to his task.

Sugar Anne was sure that her fingers were broken where Phoebe had gripped them so hard. The girl was soaking wet and moaning and thrashing as if she were truly dying.

"Shhh," she soothed, bathing Phoebe's forehead with a cold cloth. For want of a better idea, she sang a lullaby to the poor child. It seemed to quiet her for a moment.

When Phoebe began to grow restless again, Sugar Anne prayed. She prayed more fervently than she'd ever prayed in her life. *Lord, I know that for some reason you've seen fit to heap trials upon me of late. Perhaps I deserve the awful things that have happened to me, but, Lord, please, please, don't let anything happen to Phoebe on my account. Hold the fire away from us and watch over her and the baby and bring them safely through this ordeal. I'm a pitiful person to try to be helping. I don't know what to do, Lord. I don't know what to do. Help me. Please, help me.*

Oh, why wasn't Willie back with the doctor?

There was a rap at the door.

Thank God! "Come in," she called.

Willie, cap in his hands and so soot-faced he looked like a player in a minstrel show, crept in the door. "I couldn't find the doctor, ma'am. The part of Winnie where his house is was aburnin' something ferocious and the fire's moved to within a block of Broadway. Folks around there said he might be over at the park tending to some what got singed in the fire. Some was hurt pretty bad, they said. I looked. Just missed him a time or two. Want I should look some more?"

Phoebe bowed up and let out a piercing scream.

"No. Run and get some clean towels. Lots of them. And water. Bring a pitcher of water."

Her mind struggling to recall every scrap she'd ever read or heard about delivering babies, Sugar Anne stood, lifted her chin, and said, "You relax, Phoebe. We'll handle this just fine. I hear Indian women go off by themselves and squat by a tree to have their babies. Do you think you can rouse up enough to squat?"

Phoebe groaned.

* * *

"Godammit!" Cotton said, then dropped down spread-eagled on the grass beside where Webb was stretched out, resting and eating a chicken leg somebody had handed him.

"What's wrong?"

"One of my men just told me that the fire's crossed Broadway. Dammit, we thought it would act as a fire-break, but hell, it's burning two blocks on the south side."

"Holy Mother." Webb groaned. "Is it ever going to stop?"

"When it gets to the Gulf, for sure. But it should begin to play out pretty soon. There's not as much to fuel it in that part of town. I just pray that the wind dies soon and doesn't change direction." Cotton, whose hair was almost as dark as Webb's from ashes and smoke, heaved himself to his feet. "Come on. Let's get going."

"I'll be along in a few minutes. While I'm this close, I want to go by Trista's and make sure that everything is all right."

"They should have left a couple of hours ago. Anyhow, the fire didn't get past Twenty-first Street and Church. Stopped shy of her place."

"I know," Webb said. "Still, I've got this nagging feeling that I ought to go by. I'll pick up my horse, if he's still there, and meet you on the south side after a while."

Webb struck out for the house, and a block shy of it, he saw Donald driving the carriage. He hailed him and Donald stopped. "What are you doing back? Have the ladies come home?"

"No, Mrs. La Vigne and Miss Flora and my Mary are at the cemetery with their belongings stacked atop the

Spicer vaults. Mr. Underwood is looking after them. Miss Sugar Anne was to follow in the buggy with Phoebe and Willie, only they never showed up."

Webb grew alarmed. "Never showed up?"

"No, sir, but there was a host of people about, and a bit of confusion, so at first we thought we'd just missed them. But Mr. Underwood and I searched thoroughly, and we couldn't locate them. Mrs. La Vigne is sick with worry, and, truth is, Captain, I'm concerned myself. With all the excitement, there's no telling what kind are about and up to no good."

"Let's go, man." His heart in his throat, Webb swung up to the driver's seat. "Hurry."

"Yes, sir." Donald snapped the reins sharply.

When they reached the house, Webb jumped down before the carriage stopped. Shouting Sugar Anne's name over and over, he ran through the back entrance and up the stairs.

Her room was empty. The house was still.

He ran back outside, shouting over and over. The door to Phoebe's room off the kitchen opened, and Sugar Anne stepped out.

"Shhhh," she said. "Phoebe just dropped off. Don't disturb her."

"Dropped off where?" he bellowed.

"Shhhh. She's asleep. She was very tired."

"Tired. She's tired. I see." He glared at her. "Dammit, don't you know that everybody's worried sick about you? Why didn't you go to the cemetery like you were supposed to do? Phoebe can sleep later."

"Oh, hush, Webb McQuillan. You're acting like an old bear. Look." She held out a bundle of towels to him.

"What is it?"

"Why, Lord preserve us," Donald O'Toole said, "it's a baby."

Sugar Anne said smugly, "You're absolutely right." She folded back one corner of the towel so that they could have a better look. "A baby boy. And I helped deliver him."

Willie stepped out from behind Sugar Anne. "And I helped too, didn't I, ma'am?"

"You certainly did."

"It's a boy," Willie said. "His name is Timothy."

"After my father," Sugar Anne said. "Want to hold him?"

"I don't know anything about holding babies," Webb said.

"Neither did I, but I learned very quickly. It just sort of comes naturally." She looked around. "Is the fire out? Are the others back?"

Webb shook his head. "The fire's crossed Broadway and is burning toward the Gulf, but you're past the danger here. It's cut a path two, three, sometimes four blocks wide across the Island. I need to get back and help do what I can. Will you be all right?" He cupped her cheek tenderly.

She nodded. "The worst part's over. I may sleep for a week."

Donald cleared his throat. "Captain, if you think the danger has passed, I'll fetch Mr. Underwood and the ladies home."

"Do that." Reluctantly, Webb moved his hand from Sugar Anne's face. It was streaked with black. "Dammit," he said, yanking his handkerchief from his pocket to wipe away the smudges. But his handkerchief was filthy, and he only made it worse.

Sugar Anne laughed. "Don't worry about it. A bit of soot won't hurt me." She kissed his cheek. "Be careful and hurry home. I'll be waiting."

⌒ Seventeen ⌒

As the sun rose on Saturday morning, Webb paused to thank his maker that the holocaust the city had endured was almost over. South of Broadway, the fire's fury had devoured a four-block swath past Avenue M. In the ruined corridor between Seventeenth and Twenty-first Streets, only a few structures remained standing. The handsome new public school building had fallen victim to the flames, but the old Lyon School was saved.

Webb shook his head at the incongruity of it: Dr. Trueheart's residence stood unscathed, while the entire block around it was smoldering rubble. Scattered here and there among the forty ravaged blocks, five or six residences were inexplicably left intact among their wasted neighbors. It was as if God's hand had covered them—or else they were dang lucky.

The circus, which had occupied a vacant square on Avenue M, had been able to pull up stakes in time and flee the flames. And the blaze had skipped over three little cottages and Miller's Grocery Store.

At Avenue M^1/$_2$, the flames began to peter out; there was less to fuel them among the sparser buildings. The fire narrowed its course and was finally stopped at

Avenue O. It died for lack of sustenance and by the valiant efforts of the bucket brigades, the people who beat the flames with wet quilts and gunnysacks, and the fire engine placed there. It was stopped at the steps of the Nelson family's house, four blocks from the Gulf of Mexico.

Webb could see the waves from where he stood. Not a half mile from that spot, he and Sugar Anne had walked in the sand and kissed.

Had that been a mere five hours ago? A lifetime had passed since then.

Bone weary, he walked to where he'd left his horse. He doused his head in the watering trough and washed what grime he could from his face and hands, then he mounted the roan and headed home.

Home. How good that sounded.

It wasn't even his house, but it had been more of a home to him than any place he'd hung his hat in twenty-five years. And the crazy bunch that lived there were more like a family. When had that happened? he wondered. He didn't know. But he felt a strong kinship to each and every one of them. Dad gum it! They cared about him, and he cared about them.

Especially Sugar Anne.

Always Sugar Anne.

He was going to tell her the truth.

Just as soon as he got a bath and slept for about two days.

Hell, he might not even take a bath. He'd never been so tired in his life.

* * *

When she heard the door open, Sugar Anne jerked awake. She'd put her head down on Webb's bed to rest her eyes for just a moment, and she must have drifted off.

Webb stood in the doorway. His new evening clothes were torn and filthy and badly scorched in several spots; his hat was gone. His face and hands were streaked with black soot and grime. His hair was singed. Never had anyone looked so wonderful.

"What are you doing in here?" he asked.

She smiled. "Waiting for you." She rose and straightened her dressing gown. "Everybody else is asleep. I knew you'd be dirty and tired, so Donald brought the portable bathtub in here for you to use. It's filled and waiting except for the pot that's simmering on top of the coals." She went to the fireplace and lifted the kettle's handle with a thick pad. "Go ahead, strip. I'll have the water just the right temperature by the time you're done."

"I'm not going to strip while you're here."

Sighing, she glanced heavenward. "We're not back to *that* again, are we? I've seen your posterior, remember?"

"It's not my posterior that I'm worried about."

"Oh, for goodness' sakes. I've told you that I'm a modern woman." She poured the boiling water into the large enamel tub with the gold cherubs adorning the sides, then tested the mixture with her elbow. "Perfect. Come, get in before it cools. I'm going to fix your breakfast."

As she sailed past him, she stopped and gave him a brief peck on the chin, the only spot she saw that was semiclean. "Welcome home."

He grinned.

He was still grinning when he eased down into the steamy bath. "Ahhhh. Heaven."

The fancy little tub might be better suited to a lady, but it would do. It would definitely do.

Webb scrubbed with the sponge and soap beside the tub, then used the brush to scour some of the deep grime embedded in his skin. He washed his hair, then submerged his head to rinse the suds away. He came up snorting and shaking his head like a wet dog.

When he opened his eyes, Sugar Anne stood there laughing at him. "Hey!" He ducked down, making sure that his privates were covered. "Get out of here."

"Don't be such a goose. Here, let me pour this pitcher of water over you, then you can have your breakfast." She upended the pitcher over his head.

He popped straight up like a jack-in-the-box. "Dammit, that's freezing!"

"Bracing, rather." She turned her back. "It's quite beneficial. I read about it somewhere. The Swedish go out after a hot bath and roll in the snow. Or is it the Finnish? I forget. Here's your breakfast. Sausage and eggs and some bread that I warmed in the skillet with butter. And some peach preserves. It all looked so good that I brought enough for—" The words froze in her throat when she turned around and saw Webb.

He had one towel in his hands, drying his hair. Another was draped about his hips. Drops of water glistened on his broad shoulders, and rivulets dribbled down his chest, where a patch of dark hair was plastered against his skin.

Dear Lord, he was magnificent, a pure work of art. All muscle and sinew, like a Greek statue in a museum.

She went hot all over.

Her feet moved toward him. "Here," she said, picking up another towel. "Let me help you."

She put the cloth to his chest, but he stilled her hand. "I don't think that's a good idea."

Her gaze met his. "Oh? Why not?"

"I don't believe that you're that naive."

Sugar Anne smiled. "I'm not naive at all."

"Do you know what you're saying?"

She stroked his damp chest. "I know exactly what I'm saying."

"Sugar Anne, there are some things that need to be said between us before—"

"Hush. I don't need any proclamations of undying love, nor do I intend to give any." She wrapped her arms around his neck and drew his lips down to hers. "I'm discovering a whole new aspect of myself as a woman, and this is what I want now. We can talk later."

"But—"

"Later," she said, then stayed his words with a hard and hungry kiss.

Passion erupted between them like a herd of cattle stampeding before a prairie fire—powerful, mindless, uncontrollable. Frightening.

She had never felt anything like it in her life. As they kissed and caressed and struggled with her robe, she grew more and more aroused, frantic with a desire to have him take her, to consume her, to send her shooting to the sky like a blaze from the terrible fire.

There was nothing gentle in the taking. Nothing plodding or boring or perfunctory. It was exciting. Exhilarating. Incredibly astonishing. Her heart pounded; her breath raced; her body trembled with constrained tension.

When Webb stroked an intimate, sensitive spot, her

back bowed, and she sucked a long breath of air through her clenched teeth. Mercy, she'd never known anything could feel so excruciatingly divine and so deliciously wicked at the same time. She strained toward the source of her pleasure and moaned when he stroked her again.

"You like that?" he asked.

"Oh, yes," she gasped, barely able to say the words. "Inordinately well. Do it again."

He did. And laughed.

When he tossed her naked on his bed and lifted her hips in his broad hands, their eyes met. A world of longing and need and unnamed awareness passed between them, one so intense that she almost wept from the power of it. At that instant she knew that she'd waited her entire life for this moment, this man.

"Yes," she whispered. "Oh, love, yes."

He plunged into her, and she flung herself upward to meet the thrust.

When she thought that her passion had reached its peak, he took her higher still until she was sure that she would die from the pleasure of their wild merging. She clawed and bit and cried out his name as she writhed against him until she felt an energy building inside her like the rumbling, billowing fury of an inferno.

Frightened at the intensity of the sensation, she tried to stop, to draw back, but Webb would have none of it. He held her close and called her sweet names and thrust deeper still until a wondrous burst of bliss erupted from her, shattering her mind and setting her body aquiver with spasms.

She cried out and clung to him as her whole being

shook. He held her tightly, thrust a final time, then shuddered in her arms. She could feel the pulse of his seed as it pumped into her.

So content was she as they lay together afterward that it didn't occur to her to worry about anything. Not Edward, not her mission to find him, not the plight of the city. She gave the possibility of pregnancy only a fleeting thought. In all the years that she and Edward had been married, she'd never conceived. It was unlikely that a single union, glorious as it was, would result in a child.

Never had she experienced anything quite so—so heady. She still glowed from the wonder of it. Lifting up a tad, she glanced at Webb. He was sound asleep. The poor man must be totally exhausted.

She allowed herself a few more minutes of contentment in his arms, then she slipped from his embrace, stole from the bed, and pulled the covers over him. As soon as she had washed a bit, she dressed in her bedgown and robe and tiptoed to her own room.

Not that Trista and Flora would be shocked by her behavior, she thought, smiling. Given their racy pasts, Sugar Anne doubted that much would shock them, but she wanted them to be able to maintain their façade of propriety. It seemed to be important, to Trista especially. Candor about such things could wait.

The two dear ladies were both totally unaware that Sugar Anne had figured out the lay of the land early on. Although she didn't know the precise details of their former lives, it hadn't been difficult to put the general picture together from a scrap of information overheard here, an innuendo there, a bit of gossip somewhere else.

Sugar Anne wasn't nearly as appalled by their pre-

vious employment as everyone expected her to be—
saddened, perhaps, that such a life had been necessary to
survive. She even was a little amused at the thought of
those two engaged in such endeavors—but never appalled.
She was, after all, a modern, freethinking woman; as she
had assured Webb, she was not naive. But she could play
the part of an unsophisticated miss if it suited her pur-
pose, and she would fight tooth and nail to preserve
Trista's and Flora's dignity.

After she climbed into her own bed, she drew up her
knees in a hug. What an utterly delightful experience her
passionate interlude with Webb had been. Absolutely
grand. And with a culmination that she'd never encountered before. She now knew for sure that Edward had
another black mark against him.

She was not by anyone's definition a cold fish.

She giggled and pulled the covers over her head.

"I don't know how to thank you, Mrs. La Vigne," Dr.
Aiken said.

"Think nothing of it, Doctor. You have been ever
faithful to me. You're more than welcome here until your
home and office can be rebuilt."

"But your generosity is—"

"I'll hear no more of it, John. You're beyond exhaus-
tion, and you need to rest. Donald will show you upstairs
to your room. It's the one across from Mr. Underwood on
the third floor. By the time you awake, we'll have
secured clothing for you. As I understand it, many of the
merchants were spared any damage and are being very
generous to those who lost their belongings."

"Come along with me, Doctor," Donald said. "I've a

nightshirt you can borrow until you've one of your own. Captain wore it a spell when he was recovering from his wound. It's all nice and freshly laundered, and there's a bathing room upstairs if you're a mind to wash up a bit."

The doctor, who was smoke-stained and bedraggled from his long hours with the homeless and injured, nodded to Flora and Trista and followed Donald from the parlor. Flora went back to her tatting. Trista turned her attention back to the newspaper account of the terrible holocaust they had survived.

Flora glanced up from her handiwork. "Did you hear what I heard this morning?"

"I don't know. What did you hear?"

"Bedsprings."

"I heard." Trista didn't comment further.

"Hard to miss with all that moaning and carrying—"

"I *heard*, Flora."

"Think anything will come of it?"

"Like what?"

"Like them two gettin' married."

Trista sighed. "Sugar Anne already has a husband, remember?"

"Oh, shoot fire, I keep forgetting that she's not really a widow. Any way she can dump the other one? The husband, I mean, not the captain."

"I don't know. I just don't know. And we mustn't forget that everyone except you and me believes that Sugar Anne's husband is dead. I don't think that she has even told the captain."

"Shame he didn't really kick the bucket," Flora said. "Save everybody a world of grief. Maybe the sorry skunk has met up with somebody who's plugged him between the eyes."

"We can't count on such a convenient solution. I thought that I might persuade Sugar Anne to speak to an attorney to determine what recourse she has."

"Then she and the captain could get married."

Trista shrugged. "Perhaps. It's really not any of our business, Flora."

"What's not?" Willie said as he strolled in, eating a banana.

"It's not your business either, young man. Where have you been off to?"

"Been down lookin' at what the fire did. It's an awful sight to see. Tom Keenum said there's hundreds of folks without a home or a bed to lay their heads. The hotels is full and people are staying in the churches and with other families what will take them in. You don't suppose—"

Trista smiled. "I've already considered the problem. Dr. Aiken is going to live with us for a while, and I've taken in a widow lady as well. She's going to stay with Phoebe in her room and take care of the baby."

"Who's going to take care of the baby?" Sugar Anne asked as she wandered into the room, still sleepy-eyed.

"A poor widow who lost her rooms and possessions to the fire," Trista said. "She has no family and was making a pitiful living sweeping out at Lawrence Mercantile, which was destroyed by the fire."

"And Dr. Aiken is living upstairs now," added Willie.

"Trista is going to build him a new house and a new office," said Flora.

Sugar Anne kissed Trista's forehead. "You're a dear. When is lunch?"

"Lunch—well, dinner—has come and gone. Mary fixed a nice ham and left several dishes on the sideboard so that people can eat when they're up and about. Is the captain awake?"

"I don't know," Sugar Anne said. "I haven't seen him. I was going to ask you the same thing."

Flora took a coughing fit, and Sugar Anne beat her on the back. "Did you inhale too much of the smoke last night?"

"Must have," Flora said, ducking her head and covering her mouth to cough again.

"How's Timothy? And Phoebe?" Sugar Anne asked.

"Right as rain," Flora said. "I swear, I don't know how you did it, delivering that baby the way you did."

"Actually, I didn't do much except yell 'Push, Phoebe' once or twice. I don't know which of us was more frightened. I had only the most cursory introduction to midwifery in my training at the hospital. Well, actually, I didn't have any, but I heard some of the women talking, and I sort of had the general idea of what was to be done. I think I'll get a bite and visit them."

"Timmy and Phoebe are dozing," Willie said. "Least they was when I stopped by not ten minutes ago. That other one had nodded off in her chair by the fire too."

"What other one?"

"Mrs. Turnipseed," Trista said.

"The widow lady," Willie explained.

"That's an odd name. I hope there's something simple to go along with it," Sugar Anne said.

"I believe it's Louise. Such a shame that she lost everything in the fire," Flora said. "Everything. And her with only one eye, too. Now she has a new home and a new job and plenty to wear from what Mary found in the attic. Donald's taking the rest of the old clothes down to the church after a while if you want to contribute anything, Sugar Anne."

"One eye?" Willie asked, clearly intrigued.

"An accident or some such," Trista said. "Looks a bit odd until you're accustomed to it—Willie, you're not to stare, ever—but she's a kind soul, and I'm sure that she'll do an excellent job looking after Phoebe and the baby."

Sugar Anne chuckled as she went searching for food. Only this household would hire a nanny for the maid's child.

As Sugar Anne swung open the door to the dining room, something extremely large, menacing, and hairy bounded from behind the sideboard and thrust itself at her. She shielded her face with her arms and screamed just as it knocked her sprawling to the floor.

⇐ Eighteen ⇒

Willie and Flora came running into the dining room with Trista hobbling behind on her cane. Mary hurried in from another direction, Donald from still another.

"What *is* this?" Sugar Anne cried from her position on the floor, where the beast was now licking her face.

"Looks to be a dog," said Donald. "And a dirty one at that."

"Uh-oh," said Willie, his eyes wide, "looks like the jig's up, old sport. You've ruined it now."

"Ruined what?" Trista asked. "What do you know about this—this creature, Willie?"

Looking sheepish, Willie said, "Well, he followed me home. Lost his own in the fire, I expect, and I hadn't the heart to drive the poor thing away. Just look at them eyes. Don't they look pitiful and sad?"

"Not at all," Sugar Anne said. She was still sprawled on the floor with the enormous, sooty dog on top of her, and they were nose to nose. "And his breath smells like ham."

"Willie!" Trista cried after she spied the wreckage on the sideboard. "He's devoured an entire ham!"

"Yes'um. I see that. He was hungry, I expect."

"Would somebody get this—this thing off me," Sugar Anne pleaded, trying to keep her mouth away from the eager tongue that was licking great swipes across her face.

"I think he likes you," Willie said, catching the dog by the ruff and yanking. "He's real gentle, gentle as a lamb."

"And twice the size of one," Sugar Anne said as she got to her feet, brushing at the grime on her fresh clothing.

"Why ever did you bring him in the house, Willie? And him so filthy?"

"I didn't. I left him in the laundry. I guess he was lonely. Poor pitiful thing." The innocence on Willie's face rivaled an angel's.

"Lonely?" Mary harrumped. "Smelled my ham, you mean. Now just look at the mess he's made. Get that dirty creature out of the house."

"Can't we keep him, ma'am?" Willie implored, looking to Trista. "At least until we can find his owner. There might be a big reward for finding so fine a dog. Please? He looked so lost. He might even be a poor orphan like me."

Trista sighed. "Take him outdoors and give him a bath. Then we'll discuss what to do with the dog."

"What dog?" said Webb as he entered the dining room.

"That dog," Flora said, pointing.

"This dog," Willie said, wrapping his arms around the beast's neck.

"Fine looking dog," Webb said, studying the animal that was zealously licking Willie's face. "But a mite dirty."

"More than a mite," Donald said. "Let's get him out of the house and into the yard. You'll need to find a tub to wash him in."

Webb winked at Sugar Anne. "He can use the one in my room."

"Absolutely not!" Trista said. "I brought that with me from San Francisco. I spent—well, never mind. Use one of the tubs from the laundry. And, Willie, do *not* bring him inside again."

Grinning from ear to ear, Willie dragged the shaggy animal from the room.

"Just look at the mess," Mary said. "And the two of you hungry, I'll wager."

"Yes, ma'am," Webb said. "I missed breakfast."

"And lunch," Sugar Anne added, checking the sideboard to see if anything was salvageable. Nothing was.

"I've a bit of chicken left from last night," Mary said. "And some corn pudding and peaches. You sit down and I'll have a nice meal for you in no time at all. O'Toole, you'd best get moving if you're going to take those clothes we gathered to the church. And don't forget to take the cake and the box of sandwiches to Mr. Underwood and the men down at the Masonic Lodge."

Donald nodded to the ladies and followed Mary out.

Webb pulled out a chair for Sugar Anne. "Thank you," she said as she was seated. "Did you sleep well?"

"Like a rock."

Flora snorted loudly and had another coughing fit. Trista took her firmly in hand. "We're going to have to ask Dr. Aiken to give you something for that catarrh, Flora. Come, let's get back to our activities."

Sugar Anne bit her lip and kept her eyes down until the ladies left the room. "I think they must have heard us," she whispered.

"I'm not surprised. You were squealing like a stuck pig."

"Hush." She gave him a swat with her napkin. "It's

extremely rude of you to mention it. And you weren't exactly mute yourself."

He grinned, caught her hand, and kissed it. "I'll try to be quieter next time."

The thought made her go very warm all over; there might indeed be a next time. That morning she hadn't thought much further than the moment, knowing that she would soon be leaving for New Orleans. She knew that, because he was a Texas Ranger, he wouldn't be staying on in Galveston to tend Trista's business. He had made it very clear that his position was merely temporary. Since she would be going her way, and he his, there wouldn't be any complications.

But she wasn't leaving for New Orleans until Monday. Or perhaps Tuesday, depending on the train schedules and space available. Monday was two days away.

Two whole days. Or at least a day and a half. But two nights. Two nights.

She spread her napkin on her lap and smiled.

Later that afternoon, when everyone else was busy with various activities, Sugar Anne tapped on Trista's door.

"Come in."

Pushing the door open and finding Trista in bed, she said, "I hope I'm not disturbing you."

"No, no, child. Come in. I'm just resting a bit. These old bones can't take the long nights as easily as they once did. Come, sit here by me." She patted the bed. "How is our new baby?"

"He seems to be doing fine, though I don't know a lot about babies. Mostly he sleeps and makes funny faces. I think Phoebe is going to be a good mother. And Mrs.

Turnipseed is a treasure. Did you know that she had three sons of her own? Her husband and two oldest were lost in the war, and the youngest on a freighter four years ago. Now she's alone. I'm so glad she's here to help with the baby. Phoebe adores her."

"I thought that she might. Phoebe needs a mother's guidance."

Picking at a loose string on the comforter, Sugar Anne said, "I've hesitated to leave until you were recovered, but I think that you're doing very well now, and—"

"And you want to find Edward Herndon."

"Yes."

"Isn't there some way I can dissuade you from pursuing this affair? I'll be happy to hire an army of excellent lawyers and investigators to sort out the whole wretched mess. You won't have to lay eyes on the rogue again."

Sugar Anne kissed the aging hand that gripped hers. "I know that you would, and you're a dear, but this is something that I must do on my own. I swore, Trista. I swore that I would track him down and make him pay for what he did, and I intend to do just that. I only need your help to finance my search. It might be costly."

"The expense is of no concern to me. Your happiness and your safety are. Going off to New Orleans alone is the height of folly. I will be worried sick the entire time that you're away."

Smiling broadly, Sugar Anne said, "You forget that I've become quite proficient with my firearm. I'm not likely to come to any harm."

Trista sighed. "Ah, the confidence of youth. And the

foolhardiness. There's nothing I can say to dissuade you?"

Sugar Anne shook her head. "It's important for my self-respect. I *have* to do it."

"Very well. I'll give you whatever money you need for your venture—if you'll promise me one thing."

Sugar Anne smiled. "Of course. What?"

"Promise me that you'll tell the captain everything and let him accompany you to New Orleans."

"Oh, dear, I can't do that! I can't possibly. He—"

"You promised," Trista chided quietly.

Heaving a great sigh, Sugar Anne leaned her head back against the bed post. This would complicate things considerably. She had, after all, blatantly lied to him. Not only was her husband very much alive, he was a common thief! How could she possibly tell Webb everything?

"Webb McQuillan is a good man, Sugar Anne, and I've known enough men in my day to be able to separate the wheat from the chaff. I've put my entire fortune in his hands with no qualms whatsoever."

"But you entrusted your fortune to Richard Fitzwarren as well. I'm not so apt to trust men as you."

"I never trusted Richard Fitzwarren any farther than I could throw him. Augustus Kincaid always handled my affairs, but he retired and Fitzwarren bought his practice. I never liked the little snake. I was about to take my business elsewhere, and I'd told him so. That's why he sneaked in and conked me over the head. He meant to keep my business—*all* of it. But Webb McQuillan is a different breed altogether. I would trust him not only with my fortune but with your life as well. Tell him the whole story. Let him go with you. Rely on his strength."

"I'll think about it."

And she did think about it. She mulled it over for hours. She even went for a walk down to the edge of the ruined part of town and thought about it some more.

It was awful—the ravage of the fire. People were out picking through the debris, trying to salvage some small part of their lives. One woman wept when she found the head of her child's china doll among the charred remnants of her house. Its body was burned away, but the head with its painted face was intact. Her husband held her while she sobbed.

Sugar Anne found the sight so poignant. Would someone ever hold her in that way? Webb? Would Webb hold her and comfort her in a moment of sorrow?

With only the tiniest push, her imagination placed the two of them in that picture. Yes, she could envision him with his strong arms around her, giving her solace. But with the vision came a bittersweet awareness of the unsettled state of things between them.

Did she want that relationship to grow into something more lasting? Was she ready to commit herself to another man? The questions were premature, of course, but she considered them just the same.

First, she must find Edward.

That night, when everyone had gone to bed and the house was quiet except for a few creaks and crackles of the walls settling in, Sugar Anne eased open her door and peeked out in the hall.

Satisfied that she could move undetected, she tiptoed toward Webb's room, flinching when a board squeaked beneath her feet. Just as she was about to reach for the knob, the door came slowly ajar, and he slipped through the opening as stealthily as a cat.

Startled, she gasped, then clamped her hands over her mouth.

"Looks like we had the same idea," he whispered. "Your room or mine?"

"Shhhh. Yours. We're closer."

He held open the door, and she tiptoed inside. The moment it was shut, he took her into his arms and kissed her.

"I've been wanting to do that for hours," he said, brushing his lips against hers. "I could barely eat my supper for wanting to drag you under the table and make love to you."

She giggled. "Under the table? How scandalous."

"How could I help it with your toes rubbing my leg all through the fish course?"

Her eyes widened. "Rubbing your leg? That must have been Willie's new dog or maybe Mrs. Turnipseed being friendly. Those weren't my toes. I wouldn't do such an unseemly thing at the dinner table."

"Not yours? Then who—"

She laughed and kissed him again. She adored kissing him and told him so. "I think it's the mustache that is so titillating. It looks so scratchy, but it's very soft." She stroked the dark hair above his lip.

He kissed her this time. One thing led to another, and before she knew it, they were back in his bed again. This time their lovemaking was not quite so urgent or so violent, but it was just as intense.

Oh, how she loved the feel of him inside her, the touch of his tongue on her skin, the stroke of his fingers over her breasts. Exquisite. Utterly exquisite.

The fire burned hotter.

Their movements became more vigorous, and soon she was soaring again.

Soaring through the clouds and over the moon.

When it was over, she sighed and snuggled close. "I could get used to this," she murmured, drawing a circle on his chest with her finger.

"So could I."

"I really didn't come in here for this."

He grinned. "You didn't?"

"No. I—I have something to ask you. Something to tell you. Something very—I'm not quite sure how to say this."

He sat up, put a pair of pillows to his back and pulled her against him, tucking her head beneath his chin. "It sounds serious."

"It is." She took a deep breath and plunged in. "I'm married. I mean, I'm not a widow. I'm actually married. I have a husband."

She felt him take a deep swallow. "I see," he said. He swallowed again. "And exactly where is this husband?"

"By last account, New Orleans."

"New Orleans?" he asked in a calm voice that totally contradicted the reaction of his body. Her hand, which rested on his chest, felt the tempo of his heartbeat increase to a terrible speed.

Oh dear, she thought, *he must be dreadfully disturbed by what I've said.* But there was nothing to do but plunge ahead. "Yes. And I have to go there and find him."

Another swallow. "I see."

She shot straight up and turned to face him, brushing her tumbled mass of hair from her eyes. "No, you don't see. You don't see at all. Being married to him is horrible. Horrible and humiliating. He's a dirty rotten liar and a thief and a sorry scoundrel, the lowest kind of scum on earth, and I'm going to New Orleans to find him, and I may have to shoot him dead. Will you go with me?"

⚔ Nineteen ⚔

For a moment Webb was too stunned to say anything. All the while Sugar Anne was leading up to this, he could feel himself getting more and more nervous. On the one hand, he wanted to jump up and hug her and do a jig on the bed. This was what he'd been waiting for, what he'd taken a leave from his job to do, what he'd dreamed about. It had fallen right in his lap.

Edward Herndon was in New Orleans.

Lordamighty! *New Orleans!*

Webb was nearly close enough to grab that reward. He could taste it for sure.

But her revelation threw him into a real quandary. He'd always known she was married, of course. Hadn't he been bedeviled by that fact all the time his lust for her was eating him alive? And he'd known that Herndon was a thief and a general no-good son of a bitch. Hadn't he salved his conscience with that information?

The problem was, Sugar Anne trusted him and was about to spill the whole business to him, and he felt like a dirty, lowdown sneak for being who he was. Part of him wanted to stuff a rag in her mouth before she told him everything and complicated things even worse.

"Well?" she said.

"Well, what?"

She gave an exaggerated sigh and rolled her eyes. "Merciful heavens, Webb McQuillan, didn't you hear a thing I said? Don't you want to discuss it? Don't you care about the rest of it?"

"I heard." He swallowed a lump in his throat big enough to choke a horse. "Maybe you shouldn't tell the rest."

"No, I've started it, and I'm going to finish it. I know that you're probably angry with me right now. After all, I've lied to you and made you a party to—to adultery. And I know that you're a man of character. I knew that even before Trista lectured me about that fact.

"Now, I don't want you to feel one little bit guilty over the adultery part. In my heart, I'm no longer married to him. And didn't he run off with his mistress anyhow? And isn't she wearing my jewelry and spending my inheritance? Our marriage ended long ago, long before he left in the middle of the night, and me with a terrible case of influenza and practically on my deathbed, and took everything he could carry. Are you very angry with me?"

"No," he said, unable to think of another thing to say.

"You're shocked, aren't you? Disgusted. Well, let me tell you, I'm disgusted with myself, too. Disgusted and furious that Edward Herndon—that's the worm's name—has turned me into a sneak and a liar. I've never lied before in my life—well, maybe once or twice, but only small lies, the kind you tell to keep from hurting someone's feelings."

She was fidgeting something awful, and he could see that she was getting more and more worked up. He pulled her into his arms again and tucked her head back under his chin. "Shhhh. I'm not shocked *or* disgusted. A little surprised, maybe."

"Ha! I'll bet *that* is an understatement. But I want to explain."

"You don't have to do that," he said, half hoping that she'd keep quiet and not tie his rope into a bigger knot. Her coming clean was going to make things twice as tough for him.

"Yes, I do. It's important that you understand, and I need your help."

Now what the hell was he going to do?

Nothing he could do but listen. "Shoot."

With him holding her close, she spent nearly an hour explaining. Most of it he already knew, but he didn't say yea or nay while she told the story. And by the time she finished the story, he was convinced that she was telling the truth. She didn't have anything to do with her husband's thievery. She'd been as much a victim as anybody. More, even.

But she knew where Herndon was. And, much as he hated to, he had to ask. "You say he's in New Orleans?"

She nodded. "At least he was a few days before I left Chicago—which seems like forever now. I got a letter."

"From him?"

She snorted. "Not likely. It was from a nun at the Hotel Dieu—that's a hospital—in New Orleans. A man had been brought into the hospital, feverish and unconscious. A Chicago address was the only bit of identification he carried. They didn't know his name or where he was staying in New Orleans or anything. They didn't even know my name or whose address it was. The letter was addressed 'To Whom It May Concern.' Her description of the man matched Edward perfectly."

"Did you respond to the letter?"

"And tip off Edward when he came to that I knew his whereabouts? Of course not. I'm no fool. But I hoped fervently that he'd caught my influenza and was sick as a dog."

"So you don't actually know if he's still in the hospital?"

"No. In fact, it's likely that he's not. But I have a place to start looking."

"Sugar Anne, why didn't you go to the police with the information? Surely they're better equipped to investigate than you are."

"The *police*!" she sneered. "They're idiots. They're convinced that I'm mixed up in the whole thing. I told you that I was a pariah in Chicago. Even the Pinkertons think I'm guilty. That bunch has made my life miserable, may they all rot in hell!"

Webb winced, but he kept his counsel.

"I'm leaving for New Orleans on Monday," she said. "I mean to find him and the money he stole and see that every cent is returned to the rightful owners. Will you go with me?"

His mind racing, he didn't reply for a few moments. Should he tell her now? Should he tell her at all? Hell, he didn't know what to do. He had to think. The Pinkerton Agency was expecting him to come through, and he'd given them his word. He felt strongly about giving his word and living up to bargains. And, to top it off,

Amanda had wired that she would be in town on Monday for a report.

Oh, hell. Dammit to hell. What a mess. He hated lying; look what a predicament lying had landed him in. He needed time to think. Trying to figure things out now was harder than trying to put socks on a chicken.

"Well?" she said, her tone clearly impatient. "Will you go to New Orleans with me on Monday?"

He sucked in a deep breath and blew it out slowly. "Could we make it Tuesday?"

At eleven o'clock on Monday morning, Webb stood at the gate of Mrs. Glenn's boardinghouse feeling lower than a gopher hole. He still didn't know what to do. No, that wasn't exactly the truth. He knew what to do, what he *had* to do, but it pained him something fierce.

He and Amanda had been good friends for many years. When Pinkerton exhausted its leads, she had put her reputation on the line in recommending him for a shot at locating the money and collecting the reward. It was the opportunity of a lifetime for him, and Amanda knew it. She'd given him a chance at his dream; Webb had given her, and through her, the Pinkerton Agency, his solemn word that as soon as he had a line on Herndon or the money, he'd let them know. His word meant something. Hell, his word had always meant *everything*. It was a contract, a sacred trust, a measure of his character.

On the other hand, he was pretty sure that he was falling in love with Sugar Anne. Deep-down, soul-stealing, honest-to-God love. And if she had any notion that he was in cahoots with the Pinkertons, she'd have a hissy fit. Or worse. He tried to think of some way that he could break it to her gently and make her understand. He wasn't sure that there was a way. He'd sooner charge hell with a bucket of water than tell her the truth. He might lose her. And it had taken him the best part of thirty years to find her.

Shit! Of all times for him to fall in love.

But truth to tell, he had. Head over heels crazy in love. Sugar Anne meant the world to him. He didn't know what he'd do without her now. He couldn't even think about it without breaking out in a sweat.

Glancing around and seeing no one he knew, he lifted the gate latch and went inside. Amanda must have been waiting, for by the time he reached the porch, she was holding open the door. His expression grim, Webb removed his hat and went inside.

Flora was just pushing Trista's invalid chair out the door of Mrs. Cautier's millinery shop when she spotted them. Mrs. Glenn's boardinghouse was catty-corner, and she had a perfect view of the front porch. She gasped. "Would you look at that!"

Trista's only comment was a sigh.

"Did you see? Did you see the captain and that actress carrying on right out in public? Did you see?"

"I saw, Flora. Let's go on to Brown's Mercantile. I want to look at the new shipment of kid gloves."

"Gloves? How can you think of gloves when the captain is having a rendezvous with an actress right across the street? And while our Sugar Anne, so in love with him she can't see straight, is doing good deeds down at the church. I'm of a mind to march across the street and give him a talking-to, and I might snatch her baldheaded while I'm about it."

"Leave it alone, Flora."

"Leave it alone? I can't leave it alone. I'm furious. Our Sugar Anne is a gently reared young woman. She doesn't understand the ways of men, especially the handsome ones. I told her that you could never trust a handsome man, and it appears that I was right about that one. Taking Sugar Anne into his bed at night and consorting with that woman on the side. I—"

"Flora," Trista said in the tone that declared she meant business. "Hush. I'm sure that the captain has a perfectly reasonable explanation. Just because you've had a few bad experiences with handsome men doesn't mean that they're all cads."

"Fiddlesticks! And you don't believe that what you just saw was innocent any more than I do. Now, tell the truth."

Trista sighed again. "I'm willing to give him the benefit of the doubt, but rest assured, I intend to speak with the captain about this situation immediately. In the meantime, don't you *dare* breathe a word of this to Sugar Anne."

Flora made a very rude sound and pushed the invalid chair toward Market Street so fast that Trista's hair stood up from the breeze they generated.

Webb had been surprised to find a message from Trista when he returned to the office after his meeting with Amanda. She needed to speak with him immediately. Odd. They had seen each other at breakfast, and she hadn't said a word then. He had gone home right away.

He knocked at the door of Trista's bedroom, then entered at her invitation. She was seated at her desk.

"Yes, ma'am," he said. "What can I do for you?"

"Captain, I'll be blunt. What are your intentions toward my—toward Sugar Anne?"

"Beg pardon?"

"Sir, I have not led a sheltered life, and I am neither blind nor deaf. But Sugar Anne isn't accustomed to the ways of lustful men, and I won't have her hurt."

Damned if Webb didn't feel his face flush. "Ma'am, I'd sooner cut off my right arm than hurt Sugar Anne. If I'm not mistaken, I—I believe that I'm in love with her."

"Then perhaps you would care to explain your activities at Mrs. Glenn's boardinghouse this morning."

"My . . . activities?"

"Flora and I were across the street at the millinery shop. We saw you with a very beautiful young woman, an actress, I believe Flora said. She kissed you."

Webb did some fast thinking. He chuckled. "Ma'am, I can promise you that what you saw was totally innocent. Why, I've known Amanda for years, since we were kids growing up. She's like a sister to me. I'll swear on a stack of Bibles a mile high that I've never touched her any more than I would a sister. I've been helping her out on a personal matter."

"I see. Then perhaps you would like to invite this Amanda over to dinner tonight?"

His stomach fell down to about the area of his boot tops. "Well, ma'am, that's mighty generous of you, but she was just passing through. I believe that she was leaving on a train—" he pulled out his watch and studied it "—about now."

"I see. Too bad that we won't have the opportunity of meeting your . . . friend."

Webb felt like a schoolboy. Mrs. La Vigne was a sly old gal; she figured something strange was going on, but she was just barking up the wrong tree.

"Captain, I am entrusting my most treasured possession to your protection. If Sugar Anne gets hurt, I will cut off more than your right arm. Do I make myself clear?"

"Yes, ma'am. I'd say that was pretty clear. You couldn't get much clearer than that. And believe me, her happiness and her safety are very important to me. I'll take good care of her. Best I can."

They heard a loud commotion downstairs, like someone yelling and dancing around.

"Whatever is going on?" Mrs. La Vigne asked.

"Sounds like Sugar Anne," Webb said. "I'll go find out."

He hurried downstairs and found Sugar Anne in the foyer, waving an envelope and whooping and hollering like a drunk cowboy fresh off a trail drive.

"What's going on?" he asked.

"Look, just look!" She waved the paper toward him, then threw herself into his arms laughing. "A messenger just brought it."

Her laughter was infectious and he laughed with her. "What am I looking at?"

"The reward. From the train robbery. It's *enormous*. And guess what? I have a lifetime pass for first-class accommodations on the train. I think my luck has changed for sure. I'm going to the ticket agent right now and make the arrangements for our trip to New Orleans.

Right after I go to the bank. Look at the size of this draft. Isn't it wonderful? Now I won't have to borrow money from Trista."

"That's great, honey, but I need—"

She stopped dead still. "What did you say?"

"I said that was great, but I need—"

"You called me 'honey.' "

"I guess maybe I did."

"Nobody has called me 'honey' for years and years. Not since I was a little girl and my father called me that. I like it." She rubbed her nose against his, then lifted her face for a kiss.

He knew that sooner or later, they had to do some serious talking, but with her jasmine smell invading his senses and her sweet lips waiting to be kissed, he decided that at this moment he'd rather kiss than talk.

On Tuesday afternoon, everybody came to the depot to see them off except Phoebe and Timmy and Mrs. Turnipseed. Sugar Anne had told them good-bye before she left. She had hugged Phoebe and given Timmy a kiss on his tiny nose and promised to bring them presents when she returned.

"Maybe some fancy perfume for you," she'd told Phoebe. "And a toy for you, young fellow. I swear you've grown an inch since yesterday."

She had whispered to Mrs. Turnipseed, "I'll find you the best and most beautiful glass eye in New Orleans."

Mrs. Turnipseed had positively beamed—and winked with her remaining one. "Now that I look on it, that fire might have been the best thing that happened to me in many a day. Being here is like a blessing from God. And this precious little mite," she had said, stroking the baby's head, "is the grandchild I never had."

Even Willie was at the station, having wangled permission to skip his afternoon lessons for the occasion. Sport, his great shaggy dog—rather handsome since he'd been bathed and brushed—was along too, firmly restrained by a stout leash and collar.

Flora and Trista hugged her, then hugged her again.

"You have that list of names I gave you?" Trista asked.

Sugar Anne patted her black leather satchel. "Right here. I have everything. Now, don't worry. I'm not sure how long our search will take, but I'll send a wire in a few days."

Mary handed her a basket. "I've packed a few treats for you," she said. "I know you're supposed to have one of them fancy new dining cars, but you never know what kind of food you'll get. With this, you won't go hungry."

"Thank you, Mary. And thank you, Donald, for everything. Take good care of everyone while I'm gone."

"Don't you worry none, miss," Donald said. "I'll see to the lot of them."

Webb said his good-byes as well, and shook hands with Donald and Mr. Underwood and even Willie, who practically glowed at the grown-up treatment.

Amid a great deal of handkerchief waving and a tear or two, Sugar Ann and Webb boarded the train that would take them to Houston, then straight through to New Orleans. They would sleep in a Pullman Palace car, and be served their meals in the elegant new dining car that Mary had worried so about.

Sugar Anne was leaving the Island in much grander style than she had arrived.

Your days are numbered, Edward Allen Herndon. I'm on my way.

SUGAR ANNE 247

⤜ Twenty ⤛

As the carriage made its way through New Orleans, Sugar Anne said, "I remember my grandmother mentioning that street. She must have lived not too far from here, though I don't recall exactly where. She grew up in the Vieux Carré, which is the Creole part of the city. She lived here until she married my grandfather, who was an American and not at all suitable, according to her parents."

"I'm surprised that they allowed her to marry him. I always thought that the Creoles kept a tight rein on their daughters."

Sugar Anne leaned close. "I think there was some sort of scandal. Or else my grandmother threatened to create a scandal. She was very much in love with the old codger. Why escapes me. She was such a dear, but I suppose my grandfather was probably quite dashing in those days. A similar thing happened in Edward's family. His father was American and his mother was from an old Creole family, but she died when he was very young. I guess that was about the only thing we had in common."

"Then Herndon has family in New Orleans?"

"Oh no, not anymore. I think they've all died out. His

father moved to St. Louis when Edward was no more than five or six years old and became a very successful attorney there. Robert Herndon handled my grandfather's business after he left Galveston. Pity Edward wasn't the man his father was—or the man my grandfather thought he was. But Edward always could fool people. At least for a while. Oh, here's the hotel."

Trista had insisted that they stay at the Hotel Royal— "the" place to stay in New Orleans, she had said.

They were escorted to a suite with luxurious furnishings and a balcony that overlooked the Vieux Carré, and she could see the river beyond the spires. Fresh flowers filled several vases in both the sitting room and Sugar Anne's bedroom, and a large basket of fruit sat on a low table near the sofa.

Webb ambled around the rooms, hands in his pockets, looking things over. "This hotel Trista picked out is *some* fancy place. Don't believe I've ever seen anything like it." He stretched out on one of the beds and tucked his hands behind his head. "Feels just like a cloud."

Sugar Anne laughed. "This is certainly a step up from the last hotel we stayed in. Remember that terrible room in Houston?"

"Not very well." He rose, and they walked back into the sitting room.

"Believe me, this is considerably nicer. I'll leave my things for the maid to unpack, drop off some items downstairs for safekeeping, then go directly to the Hotel Dieu. I'm eager to talk with the nun who wrote the letter to Chicago, and the sooner we get started on the business we came for, the better."

"Then let's go." He offered her his arm.

Downstairs, after Sugar Anne deposited a small bag in the hotel safe, they secured directions to the hospital. It was only a short ride away.

While they waited for the hired carriage to be brought to the entrance, Sugar Anne began to fidget. Webb laid his hand on her back and made a couple of circular strokes meant to comfort her. "Ease up, honey. I know that you're having a fit to get to the hospital, but you're jumpier'n a cricket on a hot griddle."

"I know, but I can't seem to help it," she said as Webb helped her into the carriage.

They soon found Tulane Avenue and the Hotel Dieu, an imposing three-story structure with windows covered by wooden jalousies and balconies bedecked with the wrought iron trim that seemed so prevalent in the city.

Sugar Anne's heart pounded as they passed through the gate and went inside to speak to the administrator. She forced herself to be calm while she explained that she had received a letter about a patient some weeks ago, one written by a Sister Phillipa. Could she speak to the sister, please?

The administrator couldn't have been more gracious— which eased Sugar Anne's tension temporarily. She and Webb were shown to a small office to await the nun, who was busy with her duties and would have to be relieved before she could meet with them.

In a few minutes, a young woman about Sugar Anne's age and size entered. As a Sister of Charity, she wore a nun's habit, but instead of a somber demeanor, she had a sweet, laughing face with merry brown eyes and a sprinkle of freckles across her nose. Although her hair wasn't visible beneath her veil, her eyebrows hinted that it might have a decided red cast.

"I'm Sister Phillipa," she said. "Sister Agnes said that you wanted to see me. How may I be of assistance?"

Sugar Anne said, "I am Mrs. Herndon. This gentleman is Captain McQuillan of the Texas Rangers." She took the letter from her satchel and handed it to the sister. "A few weeks ago, this letter came to my home in Chicago. I believe that you wrote it."

The young nun took the now bedraggled letter and began to read. Sugar Anne grew more and more apprehensive as they waited. She reached for Webb's hand. He squeezed her fingers lightly, smiled, and winked ever so slightly.

She tried to return his smile, but she failed miserably.

"Yes," the sister said. "I recall writing this. I remember the gentleman. Is this someone you know?"

Sugar Anne took a deep breath. "Perhaps. It sounds very much like a description of my husband, who is . . . missing. I know that a great deal of time has passed, but due to very difficult circumstances, I'm just now able to contact you. Could you—could you tell me where he is now?"

Sister Phillipa glanced upward for a moment, as if in beseeching prayer. "Yes, I could." The seconds seemed interminable as they waited for her to go on. "There is no easy way to say this." The nun gently laid her hand on Sugar Anne's shoulder. "The gentleman has passed on."

"Passed on?" Sugar Anne felt the blood drain from her face, and she gripped Webb's hand tightly. "He's *dead*?"

"Yes. I'm so sorry. He was gravely ill when he was brought in, unconscious, and with a virulent fever. His disease had progressed too far when he came to us—all we could do was try to make him comfortable. He died two days after I wrote this letter. That address, tucked into his empty wallet, was our only link to his identity."

"Did he . . . ever regain consciousness?"

"Barely. He was mostly incoherent, mumbling various things. We didn't know if he was Catholic . . ." She glanced at Sugar Anne.

"He was born Catholic. The last few years . . . Well, he was not actively religious."

"Ah." Sister Phillipa nodded. "He did seem to know the rosary and found comfort in it, so we assumed that he might be. Father Antonio administered the last rites. The gentleman—what was his name?"

"Edward. Edward Herndon."

"Mr. Herndon became very agitated after Father Antonio administered rites. He—he called me 'Sugar' several times." Sister Phillipa tittered and ducked her head. "He kept saying that he was sorry and begged me to pray for his soul. And he kept talking about the St. Louis Cemetery and being buried. Over and over, he said, 'Sugar, buried by you. By you.' "

"Sugar?"

"Yes. As I said, he was mostly incoherent. Poor soul. Since he spoke so frequently during his last hours of that cemetery, and since we didn't know who he was, we used most of what valuables he had to pay for his care and rent a crypt at that same cemetery for his entombment. He wore an elegant stickpin in his tie—"

"A gold fleur-de-lis with a large diamond?" Sugar Anne said.

"Why, yes, exactly."

She nodded. "Edward wore it all the time. Other than that, he didn't care much for jewelry."

"Then there's no doubt that this man was your husband?"

"Very little, especially after your description. And you see, my name is Sugar Anne."

"Ah. It was you to whom he spoke."

She nodded and gripped Webb's hand as tightly as she could. "And our . . . parting was not amicable."

"So we inferred. He was truly repentant for whatever transgressions he had committed. We sold his stickpin for the expenses. I trust that was all right? If you want to recover it for sentimental purposes, I believe Mother Superior has the name of the dealer."

"Fine, thank you. Did he have any other possessions? Any papers? Anything?"

"Any other effects he might have carried, Mother Superior would have in her office. His clothing was new and of excellent quality, but it was beyond cleaning. It was burned."

"And you can recall nothing more that he said?"

"He was delirious, my dear. Over and over he said he was sorry, and he called for you, though we didn't understand it at the time. 'Sugar,' he said. And sometimes he said, 'Angel, by you.' And he talked of the cemetery. Even in his delirium, I believe that he knew he was dying, and he wanted forgiveness for his sins. I'm sorry. I wish I could be of more comfort to you."

"No, Sister, you've been very kind. I'm simply hoping for something that obviously isn't there. How may we find his grave?"

"St. Louis Cemetery II isn't far from here. Here, let me

write the address for you. Father Antonio can tell you the exact spot. I'll ask him. And if you will excuse me, I'll get your husband's other belongings from Mother Superior."

"One last question, Sister," Sugar Anne said. "Was it influenza?"

"Influenza?"

"That my husband died of?"

"Oh, no, my dear. It was the bullet wounds. Three of them, all serious, two in his abdomen, one in the chest. They had suppurated. The gardener discovered him near the front steps with grass stains on his knees from crawling to get here. Poor soul."

"Were the police called?"

"Oh, yes. But as I recall, they could do little without an identification. His wallet was empty, so we were sure he had been robbed. Such things happen more frequently than we like to imagine." Sister Phillipa rose. "I shall return shortly with his effects and the information from Father Antonio."

After Sister Phillipa left, Webb pressed Sugar Anne's hand against his thigh. "I'm sorry."

She sighed. "So am I. I wanted desperately to continue hating him. Now I only pity him, dying alone in a strange place with such guilt on his conscience. Perhaps I should weep, but all my tears for him are gone. I'm amazed that he showed remorse for what he did."

"I've seen men act in strange ways when they know their time is up. You'd be surprised to hear the meanest, lowdown rascals crying like babies for their mothers."

"Perhaps. Yet the comments seem odd. I wonder what

happened to his mistress. Was she the angel he spoke of? He certainly never called me 'angel.' "

Webb smiled and brought her hand to his lips. "He missed a bet."

Sugar Anne returned his smile with a forlorn one of her own. "You're a dear, dear man, Webb McQuillan. And very good for my bruised pride. Heaven knows, it has taken quite a beating these past few months. It's rather dreadful being exploited and deceived by someone who is supposed to care about you."

Webb rose and went to the window to look out, obviously discomfited by her intimate comments. For all his outward bluster, Sugar Anne thought, he was a kind, humble man—and actually rather private. Every day she cared more for him, and every day she thanked fate for placing a man of such fine character in her path. Heaven knows she'd encountered enough low types in her life.

Sister Phillipa returned shortly with a small paper bag, which she handed to Sugar Anne without comment. Accompanying her was an elderly priest, whom she introduced as Father Antonio.

The priest offered his condolences, then sketched a map to help them locate Edward's burial place. "The cemetery is only a few blocks from here," Father Antonio said. He gave them directions to its entrance.

Sugar Anne thanked both the priest and the nun; they said their good-byes, and parted.

Outside, Webb asked, "What next? Do you want to go back to the hotel?"

She shook her head. "Not yet. I want to go through this." She held up the paper bag. "And I want to go to the cemetery, I suppose, but I'm suddenly starving. Do you suppose there is a café nearby where we can get a bit of lunch? As Father Antonio was talking, all I could think of was that I wished I'd brought Mary's basket along. Very often when I get nervous, I get hungry."

Webb smiled. "We'll find a place."

A few minutes later they were seated at a charming spot that allowed them to dine al fresco in a lovely little courtyard with a fountain. Huge pots of lush plants were set about the stone patio, and others hung from the eaves of the building and from the limbs of a tree growing to one side of the enclosure.

"Oh, my, gumbo," Sugar Anne exclaimed as she scanned the menu. "I haven't had gumbo in years. When I was a little girl, we had a cook who made it often. I wonder if it's as tasty as I remember?"

"New Orleans is the place to try it. I've never eaten anything in the city that wasn't good."

They both ordered gumbo creole and a loaf of crusty bread. He asked for beer, and she requested lemonade.

While they waited for their food, Sugar Anne cleared a spot on the small table and dumped out the contents of the bag. They found a leather wallet, the one she'd given Edward for their last Christmas together, a rumpled silk handkerchief, a pair of eyeglasses, and a key.

Also in the bag was a note. It stated that the stickpin had been sold to a Monsieur DesRoches who had a shop on Royal Street. The note also said that the patient's clothes, although obviously new and of fine quality, had been burned because they couldn't be repaired. His boots had been given to the poor.

"Nothing here gives any clue to where Edward put the

money he stole," Sugar Anne said. "Nothing. He's taken his secret to his grave and is mocking me still."

"Don't give up too quickly." Webb picked up the key and looked at it. "I wonder what this fits?" He took the hotel key from his pocket and compared the two. "They're of a different make, but it's possible that this fits the door to where he lived."

"A wonderful deduction. Now, how many doors do you suppose that we'll have to try before we find the right one?" The waiter had arrived with their food, so she scraped the items back into the bag.

"I've chased a crook or two in my time," Webb said, "and I know a lot about detecting. We're not licked. For instance, the note said that his clothes were new and of good quality. What if he went to a tailor in town for a new suit?"

Sugar Anne perked up. "Of course. We need to interview tailors who deal in fine menswear. There can't be that many. Edward was such a clotheshorse. I can't imagine that he wouldn't spend some of his ill-gotten gain on finery. And I would like to redeem his stickpin. Perhaps someone might recognize it and give us further information."

"Good idea."

They discussed a number of possible avenues for exploration while they finished their meal. Their next stop was the cemetery on Claiborne, where Edward was buried.

If she thought that the dead would give up their secrets easily, she was mistaken.

What they found were rows and rows of tombs sitting above ground like miniature temples or houses, much like the Galveston cemetery where her family was buried. Some were elaborate, with pillars and scrollwork and crosses and statuary, some plain, but most were freshly whitewashed and decorated with containers of flowers long past their prime. Some had intricate wrought iron enclosures with gates; most were not fenced.

As Sugar Anne and Webb were consulting Father Antonio's map, a young priest approached them. "May I be of help?" he asked.

Webb showed the map to him. "We're not familiar with the cemetery. This was a recent burial. The lady's a . . . family member."

"Ah, yes. I know the place. It's across the way on the far side. Come, I'll show you."

As they followed him between the long rows, occasionally they passed an old tomb that had sunk a foot or more into the soft earth or one where the outer stucco had worn away, exposing the crumbling bricks beneath.

"Why are these decaying while the others are so well kept?" Sugar Anne asked the priest.

The young man shrugged and stopped in front of a weathered crypt. "Some of these tombs are quite old. Perhaps their families are gone, so there is no one to repair them or bring flowers on All Saints' Day, which is quite an occasion here. We have no local stone so the tombs are made of bricks and mortar, and our bricks are very porous, so the outside is covered with stucco. Still, after a time, the stucco must be repaired. Marble, like the slab here, is very expensive and ordinarily used only on the front to bear the inscriptions and cover the place where the tomb is sealed."

Sugar Anne leaned across the small wrought-iron

enclosure to read the family names on the marble slab bolted to the front. "How can so many people be buried in such a small area?" she asked. "These look as if they're designed for one or two."

The priest explained that after a year and a day, the remains of the individual could, if the burial chamber was needed again, simply be moved to the back—or placed down below if it was a double-decker—and the wooden casket burned. Sugar Anne was sorry that she'd asked.

But the priest seemed to delight in describing the burial practices in copious detail and even pointed out the tombs of prominent personages and the larger multi-unit tombs of certain fraternal societies, where the old boys were buried in eternal camaraderie. "Perhaps you've heard of this gentleman? Dominique You was a famous pirate, a lieutenant of Jean Laffite when they sailed the seas, but he settled down to become a prominent citizen of New Orleans. Fifty-five years ago he was buried here. And over there is a former United States senator."

"Imagine that." Sugar Anne turned a deaf ear to his discourse and trudged onward, altogether weary of the subject. She glanced at Webb and rolled her eyes. He only grinned and winked.

"Here we are," the priest said. He had stopped at a wall. "The ovens."

"The *what*?"

"The wall vaults. Sometimes they're called ovens because they resemble a baker's brick oven, as you see."

"*Ovens?* Edward is buried in an *oven*?"

"Oh, no, no, no. These are vaults. They are four tiers high here and form a wall that encloses this portion of the grounds. You see, each of these brick arches is a crypt. The front is bricked, and then marble placed over the front if the family desires."

"Which is Edward's?"

The priest studied the map again and paced five spaces down the wall. "There," he said, pointing to the top crypt, which was just above Sugar Anne's head. He handed the map to Webb, bowed slightly, and left.

For a long time, Sugar Anne simply stood stiffly and looked up at the wall and at the archway formed by the bricks. She tried to feel something, tried to wring some emotion from inside, but she felt only numbness.

"Poor Edward. There's no one left to weep for him. What a sad way to end one's life. In a rented wall oven." She sighed.

Webb put his arm around her shoulders.

With his tender gesture, her eyes stung, then a single tear trickled down her cheek. She sighed again.

"Well, at least he has a good view."

➷ Twenty-one ➶

When they returned to the hotel, Sugar Anne's tail feathers were dragging, and Webb was feeling whipped too. They hadn't made any headway finding out where the money was. Webb wondered if they would ever find it. Maybe that wouldn't be such a bad thing. Since he'd finally admitted to himself that he was crazy about Sugar Anne, not being able to recover the funds would sure take him off the hook.

Of course, without the reward money, there was no way that he could ever give her the kind of life that she was used to, with a big house and servants and a fine carriage. And clothes. He'd never seen so many clothes in his life. Her idea of traveling light to New Orleans had been a valise and a trunk that took two strong men to lift. Everything he owned was stuffed into those same scarred saddlebags he'd had for years.

Once they were in their suite, Sugar Anne sighed, and the sound was so forlorn that he hurt for her. He couldn't help but hold out his arms to her.

She walked into his embrace and laid her forehead against his shoulder. "Nothing is turning out like I thought it would. Nothing."

He held her close and stroked small circles over her back. "I'm sorry."

"Do you think that Monsieur DesRoches will be able to recover the stickpin from his customer?"

"I don't know. We'll hope for the best." He kissed the top of her head.

She pulled back, then lifted her face to look at him with those beautiful, sorrowful eyes, and he was lost again. Even knowing it was dumber than just about anything he'd ever done, he kissed her.

She tasted sweeter than honeysuckle nectar.

And one kiss only made him want another. Before he could talk himself out of it, he scooped her up in his arms, stalked to his bedroom, and laid her down on his soft feather bed.

He kissed her some more and loved her with everything that was in him.

Something dragged Sugar Anne out of a deep sleep. A knock. Loud knocking. She sat straight up in bed, both hands brushing back her tumbled hair so that she could see where she was.

She elbowed Webb. "Someone's knocking on the door."

"I know. Ignore them. Maybe they'll go away." He dragged a pillow over his head. "I need some sleep. I haven't even slept an hour the whole night."

"Neither have I. And whose fault is that?" She grabbed the pillow and whacked him. "Get up. I don't have a dressing gown in here, and I certainly can't go to the door like this."

"No, you certainly can't." He raised up and kissed her

bare shoulder blade, then lingered to nibble a path down her spine. She squealed and twisted away. "Webb, please. You have to get up and see who's knocking. It might be a message from Monsieur DesRoches."

"At this hour? I don't think a dandy like him would be stirring before noon."

Sugar Anne plucked Webb's pocket watch from the table beside the bed and squinted at it. "Merciful heavens, it is almost noon!" She sprang from Webb's bed and dragged off the spread to wrap about her.

"Coming, coming," she shouted.

Hurrying to the door, she swathed herself in the fringed and tasseled counterpane as best she could, stumbling once on a loose corner and barely avoiding a spill. Her breath was ragged as, clutching her covering with one hand, she yanked open the door with the other.

A young man in a uniform stood there, his fist raised to knock again. When he saw her, he froze and his eyes grew wide.

Sugar Anne waited.

Then she waited some more.

"Well?" she finally said.

He looked to be in the middle of a game of swinging statues, turned to marble in an odd position, his eyes bugging out like a frog's.

Webb, in hastily donned pants and unbuttoned shirt, stepped in front of her. "State your business, boy."

The youth quickly came to life, stuttering and stammering and red-faced. "I—I—I—have a message for you. From a Monsieur DesRoches." He held out a tray with an envelope on it.

Webb grabbed the envelope and slammed the door in the boy's face.

"Whatever was wrong with that young man?" asked Sugar Anne.

"Look in the mirror behind you."

She turned and was horrified when she saw her image. The long fringe on the counterpane had parted to perfectly frame her bare left breast.

"Oh, no! I'm mortified. How dreadful."

He smiled. "Not from where I'm standing." He bent and took the bare tip into his mouth.

Sugar Anne forgot all about messages and fringe. All she could think about was the exquisite sensation of teeth and tongue.

It was early afternoon before, fully dressed, they were walking along the sidewalk near Monsieur DesRoches's shop, which was only two blocks from their hotel.

"Couldn't we eat first?" Webb asked. "I'm hungry."

"If you hadn't been so lusty, we could have taken time to eat. As it is, we'll be lucky to catch Monsieur Des-Roches before he leaves. Hurry." She stepped up the pace.

"Me lusty? The way I remember it, the second time it was you—"

Sugar Anne quieted him with a smart jab of her elbow. "Shush, or that will be the last time."

Webb chuckled. "Yes, ma'am. Believe I can wait a spell for the victuals." He held open the shop door.

"I thought so," she said as she sailed past him. She smiled brightly at the proprietor. "Monsieur. Good news, I hope?"

The tall, spare man inclined his head. "Very good

news. I have recovered your husband's stickpin, and for only a few dollars more than the original purchase price."

Sugar Anne gladly paid the amount he asked from her reward funds, which were, she noted, dwindling fast. She and Webb also obtained from the shop owner the names of several of the best tailors in the city.

Taking pity on Webb, she agreed to take time to eat. To be truthful, even though they had snacked on Mary's cakes and the fruit from the hotel, she was rather hungry herself.

Perhaps it was discovering that she was a widow and not an adulteress that had lowered her inhibitions, or perhaps it was the sensual atmosphere of New Orleans, or perhaps it was because she was in love: for whatever reason, she had found herself insatiable in the bedroom. Webb didn't seem to mind. In fact, he acted quite the satyr himself. She found it delightful, but lovemaking, she discovered, tended to whet her other appetites as well. At the pace she was eating, in another few days she would be fatter than a dumpling puff.

The streetlighters were making their rounds when Webb pushed open the door of the shop. A small bell rang to signal their entry. This was the fifth tailor on their list, and due to the hour, the last that they would be able to visit until the next day. None of the previous four had recognized Edward's description or his stickpin.

Sugar Anne was growing discouraged. And tired. And cranky. She longed to loosen her corset and put up her feet. "I'm weary of this tedious business," she muttered as they waited.

"Want to go back to the hotel?"

"No, not when we're already here."

A curtain parted and a dapper gentleman of middle years stepped into the room. Sugar Anne had already learned, to her irritation, that the tailors were much more likely to speak candidly with Webb than with her. She deferred again when the gentleman addressed Webb.

Webb nodded to Monsieur Plauche and began his well-rehearsed story. "I'm Webb McQuillan of the Texas Rangers, sir, and this is Mrs. Spicer. We're trying to trace the movements of a member of her family who recently met an untimely demise. Since he always prided himself on his fashionable attire, we thought he might have visited your establishment." He gave a brief description of Edward, which could have been any one of hundreds of men with sandy hair and beard and of average size. "He always wore this stickpin." Webb produced the piece from his pocket.

Monsieur Plauche carefully studied the pin through his eyeglasses, turning it round and round in the light. "Yes, yes, I believe that I recognize this design. But, as I recall, the gentleman wore a mustache but no beard."

Of course. Edward would have shaved his beard to change his appearance. Sugar Anne's heart began to race, and she gripped Webb's arm. "Sir, we would appreciate any assistance you might offer."

The tailor glanced over his spectacles. "And how were you related to the gentleman, madame?"

"He was my—"

"Cousin," Webb finished for her.

"Cousin," she affirmed.

The tailor glanced back and forth between Webb and

Sugar Anne. "I must ask, you see, because of the . . . delicacy of the situation. Because of the . . . ah . . ."

"The lady who accompanied him," Sugar Anne added. "An actress, I believe."

Monsieur Plauche looked relieved. "Yes, an actress, I would guess. Blonde, she was. They argued frequently, even here in my establishment and at the house where I went for the fittings."

Sugar Anne's heart leapt to her throat and went totally out of control. She tried to speak and couldn't.

"The house?" Webb asked casually. "Do you have that address?"

"Yes, I'm sure that I have it among my papers. Deceased, you say? Oh, dear, and with Monsieur Beaucaire still owing a bill here."

"Monsieur Beaucaire?" Sugar Anne asked.

"Yes. Monsieur Edouard Beaucaire. Is that not the gentleman's name?"

"He often traveled incognito," Webb said. "He used many names."

"But rest assured," Sugar Anne said, "if your Monsieur Beaucaire is my . . . cousin, I will see that your bill is paid."

"Thank you, madame. I shall find the address." The tailor bowed and left through the curtain.

Sugar Anne's knees began to shake, and she clutched Webb's arm for support. "Please, please," she whispered, "let it be Edward."

Webb patted her hand. "Honey, don't get your hopes up until we can check this out. It might not amount to a hill of beans."

After what seemed forever, Monsieur Plauche returned. He handed Webb a card with an address on the back. "The house is on Dumaine, a short distance from the cathedral." He bowed slightly to Sugar Anne. "Please accept my condolences on the passing of your . . . cousin." He smiled politely.

As soon as they were out the door, Sugar Anne said, "I don't think we fooled him one bit. He knew very well that Edward wasn't my cousin."

"Probably. But we got the address. How about we go back to the hotel and try this place in the morning? I know that you're tired."

"Yes, but I wouldn't sleep a wink all night. Let's go by the house. Maybe we can find out something from the neighbors."

A few minutes later, the carriage stopped in front of an attractive home trimmed in wrought iron and with a gate suggesting a courtyard beyond the wall. The jalousied windows were dark. No glimmer of light showed anywhere. The entire street seemed quiet, and the streetlight provided only dim illumination.

Webb rang a bell pull and waited. Then he rang it again and rapped on the door. All was quiet.

Sugar Anne stood pressed against his side. "Try the key," she whispered.

"I don't have it. You do."

"I forgot." She scratched through the satchel and handed the key to Webb.

He struck a match and tried the key in the lock, then handed it back to her. "Doesn't fit."

She tried it herself. It didn't fit. "Oh, hell's bells!" she muttered, rattling the knob.

The door swung open.

She sucked in a gasp and her eyes grew wide. "It's open."

"So I see."

"Think we should go in?"

"Might be a good way to get our heads blown off."

"But this is my *husband's* house."

"We think."

"I'm sure of it. I'm going inside."

"Lead the way," Webb said with a flourish.

"Maybe you should go first. You have the matches."

He struck a match and held it out in front of him. It cast only a small pool of light. Fortunately, there was a candelabra on a table near the door. They crept inside and Sugar Anne closed the door while Webb lit a single candle of the six in the stand.

It was enough for her to see a switch for the electric lights, which she turned on.

"What in the hell are you doing?" Webb quickly turned the lights off. "Woman, you're gonna get us shot for sure."

"Nobody is around to shoot us. And if we are to investigate this house, I prefer to be able to see." She turned the lights on again.

"You'd make a sorry burglar."

"I should hope so. But this house hasn't been inhabited in quite some time." She raked her finger across the tabletop. "See? Dust. Several weeks of it, I would say."

They passed from the foyer to the parlor, a well-appointed room with expensive furnishings. Everything was in order except for a single overturned footstool and several brandy bottles strewn about on the floor by a large chair, some broken, some intact.

Webb went to the chair and squatted beside the armrest to examine it. "Looks like these might be old blood stains."

Sugar Anne picked up a bottle. "This is Edward's favorite brandy." She set the bottle on a table and started for the dining room.

Webb stopped her. "I think you should stay here and let me search the rest of the house."

"Not on your life. I'm going too."

"But there's no telling what—"

"I'm going."

"Then stay behind me." He reached into his boot for his house pistol.

"I wish that I had brought my weapon along."

"Thank God you didn't. Now, shhh. And stay behind me."

The downstairs was empty, although the kitchen showed signs of use. Fragments from a broken glass littered the floor, and several towels with rusty brown stains lay on the table beside a bowl, which was also stained and held a small amount of dark liquid in the bottom.

"What do you suppose that is?" she asked, pointing to the bowl.

"Blood. Looks like Edward—or someone—might have tried to tend his wounds. Most of the water has dried up."

Her stomach turned queasy, but she clamped her teeth together. "I see."

It seemed to her that Webb took an inordinate amount of time examining the room, the towels, and such. She studied the ceiling while he went about it. When he finally decided to leave, she breathed a sigh of relief and hurried along behind him.

He poked in this cranny and that, covering the entire downstairs. "Now the upstairs bedrooms," he said. "I'd feel a whole lot better if you would stay down here. It's liable to be much worse up there."

"I'm coming."

"Suit yourself."

They made a cursory examination of the upstairs and found a bathroom, a sitting room, and three bedrooms. There were vestiges of Edward's injury in both the sitting room and his bedroom, which adjoined it.

"You check in here and in Edward's bedroom," Sugar Anne said quickly, averting her face from the unpleasant disorder. "I'll check the other rooms."

"We don't know for sure that this is Edward's house. I didn't find so much as a scrap of paper with his name on it. We may be ransacking a stranger's home."

Sugar Anne rolled her eyes. "Surely you don't believe that. This is Edward's house, you can be sure. I'm going to check the other rooms."

She hurried to what looked to be a woman's room, off the opposite side of the sitting area. The abundance of ruffles on the bed skirt and roses on the wallpaper were a bit too gaudy for her taste. Flora would have liked it.

Throwing open the wardrobe, she found it empty except for a dressing gown with a ripped sleeve and a wad of fur—her muff! She pulled it from the bottom of the wardrobe and brushed it where it had been crushed.

Yes, it was hers all right.

At the dressing table, she found spilled powder, a stray button, hairpins, a perfume bottle, and a few other items, all left behind as if someone had packed in haste. She sniffed the contents of the bottle and made a wry face.

No wonder she left this ghastly stuff behind. It smelled like wet dog and vanilla syrup.

The chest was empty, as was the drawer of a bedside table. Sugar Anne even got down on her hands and knees and looked under the bed.

That's when she saw it: a glint of green beneath the bed.

⮞ Twenty-two ⮜

When Webb heard Sugar Anne cry out, chills went through him. He broke and ran for her. He found her sitting in the middle of the floor weeping.

"What's the matter? Are you hurt? Did you fall?" He knelt beside her and took her into his arms.

She sobbed against his shirt.

He lifted her face. "Tell me what's wrong, sweetheart. What happened?"

She held out a fist, then slowly opened her fingers. A ring lay in her palm. "It's my mother's. My mother's emerald ring. My father gave it to her when they were married. She always wore it. I thought that I would never see it again." She laid her face against his chest and wept some more.

God, he hated to hear her cry like that. It tore his guts apart. All he could do was pat her back and hold her.

In a few minutes, she took a deep shuddering breath and pulled away. "Do you have a handkerchief?"

He handed her the one from his pocket. She wiped her eyes and dabbed at her nose, which was running. He smiled and held the handkerchief to her nose. "Blow."

She honked a pretty good one, and he laughed and

hugged her against him. God, he loved her. "You all right now?"

"Yes."

"Why don't you stretch out on the bed for a minute and let me check a few more things?"

Her eyes widened, and she got that look he'd grown familiar with. "Are you mad? I'm not about to lie down on that woman's bed. I'm perfectly fine." She stuck the ring on her finger, and Webb helped her up. "I found my fur muff, but it looks as if she made off with my sable coat—and the rest of it. You didn't happen to find a diamond brooch and matching earrings, did you? They were my grandmother's."

Webb shook his head. "Sorry."

"It was too much to hope for, I suppose."

They continued their search, but they found no money or other valuables, no hiding places or any evidence of a safe. There wasn't a bankbook or a scrap of paper that indicated where money or bonds might be kept.

"I don't think that we're going to find anything else tonight," Webb said. "Tomorrow, when it's daylight, I'll come back and check again."

"*We'll* come back," she corrected.

He smiled. "*We'll* come back."

As they rode back to the hotel, Sugar Anne yawned several times.

"Tired?"

"Very." She snuggled against him.

As soon as they reached their rooms, she said, "I think I'll go to bed, if you don't mind."

He kissed her forehead. "I don't mind at all. I could do with some shut-eye myself."

She dropped her satchel on the sofa, stripped off her gloves and hat, and began unbuttoning her jacket as she headed for her bedroom. Sugar Anne might act tough as a Texas longhorn, but she'd had a hell of a day, and he could see that she was tuckered out.

He poured himself a shot of bourbon from their bar and knocked it back. He poured a second shot and sipped it while he waited. After a few minutes, he eased to her door and opened it. She was sprawled across her bed sound asleep. He shut the door very quietly, then checked his watch and went downstairs.

Their search the following morning was no more fruitful than that of the previous night. The neighbors to the left were not home; the neighbors to the right had just returned to New Orleans from an extended trip abroad and knew nothing. An elderly couple, both deaf as door posts, lived across the street and were impossible to communicate with. Their housekeeper, however, provided a bit of information.

The Beaucaires, it seemed, had a couple who worked for them and lived in an apartment at the rear of the courtyard. "One morning early, before daylight, the mistress knocked on their door and told them they were dismissed. Just like that. No warning. Paid them off and had them pack and go. Said she and the mister were going on a long trip and might not return to New Orleans at all."

"Do you know where we might find this couple?" Sugar Anne asked.

"Last I heard, they were working for the Parkers on St. Charles. I don't believe the lady told the truth," the housekeeper said.

"Which lady?"

"The blonde fancy lady what called herself Mrs. Beaucaire. I saw her leave with trunks and boxes, but I didn't see the gentleman leave with her. Saw lights on after that. Off and on for two days, I saw lights in that house."

After securing the Parkers' address, Webb and Sugar Anne went to find the servants who had worked for Edward and his mistress. They had no trouble locating them—or rather the woman, a Mrs. Fontenot. Her husband was out driving Mrs. Parker on her errands. Mrs. Fontenot was a regular magpie, who didn't care a whit for her former mistress.

"I've been in service long enough to know quality. She wasn't. The ladies in the neighborhood knew it too, and they crossed the street when they saw her coming. She hated New Orleans and wanted to leave, argued with Monsieur Beaucaire about it all the time. Mostly he just ignored her and drank his brandy. He didn't seem to be a happy man."

After a few questions, it was apparent that Mrs. Fontenot knew nothing of Edward's personal business and could be of no help. They thanked her and left.

"What next?" Webb asked as their carriage pulled away.

"Lunch. I'm famished."

He grinned. "You're always famished."

"Detecting is hard work. Let's try Antoine's near the hotel. I understand that their food is excellent."

It was. Sugar Anne had never eaten pompano with such fragrance and flavor. The sauce was superb, the vegetables tender and succulent. "I may move to New Orleans for the food alone."

"Told you it was good. Want dessert?"

"Heavens, no. I've sinned quite enough." She dabbed her lips with her napkin while Webb signaled for coffee. "What do you propose that we do now?"

"Well, we could go back and talk to the neighbors some more. We can check all the banks in the area to see if anybody recognizes Edward's description."

"You don't sound as if you think that would do much good."

Webb shrugged. "Can't ever tell, but it seems to me that he covered his tracks pretty well. Still, that money's got to be somewhere. I'm just afraid that he might have taken his secrets to his grave."

"In a wall oven."

While Webb drank his coffee, Sugar Anne pondered that awful rented crypt in the wall. Why had Edward spoken so often of that cemetery as he lay dying? She didn't recall that he'd ever had any particular attachments to cemeteries before. Of course, he'd never been so near death before. He must have stayed in that house at least two days before he sought help at the hospital.

Sugar, by you. Angel, by you. Odd, she thought. Very odd. What had he meant? And why had he chosen—

An idea struck her with the force of a lightning bolt.

She popped up out of her chair. "Webb. Come on. Hurry."

"Where are we going in such an all-fired rush? Can I at least finish my coffee?" He signaled for the check.

"You can have coffee later. We have to get to the cemetery. I just remembered that Beaucaire was Edward's grandmother's maiden name. Hurry."

He quickly paid the check, and they hurried to their carriage.

Sugar Anne urged him on so frantically that he almost collided with a poultry wagon en route, and he frightened several pedestrians within an inch of their lives. One man in a bowler jumped out of the way, shook his fist, and shouted rather vulgar comments after them.

When they drew up to the gate of St. Louis Cemetery II, Webb said, "Want to tell me what this is about now?"

"By You! Angel by You!"

"By you? I still don't understand."

"Edward's grandmother's name was Angelique Beaucaire." She scrambled down. "I'll show you. Follow me."

"Dammit, woman, you're not making a lick of sense. Slow down before you break your ankle." He grabbed her elbow. "What does Edward's grandmother have to do with this?"

"Just be patient, and I'll show you. There," she said, pointing to a tomb, "is You. Dominique You, the pirate, remember? The priest told us about him. And there," she added, pointing to the tomb behind it, "is the angel."

An angel with outspread wings stood atop the roof of a weathered tomb. The tips of both wings were broken off.

"And I'll bet you anything that—" She stopped in front of the weathered angel tomb and smiled. "I was right. Beaucaire. His grandmother's family." She leaned close to read the faint inscription on the marble. "Yes, his grandmother's name is here. His mother's, too."

"What about his grandfather?"

"He died much later. In the war. I'm not sure his body was even recovered." She ran her hand across one of the two marble slabs bolted to the tomb, one atop the other.

"No one has been buried here in over thirty years. Edward must have been the last of this line. War and yellow fever wiped out so many families here."

Webb squatted close to the front to inspect the marble. "So what do you think Edward was trying to tell the nun?"

"I don't think that he realized that she was a nun. Did you notice that Sister Phillipa and I are about the same size and coloring? I think he thought he was speaking to me. I think he was asking me to bury him here with his mother and grandmother."

"Hmmmm." He ran his fingers over the bolt. "Wonder where the money is?"

Sugar Anne's heart almost stopped. "You don't think—"

She startled at the sound of voices. Two elderly women and a younger man passed nearby. She averted her face, tried to appear inconspicuous, and waited until the sounds of their conversation died away.

"You don't think that the *money* is in there?" she whispered.

"Don't know. It's possible. This bolt looks as if it's been opened more recently than thirty years ago."

"Then what are you waiting for? Open it!"

"With people in the cemetery? Look, there comes another bunch. And we need tools to do a proper job. We'll have to come back later. After dark."

"After dark?" She swallowed.

"After dark."

When they returned to the hotel, Webb insisted that she rest while he rounded up some tools. Sugar Anne could no more rest than she could fly. She paced and she fidgeted, then she paced some more.

One thing she could do, she decided, was to be prepared. There was bound to be some danger involved with their foray into the cemetery in the dead of night. Although she trusted Webb to defend them, extra firepower seemed appropriate. She went downstairs and retrieved her pistol and shells from the hotel safe. Her umbrella was in her trunk.

By the time Webb returned, she had her outfit for their venture laid out and was considering having a light meal sent up to the suite. It would never do to have her stomach growl when they were trying to be stealthy.

"Did you find everything?" she asked.

"Yes. I left the toolbox and the lantern in the carriage."

"Do you like cold tongue?"

He raised one eyebrow. "Depends on what you have in mind, but it sounds interesting." He pulled her into his arms. "Just where did you plan to put it? And why is it cold?"

She laughed. "You goose. I meant cold beef tongue. I thought that I might have the dining room send up some sandwiches."

"Sandwiches? In New Orleans? I thought that we might try the St. Charles dining room tonight. Or we could go back to Antoine's. Wouldn't you rather have shrimp creole or trout with almonds and crab meat than cold beef tongue? I know I would."

"But we're going to the cemetery as soon as it's dark."

"No, honey, not as soon as it's dark. After dark. And after things settle down. I was thinking more of one or two o'clock in the morning."

"One or two in the *morning*?" she said, her voice rising an octave.

"Yep. And why don't you stay here and let me go alone? I—"

"For the last time, *no*. I'm going with you."

"No way I can talk you out of it?"

She shook her head. "Absolutely not."

He didn't seem at all happy about that.

Later they dressed and went to dinner at the St. Charles for a more American-style meal of roast duck and new potatoes, then had liqueurs at their own hotel and listened to the violins serenading the guests. When they returned to their suite at just after ten o'clock, she was feeling quite romantic.

Once they were inside the door, Webb drew her close and touched his forehead to hers. "We have a couple of hours to kill yet. Any ideas on how to pass the time?"

She smiled. "Perhaps we could read aloud to each other."

He laughed and swung her around. She laughed too. "Do you have any idea how much I love you?" he asked.

She stilled. "No. You've never told me."

"Never? But surely—"

"Never."

"I do love you, Sugar Anne. I'm not much good with pretty words. I can only tell you how I feel. And I feel like sometimes my heart's gonna bust right out of my chest with love for you. Your smile makes me want to laugh out loud and walk up a wall. I feel like life wouldn't be worth a plug nickel if you weren't around, and I'd rather ride through hell bareback than hurt you. I want you to remember that."

She smiled and cupped his cheek in her hand. "For someone who isn't very good with pretty words, you do a remarkable job."

He kissed her hand. "I hope you have some feeling for me. I know I can't offer you all the—"

Her fingers stilled his words. "I love you, Webb. I love you fiercely. And besides loving you, I respect you, and I trust you. That's very important to me."

He groaned with a feral sound that seemed torn from the deepest part of his being, then kissed her. His kiss went on forever, harder, softer, urgent. It sent a fever through her, and she responded with all the love stored in her heart.

He undressed her as if she were a goddess and made love to her as if she were a wanton woman. She adored every moment of it, reveled in the heat, rejoiced in the words he spoke when his mouth and tongue explored the most intimate of places.

When he finally came into her, she was raw nerves and frenzied movement. She met him forcefully and urged the same from him.

This was heaven; this was hell; this was love.

When the spasms began, she cried out and clung to him, lest she die from the pleasure of it.

When they were both spent, they held each other, nuzzling damp skin.

"I love you," he whispered. "Never forget that. Never."

"And I love you," she murmured as she drifted away.

Sugar Anne came instantly awake. The bed beside her was empty. She jumped up and ran into the sitting room just as Webb was about to open the hall door.

"And exactly where are you going, Captain?"

Webb let out a string of oaths.

"You were going to the cemetery without me, weren't you?"

"Honey, it might be dangerous, and—"

"Dangerous? I'm not afraid of corpses. And in any case, I'm perfectly capable of defending myself. Don't you set one foot outside that doorway until I'm dressed." She whirled and hurried toward her room. Mumbling came from behind her. "I heard that. And I am not stubborn, simply determined. And your foul language doesn't deter me one whit."

Since she'd laid out her garments earlier, she was able to dress quickly in a simple shirtwaist and skirt. She pinned her hat securely and picked up her satchel, which contained, among other things, her loaded pistol and her spectacles.

She grabbed her umbrella, strode into the sitting room, and announced, "I'm ready."

"What's in your satchel?"

"Essentials."

Webb snatched the bag from her hands and, undaunted by her sputtering, opened it. He pulled out the pistol and scowled at her. "You're not taking this gun."

Her chin went up. "I certainly am. You never know what sort of trouble we might encounter at this hour."

"I'll take care of any rough element. I don't hanker to get shot in the rump again."

"If you'll recall, I'm not the one who shot you in the posterior. I only shot your hat, and besides, my eyeglasses have improved my aim considerably."

Webb snorted. "Maybe so, but you're not taking this pistol." He stuck it in the side of his boot.

Sugar Anne knew better than to argue with him. A more stubborn man hadn't been born. "Excuse me for a moment, please. I forgot my handkerchief." She hurried back into her bedroom and yanked open the drawer where she'd stored her handkerchiefs. She lifted the stack and retrieved the derringer she'd stowed there. James had given it to her, claiming that the small two-shot was a more ladylike weapon. She preferred the range of the pistol, but the derringer would have to do.

Glancing over her shoulder to see if Webb was watching, she lifted her skirt and stuck the small gun in her garter. Smiling smugly, she dropped her skirt, gathered her things, and rejoined him.

"What time is it?" she asked, dropping a handkerchief into her satchel.

"One-thirty."

"Perfect. Let's go."

She wished fervently for stronger elastic as derringer and garter slid lower down her leg. She slapped her hand against the bulge, then shifted her gear to hitch gun and garter back up her thigh.

"Dammit, Sugar Anne, stop poking me with that infernal umbrella."

"I told you that I can't see. Why don't you light the lantern?"

"Not yet. I want to wait until we reach the tomb. Here, give me your hand."

"You must be half cat to be able to see in the dark. All

I can make out are some vague white shapes. I haven't any idea where we are."

He muttered some uncomplimentary things, but she ignored them, knowing that he was simply upset and concerned about her safety. She hung on to his hand and followed his lead.

The gun began to slide down her leg again so she withdrew her hand, quickly lifted her skirt, and adjusted the garter as best she could as she hobbled after him.

In a moment, he stopped so abruptly that she crashed into his back. "Did you hear that?" he whispered.

"Hear what?"

"I could have sworn that I heard someone cough."

They were very still and listened intently. The only sound that they heard was the buzzing of night insects.

"Come on," he said. "It's just over here."

She had to take his word for it. There was no moon to speak of, only a tiny sliver that provided the barest light. He stopped and set down the toolbox and the lantern.

"Might as well make some use of that umbrella," he said. "Open it, and we can partly shade the light."

Sugar Anne unfurled the umbrella while Webb lit the lantern. Then he set about unbolting the marble.

"Can you give me a hand? This damned thing is heavy."

"Certainly."

The two of them wrestled the marble from its niche, lifted the slab away, and leaned it against the side of the tomb. A brick archway was exposed; the opening was sealed with bricks as well. Webb put a chisel to the mortar and tapped it with a mallet. The bricks collapsed.

"What?"

"They weren't mortared," Webb said. "Only arranged to look like it." He moved the loose bricks to the ground. "Bring the lantern closer."

Holding the lantern in her right hand and the open umbrella in her left, she crept closer and shined the light into the opening. "What is that?"

"Looks like a coffin. A new one."

"Oh, dear. What if there's a *body* inside?"

"I'd sooner you didn't mention that." He grabbed a handle at the end and slid the coffin partway out. "Hold the lantern higher." He ran his hand over the top of the box. "Lordamighty."

"What? What?"

"Just a minute. There's a section of the top that's separate. I can feel the seam. And there's a keyhole here. Hold the light steady."

"My arms are giving out. Is it locked?"

"Yep." Webb pulled Edward's key from his pocket, fitted it into the lock, and turned.

She heard the click. "What's inside?"

"Bring the light closer. I don't have it open yet. Dammit, you're about to set my hat on fire. Move back a little."

"Well, make up your mind. Closer or not closer."

A section of the coffin top swung up, and Webb lifted a package from among the several she could see lying in the metal-lined box. The parcel was wrapped in oilcloth and tied with string.

"What do you think is inside?" she asked.

"Not but one way to find out." He cut the string and unwrapped the bundle. It was filled with stacks of five-hundred-dollar bills. "Lordamighty. Would you look at that!"

"It's the money! We've found it," she squealed.

"Hold it right there!" a deep voice boomed from behind a tomb. "Don't move."

~ Twenty-three ~

Thinking that they were about to be killed by ruffians, Sugar Anne didn't hold it at all. No way was she giving up without a fight. Heaving the lantern in the direction of the voice, she ducked behind a nearby tomb. Yanking up her skirt, she grabbed the derringer, then clawed through her satchel for her spectacles.

Webb was cursing violently, and there was a great deal of commotion—shrill noises, men yelling, and feet tramping. Her hands shook so badly that she couldn't get her spectacles on properly, and then she dropped them.

"Hell's bells," she muttered, holding the small gun in one hand and feeling around on the ground with the other.

Amid the shouting and cursing, a brute of a man approached holding a lantern aloft. "Get back," she shouted. "I'm armed."

Meaning to shoot out the light and secure her position, she took careful aim and fired. The man yelped and dropped the lantern. Whistles blew and there was more commotion.

"Norman," a man shouted. "You hit?"

"Just my damned hat!"

"Police!" the deep voice yelled. "Throw down your weapon and come out. Police! Throw down your weapon or we'll fire."

Sugar Anne froze. Police? She'd fired on the *police*? *Oh, dear merciful heavens.* She tossed her gun out from her hiding place. "Don't shoot!"

Webb continued to curse loudly and profanely. "Sugar Anne, you all right?"

"I'm fine." She tried to keep her voice even, but her teeth were chattering. She stood, hands raised. He ran to her and took her in his arms.

Half a dozen uniformed men advanced holding lanterns high. "Madam, you're under arrest," the deep-voiced one said. "Atherton, Sartor, put her in the wagon."

"But, sir, you don't understand. I didn't realize that you were policemen. I thought you were ruffians meaning to do us harm."

"Take her away."

Webb cursed some more and tried to prevent them from wrenching her from his arms, but a pair of burly gentlemen held him back and another pair grabbed her elbows.

A weasel-faced man stepped into the circle of light, and Sugar Anne's stomach sank to her knees.

Sturges, the Pinkerton man from Chicago.

An oily smile twisted his mouth. "Led us right to it, didn't you? I knew you would. Knew it all the time. Good work, McQuillan."

Every drop of blood drained from Sugar Anne's face. "McQuillan?" she whispered.

"Yes, ma'am. Captain McQuillan has been a big help. You'll be getting that fat reward soon, Captain. Fine job."

"Goddamn you, Sturges! Goddamn you!" Webb roared. "It wasn't supposed to be like this."

Sugar Anne turned to Webb and sought his eyes. They were wild. "You're with the Pinkertons? All this was for a reward?"

"No—yes. Dammit, let me explain, honey."

She stiffened her back and raised her chin. "There is nothing to explain. You're a conniving snake no better than Edward Herndon or any of the other men I've encountered. I was a fool to trust you. Gentlemen, I'm ready to go. Please bring along my umbrella and my satchel."

Webb struggled against the men who held him. "Sugar Anne, honey, please hear me out—"

Her glance flicked over him as if he were a bug. "Webb McQuillan, go to hell."

He shouted after her as the police marched her from the cemetery, but she clamped her teeth together and turned a deaf ear. She couldn't allow herself to dwell on Webb's perfidy or she would surely die.

Despite all she had endured, Sugar Anne had never suffered greater humiliation than being hauled away to jail in a paddy wagon. She was searched, questioned, and locked in a cell like a common criminal. She shared accommodations with a drunken woman in a tawdry costume and an old crone with missing teeth and a mad glint in her eyes.

Nobody believed a word she said, except perhaps her cellmates, and they were in no position to be of assistance.

"Men are sorry bastards," Sugar Anne muttered.

The younger of her cohorts roused and opened one bleary eye. "I'll drink to that. Sorry bastards every one."

Sugar Anne sat gingerly on the edge of a bunk, sure that the filthy mattress was infested with lice and bedbugs. There was nothing for her to do but pray and wait. Before her satchel and other belongings were taken away, she had given the sergeant two envelopes along with cash enough to pay for a messenger. Inside each envelope was a letter of introduction Trista had written to her close associates in the city. Sugar Anne had added her own note as well, informing the gentlemen of her circumstances.

Trista had handed her the envelopes before she left Galveston. "If you run into any trouble," Trista had said, "get in touch with these men. They wield a lot of power, and it's good to have friends in high places."

Knowing that it was unlikely that the messages would be delivered before morning—if at all—Sugar Anne resigned herself to spending the night in jail. The old hag snored in the corner, but Sugar Anne couldn't have slept a wink in that wretched place, no matter how exhausted she was.

She paced and tried to keep her mind occupied with singing songs or reciting poetry, anything to ward off memories of Webb's loathsome deceit. Pitiful moans issued forth from another darkened cell. She heard weeping and retching. She wanted to join those poor souls in their agony. Instead, she paced.

By late morning Webb was wild with worry. He had coldcocked Sturges at the cemetery and gone to the police station immediately after Sugar Anne was arrested, but she refused to see him. In his fury, he'd wired Amanda and her boss at the Pinkerton Agency, not once, but twice. By the time he received their wired responses and secured the services of a decent attorney, Sugar Anne had been in that sorry jail for almost ten hours.

Waving the telegrams and with the sputtering attorney in tow, Webb strode into the police station demanding Sugar Anne's release.

"She's gone," the sergeant said.

"Gone? Gone where?"

"With Hiz Honor, I suspect."

"His Honor? What are you talking about, man?" Webb grew more agitated.

"Hiz Honor the mayor was here before daybreak. Rantin' and ravin' he was, too. Dang near fired the captain. Busted him to lieutenant. You've never seen such bowin' and scrapin' and excusin' as they done for that little gal. Even let them two in the cell with her out—on her say-so. They was gone before you could turn around. And a good thing, too. Wasn't more than ten minutes later that one of them Italians and his lawyer showed up."

"Italians?"

"Yep. And I was some glad to tell him she was already released. I wouldn't want to tangle with any of his bunch, not on your life."

Cursing, Webb left the attorney fuming in the station and hightailed it to the hotel.

There wasn't a sign of her in the suite. Her trunk was gone. The bed was made. Not even an echo of her laughter lingered in the empty rooms.

He hurried downstairs.

"She's checked out," the desk clerk said. "Someone

came for her things quite early this morning. And here is the bill, sir," the clerk added, smiling politely. "Will you be paying cash?"

Webb looked at the paper and damn near fainted. It was more than two months' pay for a Ranger. He'd have to wire Amanda again.

Damnation, what a mess! He'd dug himself a hell of a hole, but he planned to crawl out of it some way. If he had to get down on his knees to do it, he meant to make Sugar Anne understand. He didn't plan on living the rest of his life miserable without her.

What good was the finest feather bed in the world if he couldn't share it with her?

Sugar Anne sat in her room, staring out the window, seeing nothing. Flora rapped on the door and went in. "The captain is downstairs again," Flora said. "He wants to talk to you."

"I don't want to talk to him. Tell that poor excuse for a human being to go away."

"Oh, honey," Flora said, hugging Sugar Anne to her ample bosom. "Didn't I tell you to watch out for the good-looking ones? They'll break your heart every time. I knew from the minute I saw him with that actress—" Flora slapped her fingers across her mouth.

Sugar Anne's eyes narrowed. "What actress?"

"Forget that I said that."

"It's said. I can't forget. Do you mean that you saw him consorting with another woman? When? Where?"

Flora sighed. "Trista is going to be angry with me, but since I've already spilled the beans, I might as well tell the whole story." She told Sugar Anne about seeing

Webb with the actress twice, once the day before they left for New Orleans.

"After we—after we—?"

Flora nodded.

"That lowdown, dirty, rotten scoundrel! Tell him that I said to go to hell. Tell him those very words. I never want to see his face or hear his voice again."

The moment Flora left, Sugar Anne made a dash for the chamber pot and promptly lost her breakfast.

☙ Twenty-four ❧

Sugar Anne barely made it out of bed before she was hugging the chamber pot and retching. There was a tap on her door, but she couldn't have risen that moment if her life had hung in the balance.

Trista entered without an invitation and with a cold cloth and a plate of crackers. She bathed Sugar Anne's face with the cloth. "Get back in bed, dear," the old lady said. "And nibble on these crackers."

Sugar Anne groaned. "I don't think I should eat anything. I feel like I'm dying. It must be food poisoning."

"I don't think so. Trust me on this."

Rising unsteadily, Sugar Anne crawled back into bed, then ate one of the crackers that Trista offered. Miraculously, it stayed down. She ate another and felt much better. "Thank you. I can't imagine what's the matter with me."

Trista's brows lifted. "Can't you? You've been sick every morning for over a week. Have you missed your monthlies?"

Sugar Anne nodded.

"Then I should think that you would have reached a conclusion by now."

"I'm *not* pregnant. I can't be." She turned her face away and tried to hide the tears.

"Tell me what methods you used to prevent it." When Sugar Anne was silent, Trista sighed. "Lord, deliver me from amateurs. At an appropriate time, I will educate you about such matters, but there's no use locking the barn door now. The question is, what are you going to do about your condition?"

"I'll not go to one of those awful people and have it ended. That's a terrible thing to endure. Why, I saw women at the hospital bleed to death—"

"Shhh. I wasn't suggesting such a thing, dear."

"Then there's very little that I can do except bear this child. I will never have an opportunity to have another, and I will love my baby fiercely. She will have everything that I can provide."

"Except a father. Society is very cruel, Sugar Anne. What will you do when your child is labeled a bastard and other children taunt him? What will you tell her when she comes weeping to you?"

"That's why you gave up my father, isn't it?"

"That, and because I was very young and had no way to support us. Even Phoebe realizes the stigma of bearing a child out of wedlock. Soon, she and Mrs. Turnipseed will be leaving with Timmy. I've purchased a boarding-house in Huntsville, and they will run it. Phoebe has agreed to take the name of Mrs. Turnipseed's youngest son, the one who was lost at sea. Who knows? Perhaps he was Timmy's father."

"You don't really believe that, do you?"

Trista smiled. "No, but it comforts the two of them to imagine that it might be so. But you, my dear, are in a very different situation. Your child has a father who is free to marry and who adores you."

Fury flew over Sugar Anne. "No. Absolutely not. I'll move to Huntsville with Phoebe and name this baby Herndon before I consent to marry Webb McQuillan. After all, I *am* a widow. No one need know that my husband died before my pregnancy began. If I must live with a lie, I prefer it be one of my own making."

"Won't you at least talk with the captain? Sugar Anne, he loves you dearly. I've never seen anyone in such torment. And no matter what you say, I believe that you still love him, too. I've never seen such a perfect pair as the two of you."

"I have nothing to say to the captain, and I'm not swayed by his flowers or candy or lacy cards. I've heard all his excuses a dozen times—from you, from Flora, from Willie, from Mr. Underwood, from Mary and Donald, from Phoebe and even poor Mrs. Turnipseed. He's had everyone intercede for him except baby Timmy and the dog. He is a liar and a scoundrel, and I'll have nothing to do with him."

"Sugar Anne, to be fair to the man, you played a game of deceit as well. He didn't know you when he agreed to work with the Pinkertons. It was a job—a job that would allow him to fulfill a dream. And he didn't mean for you to be arrested. He meant to give you the opportunity to return the money yourself and prove your innocence."

"Well, it didn't turn out like that, now, did it? For the last time, I'll have nothing more to do with Captain McQuillan. And don't you *dare* mention my condition to him. Promise?"

Trista sighed. "I promise."

*   *   *

Webb was at the end of his rope. He'd been to Trista's house twice a day for two weeks, and still Sugar Anne refused to talk to him. He ought to have his butt kicked from here to Amarillo for not telling her the truth long ago. But he had feared the very thing that had happened. God, he loved her so much he didn't know what he'd do without her.

He sat on the front steps trying to think of a way to talk to her. He figured that if he could ever get her to sit down and listen, he could make her understand.

Willie came out the front door with Sport. "Evening, Cap'n." He sat down on the steps beside Webb and offered him one of his two bananas. The dog lay down at Willie's feet.

Webb accepted the banana, stripped down the peel, and took a big chomp. "How's Sugar Anne?"

"About like you, I'd say. You two ever gonna make up?"

"I don't know. Not if we don't talk. But she won't see me. Trista says she stays in her room most of the time."

"Ever thought of a ladder?"

"Several times. But it won't do me any good if her window's locked."

Willie grinned. "I could see that it's left open. And stand guard at her door to see no one comes in to disturb you. For a price."

"Name it."

Willie finished his banana, then threw the peel under the rosebushes. "Banana peels are good for rosebushes."

"That so? I hadn't heard that." Webb tossed his peel alongside Willie's and waited.

After a few minutes' silence, Willie said, "I got to

thinking when Miss Trista was in that coma. You know, she's an old lady, and she could up and die on me at any time. And if she did, I wouldn't have no family at all. Now if you and Miss Sugar Anne was to get married, well . . ." He swallowed.

"You're asking if you could come and live with Sugar Anne and me if anything happened to Trista?"

"Not that I'm looking for anything to happen to her any time soon, you understand, and not that I couldn't do all right taking care of myself, but . . . yeah. That's what I'm asking."

Webb ruffled the boy's hair. "You bet you can."

"Sport, too?"

"Sport, too."

Willie grinned. "I got a plan."

It was well after midnight when Webb and Willie quietly placed the ladder under Sugar Anne's window. Webb had a rope made out of silk stockings over his shoulder— Willie had filched the stockings from a bunch that Flora was saving to stuff a pillow—and a couple of extra ones in his pocket. He was going to hog-tie that woman, truss her up, and talk some sense into her—gag her if he had to.

If this scheme of Willie's didn't work, he was flat out of ideas. If worse came to worst, he'd just have to kidnap her.

When the ladder was in place, Willie signaled that he was going to stand watch—in case Sugar Anne yowled before he could get the gag on her and everybody thought she was dying or something.

Webb waited until he figured Willie was in place, then he started climbing. He felt like a danged fool, but it might work, and he was desperate.

The window slid up noiselessly.

He threw one leg over the window sill, then the other. He was just about to tiptoe over to Sugar Anne's bed when something crashed over his head and his eyes rolled back.

Sugar Anne tied off the last knot, then picked up the pitcher and dashed cold water in Webb's face. He came to sputtering. "What—what hit me?"

"I did. With a brandy bottle."

"What did you go and do that for?"

"Because you were breaking into my room. You and Willie are about as subtle as a herd of buffalo."

"I must have a knot the size of—" He started to move his arm, and when he discovered that he couldn't, he scowled at her. "Dammit, you've tied me up."

"I certainly have. Isn't that what you were going to do with me?"

"Only long enough to talk some sense into you."

"I have plenty of sense, thank you."

"Honey, I love you. I love you more than anything in this world. I swear to God I do. Won't you please give me a chance to explain?"

"Webb McQuillan, I've heard your explanations a dozen times or more from everybody in this household. They all know your most intimate feelings."

"Did they tell you how bad I craved a home of my own, with a wife like you, and children? Did they tell you how many times I bedded down on the cold, hard ground, butt sore and weary with—"

"With only your saddle for a pillow? Yes, I heard the story. Several times. And I know how you longed for a feather bed and a house and all that. I'm sorry that you lost your family and were captured by Indians and had to live with that cruel preacher. I'm just as sorry as I can be. But the fact is, you're still a deceitful bastard no better than Edward Herndon, and I've had all the humiliation that I intend to endure for this lifetime."

"Dammit, I told Amanda that—"

"Who—is Amanda? The *actress*?" Venom dripped from her words.

"How do you know about Amanda?"

"So it's true?" she shrieked. She grabbed a pillow from the bed and beat him with it. "You good for nothing, low-down mangy skunk!" She whacked him again.

"Hold it, hold it. Dammit, Sugar Anne. You're acting crazy. What's wrong with you?"

"Amanda. Your *lover*."

"My *what*?"

"Your lover, your mistress, your paramour. Don't deny that you went to her rooms after you'd made love to me. Flora saw you."

Webb started to laugh. "Amanda? Honey, Amanda isn't my lover. She's a Pinkerton agent."

The pillow fell from her hands. "A Pinkerton agent?"

"Yes. And an old friend. We grew up together. Remember that preacher I told you about? Amanda was one of his daughters. She lit out from home not long after I left there. She's like a sister to me."

"A sister?"

He nodded. "I've never touched the woman. She was the one who steered me to the reward. She knew how badly I wanted to settle down, and she figured that this case would provide the means for me to do it. Before we left for New Orleans, I met with Amanda and told her that I couldn't go through with it. I was going to tell you the truth—though I wasn't sure how you would take it. Not too well, I figured. She's the one who urged me to continue, to give you a chance to return the money and prove that you were innocent."

"Well, it didn't exactly turn out that way, did it? The Pinkertons saw to that."

"Not the Pinkertons. Sturges. He disregarded his instructions by bringing the police to the cemetery that night. I didn't know they were going to be there, Sugar Anne. I swear I didn't."

"I believe you."

"You do?"

She nodded.

"I'm sorry that I didn't tell you the whole truth sooner."

"So am I. We could have saved a lot of heartache."

"I love you, Sugar Anne. I love you with all my heart and soul. Do you believe that?"

She nodded.

"Do you love me too?"

She nodded.

"Then what in the hell has all this been about? Why wouldn't you see me?"

"Because of Amanda."

"Amanda?"

"I won't share you with another woman, Webb Mc-Quillan. Ever."

"Honey, you won't ever have to. Untie me, and I'll show you why."

She smiled—and untied him.

He took her into his arms and kissed her.

The door opened a crack. "Everything all right in there?" Willie asked.

Webb laughed. "Everything is just fine."

And it was. More than fine.

It was extraordinary.

When they had made slow, sweet love that lasted a long, long time, they lay in each other's arms. Webb toyed with a lock of hair at her temple. "Honey?"

"Hmmmm?"

"I don't want that reward to stand between us. Come morning, I'll wire the Pinkerton Agency that I don't want it."

"Webb McQuillan, that is the dumbest thing I've ever heard you say. How are you going to support a wife and child on nothing but a Ranger's pay?"

"Well, Trista said I could have a permanent position— What did you say?"

She laughed. "You heard me. How do you think you'll like being a father?"

He grinned from ear to ear. "I think I'll like it just fine."

Galveston had never seen a wedding quite like it. On Christmas Eve, the church was full. The sanctuary was bedecked with greenery and candles and silk bows and white doves. Trista and Aunt Gaggie sat on the front pew. Mary O'Toole played the wedding march on the organ— and quite well, too.

Lucy was the matron of honor while Cotton Yarborough stood up for Webb. Flora and Phoebe were bridesmaids, with Mr. Underwood and Willie as groomsmen. Willie was so proud that he almost busted his buttons as he stood by the altar with his cowlick slicked down. Donald O'Toole gave the bride away.

And never had there been such a lovely bride, Webb thought, as he watched her walk down the aisle. Her dress was deep green velvet, as befitting her widowhood and the season, and she carried a bouquet of roses and holly. Her smile lit the room more brightly than the thousand candles Trista had ordered.

When the minister asked for the ring, Webb slipped her mother's emerald onto her finger. And when he said to kiss the bride, he almost didn't let her go.

They laughed and strode from the church as bells rang their great joy. Mrs. Southern had insisted on hosting the reception. No expense had been spared. Champagne flowed like water, and an ice sculpture in the shape of doves was rumored to have cost more than a good team of horses.

It was a grand affair, but as soon as they could reasonably make their exit, they stole away and Webb drove them home.

Home was a pretty cottage two doors down from Trista, her wedding present to them. He unlocked the front door, swept Sugar Anne into his arms, and carried her across the threshold into their new life.

He didn't stop until he reached their bedroom and laid his bride on the wedding present that she'd bought for him. A soft feather bed.

ANGEL IN MARBLE

by beloved *New York Times* bestselling author

Elaine Coffman

Tibbie Buchanan was a heavenly beauty with a dark past. Once she'd loved a man who'd ruined her. Now a gifted healer and herbalist, she swore she'd never surrender to passion again. Then Nick Mackinnon swept into town. Orphaned at an early age, Nick had made a fortune in shipbuilding, but now he wanted to build a better life for himself. The moment he set eyes on the ravishing Tibbie, he vowed he would have her heart and soul. But, ever mindful of her painful past, Tibbie would flee from love and the man who ached to free her. . . .

Published by Fawcett Books.
Available wherever books are sold.